BASIL INSTINCT

Shelley Costa

Pocket Books

New York   London   Toronto   Sydney   New Delhi

The sale of this book without its cover is unauthorized. If you purchased this book without a cover, you should be aware that it was reported to the publisher as "unsold and destroyed." Neither the author nor the publisher has received payment for the sale of this "stripped book."

Pocket Books
A Division of Simon & Schuster, Inc.
1230 Avenue of the Americas
New York, NY 10020

This book is a work of fiction. Any references to historical events, real people, or real places are used fictitiously. Other names, characters, places, and events are products of the author's imagination, and any resemblance to actual events or places or persons, living or dead, is entirely coincidental.

Copyright © 2014 by Shelley Costa

All rights reserved, including the right to reproduce this book or portions thereof in any form whatsoever. For information address Pocket Books Subsidiary Rights Department, 1230 Avenue of the Americas, New York, NY 10020.

First Pocket Books paperback edition July 2014

POCKET and colophon are registered trademarks of Simon & Schuster, Inc.

For information about special discounts for bulk purchases, please contact Simon & Schuster Special Sales at 1-866-506-1949 or business@simonandschuster.com.

The Simon & Schuster Speakers Bureau can bring authors to your live event. For more information or to book an event contact the Simon & Schuster Speakers Bureau at 1-866-248-3049 or visit our website at www.simonspeakers.com.

Manufactured in the United States of America

10 9 8 7 6 5 4 3 2 1

ISBN 978-1-4767-0936-9
ISBN 978-1-4767-0938-3 (ebook)

"AN ITALIAN FOOD MYSTERY SERIES? WHAT COULD BE BETTER THAN THIS! GET READY TO SIT DOWN AND INDULGE. . . ."
—*Killer Nashville*

Praise for the first mystery in the irresistible new series from **Shelley Costa**

YOU CANNOLI DIE ONCE

"Intriguing. . . . A nicely crafted mystery about murder, opera, and delicious, mouth-watering Italian food."

—*RT Book Reviews*

"The heart and soul of this book is the warm relationship between Nonna and her granddaughter, Eve."

—*Reviewing the Evidence*

"Fun, delightful. . . . This laugh-out-loud tale combines a murder mystery with an entertaining picture of an Italian restaurant and delicious glimpses of its larger-than-life staff."

—*The Reading Addict*

"Entertaining and delightful."

—*Spotlight Reader*

"I enjoyed the author's style and humor . . . and look forward to more adventures at Miracolo."

—*I Love a Mystery*

Also by Shelley Costa

You Cannoli Die Once

For Aunt Gem—
more beautiful than Eve,
more elegant than Maria Pia,
and more fun than all the others—
with love always

Acknowledgments

To my dear Italian family of cooks: Pia, my own nonna, at whose table I first tasted stuffed artichokes at the age of three; my talented chef cousins, Lisa, Susan, and Andrea (thanks, Lisa, for letting Choo Choo use your delicious Gorgonzola recipe); and my aunt Gemma, who first introduced me to bagels and lox. Not every great thing is Italian.

1

At 9:41 p.m. on June 16th I uttered those fateful words: "How bad can it be?" If you didn't tumble out of your crib just yesterday, surely you know that the universe hears those words as a challenge. So it sends you a hurricane or a tax audit or a new man who still lives with his mother. Even so, I didn't see it coming.

As the head chef at Miracolo Italian Restaurant in Quaker Hills, Pennsylvania, I had just been plating an order of *vitello alla Bolognese* when our best server, Paulette Coniglio, one of those sturdy middle-aged women with wedge cuts and expensive highlights, handed me a violet envelope. Telling me someone had left it on the table, wedged between the salt cellar and the ornamental bamboo, she arched an eyebrow, smirked, and flipped the envelope at me the way a cop hands you a ticket for speeding. Not that I would know.

Our eyes met.

I took the envelope gingerly between my slightly greasy thumb and forefinger and gave it a look. Navy-blue calligraphy on card stock. Back flap sealed with a round blob of navy-blue wax embossed with the letter *B*. Addressed to Chef Maria Pia Angelotta—my nonna (Italian for annoying grandmother), who owns Miracolo.

"So who left it?" I asked.

Paulette rolled her shoulders to get the kinks out. "Two well-dressed women who knew enough to get the Barolo with the veal." I like this woman for a couple of reasons. First, she used to date my father Giacomo (Jock) Angelotta, and she stuck around even after he didn't. Second, she is the field commander you want in all the battles of daily life.

"Ah," I said ruminatively, "foodies." Wine selection is always the giveaway.

Paulette's gaze swung to my cousin Landon, my sous chef, who was garnishing an order of his profiteroles—think cream puffs—and doing the famous two-handed hat lift from the Bob Fosse number "I Wanna Be a Dancin' Man." Her eyes narrowed. "Mm," she hummed, shaking her head slowly, "something more."

"More than foodies? What could that be?" I was

at a loss since I had been so busy during the dinner rush that I hadn't peeked my head out of the kitchen even once. I wiped my hands. "Did Maria Pia recognize them?" She'd been swanning around the dining room all evening. My grandmother sincerely believes our customers come because of her. The rest of us believe they come in spite of her.

"I don't think so." Paulette is my ally in my ongoing effort to keep the dragon (Maria Pia) at bay in the business of the restaurant, which is why she always keeps me in any loop reassuringly ahead of my wild-card granny.

I brought the violet envelope next to my ear, squeezed it between my fingers, and then held it up to the overhead lights. "Well," I said philosophically, "it's not ticking, oozing white powder, or holding cash, so I think I'm losing interest."

She held out her hand. "I'll give it to Maria Pia."

Which is when I said with a shrug, "How bad can it be?"

I found out just two minutes later, when my grandmother flung open the double doors and stood there dazed, the opened envelope hanging loosely between her fingers. Out in the dining room the regulars were tuning up, trying to find an A they could agree on. They're amateur musicians who several years ago decided Miracolo is the perfect place to try out their stuff. In public. To get the picture, think squatters with musical instruments. Maybe none of them has a garage.

Landon and I turned to our grandmother. "It's happened," she croaked, her arms pushed quivering against the double doors like she was trying to launch a lifeboat from the *Titanic*. Her face was ragged.

"What?" I asked her, as I plated an order of risotto. "You finally been invited to a baby shower?"

"It should only be yours," she answered kind of automatically, in a strange voice, staring past me. On my nonna, it's hard to tell the difference—just by looking at her—between alarm and ecstasy, which must have somewhat complicated her love life with my grandfather, the sainted Benigno.

At seventy-six, Maria Pia Angelotta is pretty much what you'd call a babe—with wrinkles. These she slathers nightly with half a dozen different creams labeled "crèmes" to jack up the price. She looks a lot like Anne Bancroft, those big, wide-set dark eyes, that broad and sensuous mouth. From her I got my good legs, something she never lets me forget, although hers are shorter, something I never let her forget.

"Then what, Nonna?"

"It's Belfiere."

"Who's that?"

"It's *Belfiere*."

Which didn't clear it up. "And Belfiere is—?" I prompted her slowly.

Nonna got testy. "Have all your pants cut off the circulation to your brain?" She believes I've ruined all my chances at a niceItalianboy by preferring pants to skirts. I resist telling her that niceItalian-boys have no trouble getting past garments of any sort. And I do mean getting past. "Belfiere is the oldest culinary society in the—the—world."

Landon and I exchanged a look. His said: *Do you think it's time to take her in for an evaluation?* Mine said: *I thought this blessed day would never come.* Then Landon cranked up his help-me-to-understand manner. He leaned in toward her and said, "Kind of like the American Culinary Federation, Nonna?"

I crossed my arms. "Or . . . The American Cheese Society?"

She hit us both with the violet-colored invitation. "No, you ninnies, not at all like those." This was followed with a spray of sentiments half in Italian that—from what I could follow—compared Landon and me to that traitor Little Serena, her other granddaughter, whom she likened to bread made with expired yeast and then taken off to the woods by non-Italian wolves. (But then, my Italian is a little rusty.) All Little Serena had done was to come out of the closet and declare her kitchen orientation—"I don't cook"—upon which she blew town to work a ride at Disney World.

I held out my hand. "Can I see the invite, Nonna?" *Nonna*, a soft little nursery rhyme kind of word. Makes you picture some mild-mannered smiling human cushion that shells peas, slips you five dollars if she thinks you studied your catechism, and uses her loose dress as a dish towel. But this would be somebody else's nonna, not mine.

She glared at me. "Of course you can't see it. It's not for the uninitiated."

Landon went for logic. "Well, you're uninitiated."

She gave him the look she usually reserves for overcooked pasta. "Yes, but I am among the chosen." And then, as Landon and I stood there, Maria Pia Angelotta got intense, which is definitely her default setting, clutching the invitation to her generous breast. "Belfiere," she explained in the hushed tones usually reserved for deathbeds, "is two hundred years old. It's a"—she slanted a suspicious look at Li Wei Lin, our young Chinese dishwasher, as though she couldn't be absolutely sure he wasn't a spy—"secret society of no more than fifty chefs—all women, no men—and you can't apply to become a member. You are selected by a secret process." Her already large, expressive eyes widened. In awe, I thought. Maybe fear. Hard to tell. "And inducted in secret."

It took a lot for Landon not to roll his eyes. "We get it, Nonna, it's very hush-hush."

"Well, what do they actually do, these Belfiere ladies?" That was me.

"Do?" Nonna gasped. "Do? They don't have to 'do' anything. They just"—and here she exhaled reverently—"are."

"Well," I said, scratching my head, "are you going to have time for this—this—secret cooking club? I mean, the restaurant kind of, well, needs you." Was I crazy? Maybe Belfiere was the perfect excuse to get her out of my hair . . .

Chef Maria Pia Angelotta pulled herself up straight and gave me a stony look. "You don't understand. This is not some little club for"—her fingers twiddled the air in the Italian gesture that says *You are so inconsequential, even my fingers are bored*—"tap dancers or hairdressers." Are there really such things? "Belfiere is the greatest honor in all the world for a woman chef. If you are called," she said, rippling an eyebrow at me, "you go."

Landon got alarmed. "What do you mean you go? Is it a commune? Do you have to sell all your stuff and go live with them?" He was winding himself up, all right, but it was alarm I happened to share. "If so," he finished with a self-conscious little laugh, "I get the art deco blue mohair armchair. Please, oh, please. Just remember I'm your oldest grandchild."

He pursed his lips and I elbowed him in the ribs.

"I'm not going anywhere," she said imperiously. Then she lifted the invitation and scrutinized the printed instructions. "That's not how it works. Tomorrow will be busy. I start preparing for the special meal I cook as part of my initiation—so we'll be needing extra help."

Landon groaned. "Extra help?"

"Cooking? Serving? What do you mean?"

She waved us off, lost in a daydream about hobnobbing with her fellow wizards. "Belfiere," she said, choked up, "I can hardly believe it. I only wish Benigno had lived to see it," she finished with a magnificent sniff. Then she bit her lower lip and stared at a far corner of the ceiling. "So much to do," she said, turning away, tapping the invitation against her hand. "First thing tomorrow," she announced, "I get my Belfiere tattoo."

Tattoo?

Maria Pia Angelotta?

The woman who, on the subject of body art, runs the gamut from nausea to horror?

Little did I know that before the week was up, I'd be seeing another Belfiere tattoo—on a corpse.

If this Belfiere cooking society was enough to get my squeamish grandmother ready to run off and get inked, already I didn't like it. Neither did Landon. I could tell by the fact that in the last thirty seconds he had left traces of mint leaves and chocolate shavings in his otherwise perfect hair.

We followed her back into the dining room, where the last of the evening's customers were weighing the effort of pushing themselves off their chairs against hanging around for the first set played by the late-night regulars. Our cousin Choo Choo Bacigalupo, the maître d', dimmed the lights and smiled suggestively at his crush, our server Vera Tyndall.

Paulette and Mrs. Crawford—a mysterious pianist who I suspect was named Mrs. Crawford at birth—could tell something was afoot from Landon's hair and the fact that my black toque had fallen over my eyebrow. The two of them shot us questioning looks. Jabbing my finger at the violet invitation in Nonna's hand, I mouthed, *Get the card* at them.

Paulette improvised. "Is that a cockroach?" she exclaimed loudly, stalking over to a dark corner behind the bar, where our octogenarian bartender, Giancarlo Crespi, was slicing lemons with manic ferocity.

"Where?" gasped Maria Pia. She quickly glanced around to see what effect this discovery was having on business—zero—so she headed toward the corner still clutching the violet invitation from the good crackpots at Belfiere. There was a chance she was planning on using it to address the problem, but I looked pleadingly at Mrs. Crawford. Which was when, without a ripple of change in her expression—courtesy of a theatrical supply house—our pianist performed the arpeggio that routinely opened my grandmother's favorite song, "Three Coins in a Fountain."

All interest in an alleged cockroach evaporated.

Maria Pia fanned herself demurely with the invitation, acting as though her nightly mad interpretive dance to the fountain song had been vigorously requested by the crowd. There was no crowd. There was a red-nosed businessman hoping another split of champagne would cure the eye-rolling boredom of the young redhead with him. There was a table of five flashy women who kept trying to top each other's bad-boyfriend stories but had dressed with enough dazzle that they were probably secretly hoping those boyfriends would walk in. There was a very pregnant gal thumbing through a baby name book and disagreeing with everything her husband actually liked.

No one was clamoring for my nonna's expressive whirling that made me have to increase our insurance coverage. But, with a theatrical flourish, Maria Pia set the invitation down on an empty table and launched into the song. She got as far as "Three—" and was sucking in a big breath when our singer, Dana Cahill, came motoring up to her, shouting, "No, no, no!" At that moment, Landon oozed by the table, snagged the violet card, and disappeared into the kitchen. I knew he was heading to the office at the back, where he'd make us a copy of this piece of mail from Belfiere that was already smelling like five-day-old mackerel.

Dana smiled indulgently at Maria Pia and drew her aside, out of earshot of the late-night regulars, who appeared to be moping. "Don't you remember what week this is, M.P.?"

To which my bemused grandmother said, "Heh?"

Dana smoothed her bobbed and dyed black hair (as if it ever got wayward) and licked her vampirish red lips. At that point I noticed she was wearing a sleeveless black sheath I think I saw at Saks in the Donna Karan collection—and a black armband. Who died? Knowing Dana, it could have been the death date of some obscure Russian poet— anything to throw out there if someone asked her about the cloth around her upper arm. She chooses her dramatic effects and then digs up a plausible reason for them.

"It's Grief Week," she said in a way that reminded me of a nun in fourth grade when some poor boy couldn't name the ninth Station of the Cross.

My grandmother looked puzzled.

Dana spoke up, enunciating each syllable as though my nonna's singing her signature song was second only to the problem of her ear wax. "*Setti-man-a do-lo-ro-sa*, M.P. Grief Week." For someone wearing a black armband, she was also sporting about two pounds of gold jewelry.

I could tell Maria Pia Angelotta was close to strong-arming the slight Dana Cahill out of her way with a rebuke for keeping my nonna from her following. "I must give them"— she slapped a hand on her breast—"what they want." (In that case, Nonna, grappas all around.)

But Dana hung on to her, and went on to remind my thwarted grandmother that the third week in June honors the losses suffered—in a bizarre coincidence—by the regulars during that week. Different years, same week. It all came back to me. It was the third week in June when the clarinet's wife left him, the mandolinist's son died in a road accident, the drummer's mother succumbed to a bee sting, Giancarlo Crespi's father died on Okinawa during World War II, and Dana Cahill's basset hound, Booger, died (probably just to stop answering to that name).

So, in a show of solidarity, which annually drives away customers, the Miracolo late-night regulars take the opportunity during the third week in June to play maddeningly mournful music. If the song features justice gone awry or star-crossed love, they were all over it. And if it wasn't already down-tempo, they'd work their antimagic on it until it was.

Maria Pia glowered at the hangdog regulars who were no doubt thinking that "Three Coins in a Fountain," while full of longing, was still not appropriate for Grief Week. "Oh, all right," she spat, graciously. At which Mrs. Crawford lifted her fishnet-gloved hands from the keys and we watched the regulars launch into their first number. I had just identified it as a dirge probably played for wailing crowds at state funerals in Kazakhstan, when Dana leaned in to me. "I love what they do with 'Teen Angel,'" she whispered, scratching underneath her black armband.

Out of the corner of my eye, I saw Landon slipping the invitation from Belfiere back to the spot our Nonna had left it, just as she—with no coins to toss in a fountain, due to Grief Week—seemed to remember she had set it down, and turned to retrieve it. Landon patted his pants pocket, which I took to mean that he had stashed a copy there, and I looked at him quizzically. Blinking, he mouthed a big exaggerated "Wow!" at me. So he had read it.

I wasn't reassured. "Not sticking around for 'Ode to Billie Joe'?"

He pushed behind our grandmother and did a

tense head shake at me as he headed toward the kitchen. "Wait till you see it," he whispered.

"That bad?"

Staring, Landon kept walking. "No good can come of it," he intoned.

Between us, Landon and I managed to clear Miracolo out by 11:52 p.m., well before its usual closing time. Grief Week was just going to have to be a tad less grief-filled this year. Landon and I had crazy cooking societies to discuss before collapsing into our beds. Dana was sitting hunched on a bar stool clasping a cordless microphone and singing the final strains of her spin on "Billy Don't Be a Hero" (her third splatter platter in a row), sung as what I can only call a breathless lullaby. When one of the drummer's sticks slid off his plaid Bermuda shorts, I saw he was fast asleep.

Leo, the electric mandolin player—and the only musician regular I knew by name—was gathering up the pictures of the subjects of Grief Week from the end of the bar, which had become a shrine. Pictures of a swaybacked basset hound apparently wondering what the hell was wrong with the human who would name him Booger. A young marathoner. An out-of-focus shot of a crew-cut GI caught mugging for the camera on a beach in the

South Pacific. A stiff wedding shot of the clarinet-ist and his bride, who had eyes for the best man. A long-haired girl in a purple miniskirt holding her young son in one arm and pointing out a zoo giraffe with the other.

Maria Pia was carried along with the rest of the staff, who warbled their good nights, and I finally gave Dana a little shove, which she interpreted as some kind of Girlfriend Gesture and responded affectionately with "Oh, you!" But at least she went out the door. Landon killed the lights, I locked up, and together we headed across Market Square to Jolly's Pub, which stays open until 2 a.m.

The downtown commercial district in Quaker Hills, Pennsylvania, consists of shops and businesses lined up on all four sides of the three-acre green space called Providence Park. Right across the street from us is Jolly's Pub, owned by a second-generation Brit named Reginald Jolly, who, if you happen to come during the slow period, between lunch and happy hour, you might catch trimming his pencil moustache. I think of him as the anti–Maria Pia—he's as inscrutable and self-controlled as she is generally Out There. They approach each other warily, which is wise, and not often.

Landon flicked open the top two buttons of his shirt as we loped across Market Square and headed straight across the park. My little hemp tote

slapped against my right hip as I dodged benches
and playground equipment. "Hi, Akahana," I
called to our wandering Japanese philosopher, who
was stretched out on the kiddie slide, reading by
the halogen light of a headlamp. I could tell by her
grunt that she was pondering the origins of consciousness, her favorite late-night activity.

The entire front wall of Jolly's Pub had been
buzzed up and out of sight, like a garage door, and
the drinking crowd had spilled out to scattered
tables fronting Market Square. Inside was a long
bar that gleamed like a grand piano and café tables holding battery-op candles that even flickered
like the real thing. No Grief Week on this side
of the square. Glasses clinked. Voices topped each
other. Late-night laughter sounded like surf. The
scent of Scotch perfumed the summer air. Floating close to the tin ceiling was the sound of Bob
Dylan singing "Subterranean Homesick Blues."
Maybe I could just hang out at Jolly's for the rest
of Grief Week.

Landon and I grabbed a table, signaled two short
ones to Jeanette, the bartender, and we sat. Listing
over to one hip, he teased the copy of the Belfiere invitation from his pants pocket. Landon is probably
my best friend and the closest thing I'll ever have
to a brother in this lifetime. After my mom died
when I was nine and my father—Maria Pia's oldest

son, Jock—took off for parts unknown when I was fifteen, Landon's dad gave me a home, partly to keep me out of his mother's clutches. It almost worked.

He slid the paper across the table to me.

My fingers walked over to it and slowly drew it back toward me.

After about three seconds, Landon erupted into fits of exhaled air and pulled his chair around so he was shoulder to shoulder with me. I smiled at him. Bullets leave guns slower than my beloved cousin reaches the limits of his patience. "Oh, here," he cried, as if I'd bungled the unfolding. In what looked like one motion, he unfolded the copy of the Belfiere invitation, smoothed out the creases, and spun it to face me.

Centered across the top was what looked like a coat of arms. To me, the shield was shaped like a funnel, which I suppose made more sense than something you'd carry into battle. Even on the worst days, the kitchen at Miracolo didn't get *that* bad. In the upper-right quadrant were three silver knives with identical ebony handles laid side by side. A carmine-colored slash ran diagonally from there down to the lower-left quadrant, where a black mortar and pestle was pictured. Running below the funnel-shield was a scroll with the words *Numquam Nimis Multi Cultri*. Possibly Latin for Crazy Cooking Club?

And then I read:

The Society of Belfiere
~ honoring the gustatory delights of life and death ~
welcomes you as a member
You will first undertake to receive the traditional 3cm *B*
tattoo in Bastarda font on the wrist of your stirring hand
You will prepare an exclusive evening meal for 50 guests
on Friday, June 20, at 9 p.m.
You will provide yourself with the traditional Belfiere
gown in midnight-blue satin for your induction
on Sunday, June 22, at 10 p.m.
at 7199 Gallows Hill Drive
Pendragon, Pennsylvania
You must arrive and depart alone
You must perform all instructions faithfully
and
In all things pertaining to Belfiere you must observe
omertà
We are 200 years old and our traditions are known only
to ourselves
In matters of our history we are Clotho
In matters of ourselves we are Lachesis
In matters of food we are Atropos
We are Belfiere

I shuddered.

"I know!" whispered Landon, his green eyes wide. Then he waved the paper under my nose.

Our Scotch arrived—Laphroaig for me, Oban

for Landon. We were staring at the amber liquid while Dylan sounded so close he might have been at the very next table, and for sure he was the only one at Jolly's making any kind of sense. *You don't need a weatherman to know which way the wind blows*. Whatever this whole Belfiere thing was, Maria Pia Angelotta had unquestioningly bought into it, so the prosciutto was about to hit the fan.

"Our fortress has been breached," I told Landon moodily, picking up my drink.

"The barbarians are at the gates," said Landon, lifting his drink, adding, "and they are *so* wearing last year's fashions."

"Dwelling on the line about the midnight blue?"

"Well"—he lifted his elegant shoulders—"coupled with the satin . . ." and he punctuated his scorn with a little sound that went something like *"Puh!"*

I took one sip I let slosh from side to side, then knocked back the rest. As I winced and writhed, I got out, "I mean, what's their brand? On the one hand, bastard tattoo fonts—"

"On the other," said Landon, sipping, "an elegant dinner for fifty. I agree. And girlfriend"—he slipped an arm around me—"let's not even touch the"—here his voice dropped—"*omertà* line."

Omertà is the code of silence. Usually reserved for certain Italian neighborhoods. Usually understood as the cost of doing business with certain Italian businessmen. Or getting the business from certain Italian businessmen. Violating *omertà* is usually punishable by listening to Dana Cahill sing Motown. But the fact that Belfiere members were bound by this code of silence gave me the kind of creeps that had nothing to do with Sandor the toothless floor mat delivery guy offering to try out the mat together. "And then," he always finishes with a leer, "let's see what happens."

I signaled for a second shot. "There's a lot of death talk in this invitation," I pointed out to my cousin. "*Omertà*, the Three Fates—"

Landon snatched the paper. "'The gustatory delights of . . . death.'" He shivered. "What are they talking about? What are those?"

Indeed. I waved around my empty shot glass.

Landon went on, "Is it some kind of depression support group?"

"Or do they believe in some kind of epicurean afterlife, or—"

Landon caught my drift. "Or . . . does Belfiere 'help' you on your way? Is it an assisted suicide cult?"

My eyes roamed the walls of Reginald Jolly's pub, which featured framed map reproductions of England all the way back to when it was called Anglia and centurions only dreamed of a future that held pizza. Why all the enforced silence, the secrecy, the mystery, the lonely initiation ceremony out somewhere in the boondocks? What had Nonna gotten herself into? Yes, there were times when I wanted to kill her, but that was my own rightful fantasy, not anyone else's.

When I fell off the stage of the New Amsterdam Theatre on October 23, 2009, where I was in the chorus of *Mary Poppins*, and I broke my leg, I needed a living. And Miracolo is like a hereditary obligation. We Angelottas have been pounding veal senseless for the past eighty years. That alone is the "miracle"—that we're still cooking, still making money, still not throttling each other. So I caved. And I cooked. Caved and cooked. Nonna purred for weeks.

Finally declaring the Miracolo culinary tradition safe in my hands, she announced she was retiring. The rest of us—which included vendors, customers, and neighboring shop owners—feigned everything from disbelief to operatic distress at the news. Little did we know that my nonna's idea of retirement pretty much meant having none of the actual responsibilities of the restaurant while still being every bit as annoyingly present as before, telling Landon he chops like a girl, or Choo Choo that goatees are all fine, well, and good for quadrupeds, and me that I could sell my gnocchi to anyone in the mob looking for the perfect thing to tie to, oh, something they want to keep from floating.

But she was our nonna. She gave me a job when my whole dancing career fell off the stage right along with me. And to this day I am still pretty sure she didn't push me. But late that night on the day Maria Pia received a command—for that's really what it was, not an invitation—to tattoo herself with the sign of allegiance, to feed fifty all dressed alike in a Belfiere costume, to show up alone and friendless for a strange initiation ritual, and to understand the absolute need for secrecy . . . danger prickled my skin like the humid June night. I didn't like any of it. Not one bit.

Finally, without looking up at Landon, I spoke slowly. "Or is Belfiere . . . a murder club?"

2

By 10 a.m., with a mug full of French roast and a chocolate croissant on board, I checked in with Landon, who had already done an online search for Belfiere—surprise, no website. This group sounded like you'd have to pry it open with a crowbar, so these were not folks who hoped to entice visitors to click on their history, their members, their projects, their photo gallery, or driving directions to Dracula's Castle.

While he talked, I watered my blue geraniums on the grass next to the little two-by-two-foot porch of my Tumbleweed Tiny House, parked on its utility trailer on a patch I rent on a lot owned by a Philly choreographer I know. One hundred thirty square feet of living space, cedar siding, tin roof—by me, that's as much home ownership as I can stand.

Like Landon, I had spent the morning with my laptop, slowly chasing down even the slightest of hits on the word *Belfiere*. I found a Bruno Belfiere, a self-styled poet in Bayonne, New Jersey. I found a chichi hair salon in Dubuque, Iowa. I found a Bargello pattern on a handicrafts website. And I found an AKC prize-winning English bulldog in Charleston, South Carolina. But there were still a few more hits to check out.

Landon had more luck. He did a reverse lookup from the White Pages—"Am I the sleuth, or what?"—and came up with a resident at 7199 Gallows Hill Drive, Pendragon, Pennsylvania.

One name: Fina Parisi.

Then Googling the name Fina Parisi showed him, at least, that we were in the right ballpark. The Parisi woman competed in a past season of *Top Chef* (she lost the elimination challenge because she had never seen a grit, let alone cooked one) and is part owner of a French restaurant in Larchmont, New York. While living in Larchmont (Did she retire and move to Pendragon? And was it a problem I had never heard of this town?), she served on a committee to raise funds to build a school garden in Bardstown, Kentucky. She was trained at the International Culinary Center in Parma, Italy. Back in the early eighties she played lacrosse in high school on Long Island. She voted Independent, donated regularly to Heifer International, took fencing lessons for the past seven years and preferred foil to épée, and was a sucker for dachshunds.

Well, neither Landon nor I could find fault with any of these pursuits and accomplishments—and the dachshund thing seemed particularly sane—but we decided our pal Fina Parisi could use a closer look. Perhaps she was just letting the Crackpot Cooking Society use her home for a meeting or two. Or, all right, all right, maybe Belfiere is just a bunch of harmless, doddering old chefs who had turned in their toques for wide-brimmed hats with fake peonies. Maybe the secret sign was raised pinkies over china cups of English breakfast tea. Maybe Belfiere was just a kind of Junior League for old cooks and Maria Pia wasn't in any danger.

And then I remembered their coat of arms: three knives on what looked like a field the color of dried blood. Landon and I would keep digging, dachshunds aside. After hanging up, I threw on my work clothes, the "Miracolo look," which consisted of sleek summer-weight black pants and (only because it would be hidden beneath my chef jacket) a deep V-neck, ruffled white blouse you could probably kind of see through even if you were standing in a dark room. I added a black single-breasted suit jacket and—grabbing my brand-new, too expensive leather portfolio—headed out the door.

I had business out at the Quaker Hills Career Center, and I wanted to get it done before needing to turn up at the restaurant for a day in the life.

Cranking up the A/C, I picked up County Highway 8, thinking about how I'd got roped into a new gig. Even though our nonna retired from cooking when I stepped up after my accident, Choo Choo says she's still adjusting to a reduced role in the world of Miracolo. Maybe that explains her bedazzled response to the invitation from the Crackpot Chef Club, aka Belfiere. And true, her boyfriend had wound up murdered just three weeks earlier, which left our nonna with some time on her French manicured hands.

But for years now Landon and I have watched Maria Pia Angelotta do mortally embarrassing interpretive dance to the music provided by our ragtag group of late-night regulars and wonder how Choo Choo defines "reduced role." But he tends to take a more generous view of the grandmother we share. I think, in retrospect, that Choo Choo Bacigalupo's relaxed attitude toward everyone and everything is what explains why I was now swinging my beloved old blue Volvo sedan into the parking lot at the Quaker Hills Career Center, where they teach firefighting, welding, computers, welding computers, whatever "automotive technologies" may be, and . . . cooking.

Falling in love with Vera Tyndall, one of our servers, led the three-hundred-pound Choo Choo Bacigalupo to join Weight Watchers. Losing ten pounds pretty quickly led to his receiving a Bravo Sticker at his weekly meeting and deciding there was nothing he could not reasonably do. But with Choo Choo, "doing something" invariably meant getting someone else to do something. I could practically see his thoughts writ large on the black-board of his brain: a fine two-hundred-ninety-pound example of a male Bacigalupo would now undertake to give back to the community.

Just how this played out was by Choo Choo's talking me—whose vision of civic-mindedness consists of not throttling my nonna— into teach-ing a four-week cooking class through the Quaker Hills Career Center. He wheedled, he cajoled, he invoked *Stand and Deliver*, he referenced *To Sir with Love*, he was majestic in describing what he deemed my moral obligation to pass on my gifts to the noncooking youth of America. Here's how I heard the bottom line: I could earn a pittance and impart my skills to a few less-than-stellar students who would rather be watching Paula Deen. For reasons still very murky to me, all this sounded as good as Landon's creamy *panna cotta*, and I signed on.

I'd like to say it was the beginning of the end.

But that would be an understatement. And unfair to the problem of Belfiere.

So, before I had to turn up at Miracolo to receive the day's order of farm-fresh produce from my second cousin the flaky Kayla Angelotta, owner of a farm she calls Kale and Kayla Organics, which tells you something about what she considers clever, I entered an office labeled *Admin*. There, a fifty-year-old woman with beauty parlor pouffed hair and a pink polo shirt emblazoned with *Quaker Hills Career Center* like it was a muffler shop, handed me my class list for Cooking Basics (taught apparently by someone called Staff).

I wondered if Choo Choo got a finder's fee for delivering me.

When I asked her whether there would be an orientation for new faculty, she stared me down. "You get paid on the fifteenth and thirtieth of the month," she said. "Keep your valuables with you at all times. If you leave it, you grieve it." Then: "Consider yourself oriented."

"And"—here I was winging it—"if I need to consult with the dean of students . . . ?"

"Well, that would be someone at some other institution," she drawled, getting all fake-sincere, "so you might have a hard time getting an appointment."

At which I gathered up my papers—well, paper, since all Muffler Miss, whose desk nameplate said she was Courtney Harrington, had given me was the class list (personally, I was thinking this *strega*—Italian for witch—had stuffed what was left of the real Courtney Harrington in a foot locker)—and slid them professionally into my portfolio. Then I fake-smiled her right back and headed out to the parking lot. Inside the car I studied the names like they held the secret of spinning straw into gold:

Renay Bassett
Frederick Faust
Will Jaworski
Slash Kipperman
Georgia Payne
Corabeth Potts
Mitchell Terranova
L'Shondra Washington

Eight lovelies. Mitchell would be the class clown. Corabeth would be the shy violet. Renay would be secretly pining for Will, who would be the quarterback—wait, did the career center have a football team? Just as I was sliding into a sweet little reverie about which of my brood would be the first to set a polished red apple on my desk, I checked the time, yelped, and headed lickety-split back to town.

It's not that I was worried I'd miss cousin Kayla's

delivery, it's that I was worried she'd get there and just hang out in my restaurant without adult supervision. The last time that happened she had a three-night fling with my lawyer, Joe Beck. And the time before that she managed to set off the sprinkler system. I don't know which infraction made me madder.

Sure, water everywhere was a mess and a nuisance, so that was bad. But Joe Beck was, well, Joe Beck—kind of the human equivalent of Landon's best cassata cakes, and someone I think deserves better than a woman whose conversation runs from how garlic has a soul to the best time she ever had in the back of the Kale and Kayla Organics van with a man. (This account changes monthly.)

I have no personal interest in the Beck Stakes, really, because although he came in reasonably handy when Nonna was arrested for murder, (a) I don't think it's wise to give a new meaning to the term legal aid, (b) I couldn't get the visions out of my head of my lawyer finding organic things to do with the flaky Kayla that had nothing to do with farming, and, well, (c) I don't think he likes me.

During a drowsy afternoon of dinner preparations, the day after the Belfiere invitation arrived—and the day before I was scheduled to walk into a classroom at the Quaker Hills Career Center—Choo Choo found me in the kitchen, thumbing through our collection of family recipes, hunting for an entrée special for the next day. The summer sunlight crowded through the skylight and I could watch sun specks dance in the steady thrum of the circulating fan. I really wasn't getting very much done.

"You got eight," he announced cryptically, smoothing his cuffs. I looked up. "I checked online." Li Wei was perched on his stool, reading a book on the history of video games. Sometimes he just shows up when he's off the clock—I think it started after Choo Choo called him an honorary Angelotta and stenciled *Lee Way* on the back of his stool.

Landon was humming away—the clear sign that he's experimenting—while grinding and toasting a pound of shelled hazelnuts. Since his signature dish, *panna cotta*, was on the specials menu for that night, I was betting the toasted nuts were destined for the creamy custard. He caught my eye at Choo Choo's cryptic announcement that I had eight. Ever since he developed an effervescent crush on our sommelier, the delectable Jonathan, Landon has promised me that—unlike Choo Choo—*he* would not celebrate any romantic success by casting his beloved Eve into the Great Unknown. Then he wisely made himself scarce while Choo Choo's Give Back to the Community phase flourished.

"Eight what?" For a second I worried he was referring to zits, but I couldn't figure out how that observation would have made it to one of the popular cyber-squeal places yet. But with the fan lazily spreading golden sun specks and the aroma of toasted hazelnuts, I hardly cared. If there's a heaven and it doesn't include toasted nuts, then it's not what it's cracked up to be.

"Students," said my scrupulously bald cousin. The tip of his Weight Watchers Weekly Tracker peeked over the top of his breast pocket.

"I know. I picked up my class list. Is eight good?"

"Well . . ." He narrowed his eyes and looked like he was pondering the third law of thermodynamics while Li Wei elegantly turned a page and Landon's fingers fussed. Then Choo Choo came to a conclusion. One strong, black-sleeved arm swung open one of the double doors leading back out to the Miracolo dining room. Where was he going?

Out of the corner of my eye I caught sight of Maria Pia, dressed in one of her signature Lucy Ricardo dresses she "summered up" with a wide cinch belt in Florida pink, talking to herself as she motored around the cool, dark dining room with a clipboard, her right hand looking like a big paw in a glove, planning what Landon and I were calling Friday's "hazing" meal for the Belfiere cultoids.

The fact that she appeared to be weeping quietly had nothing to do with Grief Week and everything to do with the trip with Choo Choo to the tattoo parlor in Philly that morning. She had returned with every spray, lotion, powder, cream, and ointment in a product line called Ink-Me-Gentle, designed to settle down skin with a new tat. These, Choo Choo reported, she applied simultaneously, then pulled up one of Choo Choo's biker gloves to cover the site. Choo Choo thought the *B* in Bastarda tattoo font really looked very nice.

So Nonna was inked, which was more than I could say about myself.

If Landon and I were going to bring her to her senses about goofy cooking societies, we were going to have to act fast.

I got impatient. "Well, what, Chooch?" I called after him. "Is eight good?"

"Well," said Choo Choo, an octave higher, "it's probably a very good thing, considering four of them"— he turned and was already halfway out of the kitchen—"are from cribs."

And he was gone.

Four of them are from cribs? How young does the Quaker Hills Career Center take them? I looked at Landon, who wrinkled his nose at me—he didn't have the answer—and even Li Wei shrugged, without so much as a glance. Me, I turned back to a page of ziti recipes, wondering if there was anything at all I could do with penne pasta that did not involve either baking or chilling. Stuff them with hazelnuts? No? Almonds, then?

What with a new gig looming as a college (Was it fair to say?) professor, I could feel myself sliding into a weird think-outside-the-recipe-box mood. *Don't just anticipate the unexpected . . . create it.* Let that be the motto for Professor Eve Angelotta, undergraduate dance major at Sarah Lawrence, chef by default.

So, it was in that mood on a lazy summer afternoon at Miracolo that I decided that my four young students out of cribs were just precocious. Supersmart and keen to chop. Yes, that was it. Fresh off solving the murder of Nonna's boyfriend, I chuckled softly, what *couldn't* I handle? Eve Angelotta: Pasta professor. Crime solver. Handler of grandmothers. Broken-legged chorus girl. Maker of cannoli to die for.

All terribly important skills.

As Landon, humming, let hazelnut morsels fall through his long fingers, I could tell we were both luxuriating in our little lives and jobs and sexual fantasies. Without so much as a word, we kissed the air near each other's cheeks. I stretched, ran my fingers through my wavy auburn hair, and believed in that moment at 1:23 p.m. that my world was under, well, control.

I'm glad I noted the time.

Control of my world was about to disappear as fast as Landon's brand-new *panna cotta alla nocciole*—hazelnut custard.

While cousin Kayla, dressed in her light patchwork overalls and gossamer pink top—how does the woman actually farm?—argued with Landon over the day's botched delivery, Nonna breezed into the kitchen with her mascara smeared and her clipboard clapped awkwardly against her chest with her non-bear-paw left hand. To the others she delivered one solemn nod; to me she murmured, "Eve, please," and jerked her head toward the Miracolo office down the short corridor at the back.

Dutifully, I followed her and closed the door behind us as she tottered over to the white oak and mahogany desk near the wood-shuttered window on the far wall. She collapsed into the leather swivel chair with a squeak. I couldn't tell if it was her or the chair. Blinking, she set her right hand on the desk, where it lay there looking like a Darth Vader body part, and she went on to ignore it. Like it was somebody else's paw, somebody else's tattoo, somebody else's mound of creams and ointments.

In her left hand she held a fountain pen as though it was a dart, that's how unfamiliar that hand was with writing tools. "Here is the menu for my special meal for"—she actually looked around like possibly Li Wei had slipped into the closet—"you-know-what this Friday night." She glanced at her clipboard.

I listened as she rattled off in a single breath what sounded like Scallop Fritters with Roasted Chioggia Beet Carpaccio, Sestri Salad with Grappa and Fig Vinaigrette, Saffron Risotto alla Milanese, Saltimbocca, and Granita di Caffè con Panna. At which she drew a breath, pushed back her lustrous salt and pepper hair with her Darth Vader mitt, and waited for a comment from me. Her expression was a blend of haughty and fearful. I suggested adding some *biscotti all'anaci*, as the anise flavor would blend nicely with the coffee sherbet. Otherwise, I told her with a respectful dip of my head, a gorgeous menu.

"Grazie," she whispered. Then she rambled incoherently about how we'd need at least two other servers and another rock solid sous chef for Friday night, no arguments. Although my mind was whirring along figuring the net loss of providing fine, free eats to Nonna's new sorority—not to mention all the lost revenue from other customers, considering we'd have to close for the evening; not to mention having to pay three extra staff for this gig—I said, "Of course" without a hint of good Italian ire in my voice.

She seemed relieved.

"Let me see your tattoo, Nonna," I said, stepping closer.

She looked pained, but extended the mitt to me and turned her head away. I slipped off Choo Choo's black biker glove and pushed aside a layer of white Ink-Me-Gentle goop, and there it was. An artistic three-centimeter blue *B* in what was apparently Bastarda font. I toggled my head as I gently rotated her wrist. "I think it looks good, Nonna." With one fingertip I slid the goop back over the tattoo and eased the mitt back into place. "It'll heal, you know."

Her whimper seemed doubtful on that score.

I found myself wondering if she was regretting her invitation to join Belfiere. Very slowly, I started to ask, "Nonna—do you—"

She held up the mitt. "Don't even say it, Eve. As if I could—ever—ever—as if a little tattoo is enough to make me—" At that I lost her in a flutter of eye blinks.

"Okay, okay. I get it."

She gained strength. She snorted. She was back.

Then I crossed my arms. "Landon found out who lives at 7199 Gallows Hill Drive in Pendragon."

Suddenly my nonna went red in the face and started to stagger to her feet. "You looked?" She sounded like she had just washed up on a desert island and was struggling to catch her breath. "You read my invitation? Shame on you! Shame—"

In another minute she'd wrestle with a desire to slap me with a lusty *malocchio*—an Italian curse that generally explains sudden and intractable cases of warts and hairlessness. Mind you, not even Little Serena, that happy heretic, had deserved a *malocchio*. When the "other" granddaughter declared she Didn't Cook—"Why the hell should I spend the time making food when I can just pay for the food other people cook like, say, at the Kroger's?"— Maria Pia was so distressed that she actually looked for a support group for Fine Italian Chefs Whose Grandchildren Don't Cook. She ranted when she couldn't find one, and it was the closest she ever came to burning a *risotto alla Milanese*, but even then she wasn't flinging around *malocchio*s.

Finally, when nothing seemed to help, Little Serena Bacigalupo got flung into Maria Pia's blind spot. It's not that she forgot her. It's kind of like the blind spot in the car when you're driving down the highway. You know that motorcycle's there; you

just can't see it. I was pretty sure a grandchild—
any grandchild—lived in a *malocchio*-free zone, so
I didn't hesitate to tell Nonna about eyeballing her
invitation from Belfiere.

"Nonna!" I said firmly. "Landon and I have
your back whether you like it or not. In fact," I
added, "whether we like it or not."

She narrowed her eyes. "You must never divulge
what you—"

I waved a hand at her. "Fine, fine, no problem,
believe me."

Even though she was squirming in her chair, she
gave me the eyelash flutter that always tells me she
knows she's either lying or about to tell me something she knows I'll hate. "I am telling the staff"—
here she laid the mitt against her chin and tried to
look dignified—"that Friday evening we're entertaining my"—flutter, flutter—"mah-jongg club."

I slapped my forehead. "Mah-jongg club?
Nonna, you don't even play mah-jongg."

She tried to fold her hands and gave up. "They
don't know that." I was about to make a crackpot
pitch for honesty, but then she added, "You read
the invitation, shame on you. So you saw the line
about *omertà*. I just don't know how far it goes. So
I'm not taking any chances."

She had a point. Mah-jongg club it is, then.
"As for the owner of the house where you're being

initiated . . ." I had her complete attention. "The name is Fina Parisi."

With a sudden step backward, Nonna landed in the leather swivel chair. "Are you sure?"

Something changed, but I couldn't tell what, exactly. My eyes slid away from her, trying to understand what was different. "Yes. Fina Parisi," I repeated. "That's the name."

Maria Pia Angelotta gazed past me. "So," she said finally, barely above a whisper, "Fina Parisi is La Maga of Belfiere."

"The what?"

"La Maga. The chef of all chefs." Her brown eyes closed softly. "The supreme conjuror of gustatory delights—"

"Ah, of life and death."

She shot me a dark look. "La Maga is in charge for three years. And chosen"—here my nonna indicated something rather mysterious with her big mitt—"in a very complicated process."

"Let me guess. Is it secret?"

She squared her shoulders. "You have no respect."

"I have respect, Nonna. When it's something that lets me look at it. But not this. Not Belfiere. I'm sorry," I temporized. "Not yet."

But my grandmother wasn't listening to me. Instead, she had a faraway look in her eye. "Fina Parisi," she said slowly, her voice dripping in a thin stream like melted chocolate into Landon's ricotta pudding.

I lifted my chin. "Who is she?"

"Fina Parisi," said Maria Pia Angelotta, looking me with a strangely neutral expression, "is that *strega* Belladonna Russo's daughter."

Belladonna Russo, who owns a restaurant in New Brunswick, New Jersey, is Nonna's culinary archenemy. Exactly how this came to be so, I'm not sure. All I know for a fact was that they trained together and the bad blood began in their Advanced Sauces class. There was an unfortunate hair-pulling incident followed by a takedown in a puddle of flung béchamel sauce.

Now, the fact that the daughter of this archenemy happened to head up the Crazy Cooking Club at the precise time when Maria Pia Angelotta was invited to join was somewhat worrisome to me. Was Nonna being set up? And, if so, set up for what? I was baffled, all right, but fencing and dachshunds aside, Fina Parisi screamed for more digging. Why, after all, was this Fina person—a *Top Chef* finalist, after all—living kind of in our neighborhood? Bucks County, Pennsylvania, is a little far from where Fina Parisi has a part interest in an upscale place in Larchmont.

Landon, who had disappeared for a while, came back a little later than he usually shows up for work, and he was toting his laptop. Since Maria Pia had gone home early to call vendors for the Friday-evening soirée—she insisted it had nothing to do with avoiding all the merriment of Grief Week here at Miracolo—the office was empty. Landon was looking freshly showered and shaved, but so quiet and distracted that even a megawatt smile from the delectable Jonathan got little more than a thin smile from my cousin. And when no Fosse steps find their way into whatever he's doing with a utility knife or spatula, I know something's amiss in Landon Land.

At a break in the mid-evening reservations, Landon touched my shoulder and led me back to the sumptuous brown leather couch in the office. The very scene of the crime where Kayla Angelotta had consulted my lawyer Joe Beck on matters of sex. Landon and I sat, knee to knee, and he powered up the laptop, basking in the Wi-Fi. "Look what I found," he said, tapping quickly across the keyboard.

"What?"

"I decided to try different ways of spelling Belfiere, just in case we were missing something, you know?"

I nodded.

"When I typed in Belfiere and spelled it with a

final *i*, here's what I got." He scrolled down. "Well, it's a blog for victims of cults. Nothing very official. Just a cyber support group." Landon turned the screen to face me. "Here's a post from a couple of years ago. It's still up."

I scanned it quickly, saw it was signed "Anna T.," and then—with my heart pounding—I read what she had to tell us about Belfiere:

OMG I think I'm going to die, I think they'll come after me, they're so crazycrazycrazy. I couldn't take it anymore at the meeting last night when they were doing the poison guessing game or whatever they call it in Belfieri when you have to decide which dish has the poison only by smelling and looking and then you actually have to taste one of the other dishes!!! And then that one member collapsed and I started screaming. I think they know they made a mistake with me but they never let you go, never let you go, and all I could do was run. I'm too scared to go to the police because of the code of silence. The next day there was nothing in the papers, I looked, nothing online, nothing anywhere about the member who fell over and died. What did they do with her? OMG what did they do with her?

3

"Eve!" came a voice from very far away. "Eve! Snap out of it already!" It was Paulette and she clamped a hand around the pastry tube I was apparently using to squeeze Kahlúa cream over a veal chop. Which was pretty much how the rest of the evening went in the Miracolo kitchen after the revelation of Anna T.'s hysterical blog post. Landon wasn't doing much better, ladling pomodoro sauce over an order of tiramisu. There are truly limits to what you can reasonably expect from heavenly San Marzano tomatoes.

The customer actually liked what Paulette explained as *vitello alla Kahlúa*.

All I could think of was the "poison guessing game" Anna T. had mentioned. Nonna had a pretty good nose, but it was, after all, a seventy-six-year-old schnoz and maybe not quite up to the deadly task, flared nostrils aside. And if you could tell poison just by looks and smell, you really have to wonder what accounts for so many murder-by-poison victims over the centuries. No, Belfiere wasn't just dangerous—there was something downright, oh, nihilistic about them. They set up life-threatening outcomes (the delights of death) out of some conviction that nothing means anything. Not even beautiful food. So, in Belfiere World, bring it on. Guess the poison. No? Wrong? Thrill to the dire pleasures of your fatal mistake.

These are people I do not understand.

When Paulette wiped her feverish brow with a white linen napkin and announced the last of the dinner crowd, I sank quivering against my Vulcan stove and pulled off my toque. Dragging my sorry legs through air that felt strangely like wet concrete, I found my way over to Landon, who was collapsed at the waist over the stainless steel prep table. Worn out, we clung to each other and whimpered just a little. I told him I was going to call Joe Beck for advice. And Landon told me he'd have Paulette close up for the night. Neither of us could bear the thought of getting through an evening of Dana Cahill and Grief Week.

I grabbed my hemp bag from the hook and found my way along the south side of Market

Square to my Volvo. I felt strangely aware of my hips and totally unaware of my legs—the way you usually do when you're trying to ambulate on the wrong side of four drinks—and I made it to the car, falling into the front seat. No drinks, but no dinner, either. I tugged open the glove compartment, figuring on downing my emergency stash of pico de gallo chips. Empty. Empty. The universe is just that cruel.

Driving home was a slow and pathetic process as my eyes strayed to what seemed like every circle of streetlights hazy and swollen from the humidity. I was never so happy to see my Tumbleweed Tiny House, and the peaceful rasp of the crickets was all the welcome I needed. It wasn't until I locked the door behind me and climbed up to my sleeping loft in the dark that I called Joe Beck. I needed another head on this whole Belfiere thing. Not just another head—I needed Joe Beck's. What could we do to keep Maria Pia out of the sick clutches of these homicidal cooks?

Answer, answer, I willed him, flat out on my mattress, my eyes crinkled against the shadowy sight of the slowly rotating ceiling fan.

No Joe.

No Joe.

I was unreasonably disappointed. Then I got his voice mail, which made me wonder what he was doing at 10:45 p.m. that he couldn't answer his phone. I refused to let the image of my flaky cousin Kayla wave like seaweed into my consciousness. "Joe," I said, going for a got-my-act-together voice I hoped would entice him to call me back, "It's Eve. Got a problem"—damn, my voice broke at that understatement—"and I need your advice ASAP." Sound breezy, no big deal, tomorrow, day after, whenever, bro. "Joe, I really need the help," I squeezed out before my throat tightened right up and the "thanks" that came out was just a pathetic squeak. I'm pretty sure I managed to hang up. And then the unthinkable happened . . .

I fell asleep.

Day One of summer session at the Quaker Hills Career Center. After a restless night—and no return call from my erstwhile lawyer—I stood with my eyes closed in my tiny shower and just let the hot spray rain all over me. It was definitely a day when that shiny red polished apple was needed. Anything for the sake of distraction from the problem of Belfiere and my brainwashed nonna. Come on, Mitchell Terranova, make me laugh. Okay, little Corabeth, don't be afraid, I bite only shiny red polished apples. And Renay, honey, strictly between us, all you're missing with Will is him as a fat forty-year-old who yells from the bleachers at your kid's coach.

I had much to share beyond knife skills and basic sauces.

For my first day's outfit I chose a teal blouse with a decent V-neck and a white skirt that had some nice flow to it, and I threw my white chef jacket and toque into the car. Munching a rice cake slathered with peanut butter, I backed out of my gravel parking spot and headed out Highway 8, thinking how best to handle the likes of Courtney Harrington should I run into her. The Belfiere poison guessing game came to mind. I figured I had an edge over Courtney. And I have to say, it was a bit of a kick to see a full parking lot at QHCC and realize I had a part in it.

Clutching my pricey portfolio—which held my syllabus and my personal set of knives—I struggled into my jacket and headed for the front door. As a couple of others dashed by me, I flung around my slumming-aristocrat smile, then I found my way through a maze of hallways, wondering why nobody seemed to be around. Finally, I stood outside the closed door of Room 12, labeled Kitchen Classroom.

"Angelotta!" barked someone.

Let me guess.

I turned. Courtney Harrington came power-walking toward me. Was there more to my new faculty orientation than she remembered yesterday?

"You're twenty minutes late! What've you got, Cookie Girl, a PhD? Think this gang will wait around for you?"

I jerked my wrist up to my face: Ten-twenty a.m. "But class starts at ten-thirty!" Was she going to give me a detention? Could she do that?

"Half an hour earlier on day one. Didn't you read the employee handbook? Very nice," she said in an oily way and breezed right past me.

"What employee handbook?" I called after her. *Strega.*

She disappeared around a corner.

I squared my shoulders, held my portfolio in what could only be considered a professional way, and with my hand gripping the doorknob, took that moment to consider my opening remarks. *Good morning, I'm Chef Eve Angelotta of Miracolo Italian Restaurant, and I'll be teaching you Basic Cooking Skills.* Reliable, informative, maybe a little predictable. Or I could go with *'Sup, dudes, and the name is Eve— we're gonna chop till we drop, you better believe.* That one was younger and hipper than I ever was. But maybe Renay Bassett and the others didn't need to know that.

Maybe there was a third alternative . . .

Undecided, I took a big breath and swung open the door to the Kitchen Classroom.

Which was when a bunch of lighted matches, arcing through the air, damn near hit me.

Over the next ten seconds I hooted and yelped as half the class fell out laughing. Landon would be so proud: I did a whole routine of Fosse sidesteps just trying to keep my clothes from catching on fire. I felt wild-eyed, watching the final match burn itself out and fall to the floor. With one hand I slammed my portfolio down on the prep table and clapped the other to my chest. Someone whistled. After a second of catching my breath, I ditched my first two choices for opening remarks and went with a third alternative.

I don't know what I was saying, but it was mostly in Italian, which I discovered wasn't as rusty as I had thought, and partly in some Mandarin dialect. Apparently everyone in Room 12 had had at least two semesters of both languages at Quaker Hills Career Center because they seemed to understand everything. I do think it helped that I punctuated my remarks with repeatedly slamming my portfolio on the prep table with both hands and gritted teeth. When teaching on the postsecondary level, it's very important to use visual aids whenever possible.

A series of knocks at the door was followed by the visage of Courtney Harrington, who—much to my satisfaction—looked a little pale. She asked if everything was all right. I shot her the dazzling smile I usually reserve for third dates that are going exceptionally well and explained that we were just going over the ground rules—good group, good group— and that my first impression was that my pupils were afire with a desire for knowledge. (Behind me, nervous laughter.) Muttering, she disappeared, and when I was absolutely sure she had power-walked her way out of earshot, I turned on them.

There were enough face piercings in that room to melt down and fashion into everyday flatware for the White House. In addition, there were a couple of studded collars and at least one leather corset. Wordlessly, I opened the box of my personal knives, chose one, held it up to the light, and then plunged it into the butcher block. There were a few gasps. Mine included.

Then I handed the class list to a small blonde who looked a little older than the others and seemed to have some self-control. Which was more than I could say for myself at that moment. "Read it, please." My eyes slid over the others. "When you hear your name called"—here I flicked the knife just enough to keep it swaying, then crossed my arms—"tell me who's responsible for the matches."

You could have heard a burning match drop, the place got so silent.

The blonde started down the list. *Renay Bassett*, she read out nice and loud. Like she was bringing charges against Marie Antoinette. It was as far as we'd get. My fantasy girl with the crush on the quarterback turned out to have heavy red bangs, blue hair, a nose ring, a tongue stud, and a tattoo of a python around her neck. Her orange T-shirt said *Girls Do It Better*, which seemed to lay to rest the whole quarterback thing.

She stared at me and said she didn't do it. I was about to have the blonde move on, when Renay added that she was sick of the crap from Mitchell and Slash and when were they going to grow the fuck up anyhow. At that, she yanked a toaster out of its socket and hurled it at a smirker with dreadlocks down to his scrawny ass who was perched three seats over from her—presumably Mitchell or Slash.

In the next ten minutes, certain things became clear. Frederick Faust, Georgia Payne (the little blonde), Will Jaworski, and L'Shondra Washington were actual students at the Quaker Hills Career Center. *Aspiring chefs, even*, announced L'Shondra in her white caftan and bright blue headband, *not like these CRIBS nut-job slackers*. At which Frederick, Will, and L'Shondra all glared at the nut-job slackers.

Georgia just stroked her neck ruminatively and gave me a look that said, *Cribs will be Cribs*. Which was when the fourth girl, a six-foot tall, 225-pound monument to late adolescence, what with her short dyed red hair separated into about a dozen ponytails sporting rubber bands with little grinning skulls, got to her size-12 feet.

This was Corabeth Potts, and she was wearing a silver tube top that could gift-wrap a Michelin man, and short plaid shorts. As she turned to head over to the fallen toaster, it became clear the shorts were not doing the job, assuming the job was to cover the flesh. With high-cut legs, a good deal of Cora was open to inspection.

And what was on view was a tattoo across her entire backside that looked like a very detailed inking of an action scene featuring Death Eaters from one of the later Harry Potter books. Only Corabeth must have had it done when she weighed considerably less, because now the Death Eaters and wizard kids all seemed to be sloping off the mountain of flesh in a kind of group disaster and disappearing toward the thighs.

When I questioned Mitchell (dreadlocked smirker) and Slash (frighteningly normal-looking lad with buzzed brown hair and a T-shirt that declared *I'm a Mess*), we settled the matter of the flung and fiery matches—them—and the definition of CRIBS, which apparently my cousin Choo Choo already knew. CRIBS stood for the Callowhill Residential Institute for Behavioral Success. Which obviously meant the Callowhill Residential Institute for Behavior Problems. Only the acronym for that wasn't as good. The place had an "understanding" with Quaker Hills Career Center that resulted in the oldest CRIBS students being able to take some classes in exchange, I'd guess, for not burning the building down. Oh, they were going to burn the building down anyway; now, at least, maybe they'd land jobs in the prison kitchens.

While I pondered punishment, while I pondered consequences, I tossed beautiful red, ripe tomatoes—the best of Kayla—to each of them and discovered a new problem. How would I ever teach this wild and sketchy group to slice a tomato properly if I wasn't going to let them use knives?

When Landon had said in a sepulchral voice that *No good can come of it*, he might as well have been talking about my Basic Cooking Skills gig. But in just the first session with these seventeen-year-old sociopaths, I actually discovered the solution to the problem of additional help for Nonna's big spread for the other set of maniacs presently in our lives.

Georgia Payne actually knew how to wield

a knife in no way that involved a felony in fifty states, and Corabeth Potts was surprisingly quick and graceful and seemed to pick up the rhythm of the kitchen. Slash and Mitchell failed tomato slicing—granted they were handicapped by the cheap plastic knives I dug out of a drawer for the two of them. I didn't care.

I was undecided on my approach to these two.

I could Mother Teresa them. It might be the high road, but the high road was as littered with saps as the low road was littered with less likable saps.

I could outtough them. I'm not quite sure what that would entail, but I think it would have to include weapons more impressive than my cheese grater.

I could scare them. I would hint at consequences that might imply the loss of body parts. I would conveniently let slip the indebtedness of Don Lolo Dinardo to me for performing the Heimlich maneuver on him when his *scungilli* appetizer was literally taking his breath away. As I yanked open my car door when the first class meeting ended without that *strega* Courtney Harrington having to call the fire department, I found I was liking this total fiction about a mythical goodfella named Don Lolo. Mitchell Terranova and Slash Kipperman (who informed me that he was to be called Slash the K, the little brat— I silently added the brat part myself) may be seventeen-year-old sociopaths, but they were still just seventeen-year-olds.

I could most definitely play with their heads.

So, when class ended, I kept Georgia Payne and Corabeth Potts around. Corabeth let me know she was anxious about missing the bus back to CRIBS. I thought this concern showed some good stuff in the big girl. She was actually sweating a little. Narrowing my eyes, I had a moment wondering whether she was either high or snowing me, but thought not. Narrowing my eyes again—this time, trying to picture her dressed in the Miracolo look—I thought I could work with this girl.

So, I brought on the temporary help.

I hired Georgia—who mentioned she was hoping to get back into kitchen work after being away for a while— to be a second sous chef for the next few days. She seemed pleased, ready to show up at Miracolo the next day, and reasonably well dressed, without any part of her backside telling whole chapters of, say, the Tolkien trilogy. Corabeth I would turf to Paulette and Vera for a nuclear makeover that would find her waiting on customers before she could say Callowhill Residential Institute for Behavioral Success. I'd call the stalwart folks at CRIBS and square it with them. Georgia even offered to pick her up on the way to Miracolo later that afternoon.

On a mission, I swung by Target and shopped

for the Corabeth makeover. A size-16 pair of black pants with elasticized waistband. A white Oxford button-down shirt in XXL. And a box of Nice 'n Easy hair color in black, but then I thought the effect would be a little too Lily Munster, so I exchanged it for ash blonde. If Corabeth kicked up rough at the changes, Paulette would have to make it clear these were, well, conditions of employment. She needed to conform to the Miracolo "look." Which I secretly believed was tiresome, but while Maria Pia Angelotta was in charge, what are you going to do? Black pants, white shirt.

In just forty-eight hours, the Miracolo "look" would also include murder, but for now, as I slung the Target bag into my car, we were keeping it down to nothing more than pants and shirts. When life was still simple.

Halfway back to my place, my phone sang out some Scott Joplin ragtime at me, and I picked up. "Hey, Eve," said the caller. "It's Joe Beck." He always tells me his whole name, like I'm not going to recognize his voice, or he's distinguishing the Joe he is from all the other Joes I must know, or he's not quite comfortable being on just a first-name basis with me.

"Hi, Joe Beck. I've got a problem."

"You mentioned."

He didn't sound nasty about it, so I forged ahead. "It's my nonna."

"I figured."

In an acquaintance of just one month, already he got the picture of life in the Angelotta brood. Life happens to Maria Pia, and all the rest of us scramble around trying to push it back or just jump out of its way. In a sense, I suppose, life was not unlike lighted matches being flicked at you. "It's a long story," I told him, which is when I discovered that I thought it was.

"Highlights?"

"Oh, possible homicide, reckless endangerment, abuse of a recipe . . ." Was there no end to the stuff I was inventing that day?

Silence. "Just tell me now," he said finally. "Any withholding of evidence?" Ah, Joe Beck. He of the long memory when it comes to my more problematic moves. But then, it had been only three weeks since the infamous bracelet incident during my last murder investigation.

"Not as of this time," I hedged, reserving the right to withhold. Evidence, information, taxes, affection.

"Any breaking and entering?"

"Hey, bucko, you were with me!"

"To keep you from committing a felony."

"Do we really want to split these particular hairs?" I said patiently.

Then: "Free for lunch?"

"Are you asking, or just telling me you have no social life?"

"Asking."

"Because I'm sure Kayla's available." Low, Eve, low. He had shown remorse. Or, at least, a degree of embarrassment.

With a sigh, he explained, "This is a business lunch."

"Oh." More lighted matches. "I knew that."

"My place in twenty?"

And then I got prissy. "I thought you said it's a business lunch." Was this the same woman who had plunged a Wüsthof knife into a butcher block not all that long ago? Maybe I should ask Renay where she got her python tattoo . . .

"It is. I mean my office."

"Of course."

Then his voice spiraled up in confusion. "I mean, I assume you want my legal help, right? I mean, this isn't just a social call, right?"

"I believe I paid you a retainer." Which was somehow beside the point, but I was fast losing a grip on the point . . .

"One dollar."

I sounded haughty. "Will you be needing more?"

He laughed. "Than a buck? Depends on what I have to do for you, Angelotta."

Was the man actually flirting with me? Or had it

really been that long since my one-off and misguided back-office romp with the FedEx guy that anything sounded sexy? "Well—" Why was my brain drifting to the leather couch in the Miracolo office? Was I truly no better than my flaky farming cousin?

"See," he went on, "you could have said it's a social call, and then wormed the legal advice out of me anyway."

"Oh, you'd like that, wouldn't you?"

"Huh?"

"You should be so lucky," I said with some spirit that really pretty much put me on a level with L'Shondra and Renay. "If it's ever a social call, Joe Beck, you can be sure I'm not there—" I searched for the stuffiest words I could find—"under false pretenses."

"Good!" said Joe Beck. Then, with a smile in his maddening voice, he added, "I'll look forward to it. Now, what say you swing by Sprouts and pick us both up something for lunch. And, if you're worried about our lawyer-client relationship staying pure, I won't even offer to pay you back."

"I should hope not." What just happened here?

"I'm at 1220 Franklin Crescent. See you in twenty." With that, he hung up.

After multiple calls to Choo Choo, to begin the extravagant reaming I had in mind, went unanswered, I decided it was probably better done in person. Although it may involve a bit of a foot-race. Note to self: Bring tennis shoes and a cheese grater. I swung by Sprouts—a trendy veggie restaurant, all of whose sandwiches are named after food warriors—just up the street from Miracolo. For Joe Beck I ended up with a Michael Pollan gluten-free wrap with locally grown, seasonal, and not too many vegetables, and for me I got an Alice Waters bagel with goat cheese schmear topped with sprouts grown by schoolkids. Then I swung by Starbucks and got two Ventis of the real thing, bold and black.

Two miles south on East Market Street, I turned west onto Franklin Boulevard and hit construction, where I waited out the lethargic (not to mention cryptic) hand signals of a hard-hatted gal planted on the blacktop in the bright June sunshine, and turned at last onto Franklin Crescent. The Crescent was a new three-story "colonial" office complex, where the developers were hoping you'd overlook the exterior glass elevators and underground parking warren in their attempt to make you think you were back in William Penn's day. It turned out Carson and Beck, Attorneys at Law, were on the first floor of the second building, which I could get to through a beautiful brick archway and then a courtyard with a fountain I was pleased to see did not depend on cherubs peeing.

At that moment—in that place—I felt very far away from Miracolo and the Quaker Hills Career Center. There's something about the smell and sound of a fountain that makes me feel like I've landed on my time-traveling feet in a piazza somewhere on the Mediterranean. The sun, overhead, was glancing off the arc of the spray. It's irresistible. I dug into my hemp bag and came up with my change purse, which actually held more than three coins, but that's all my fingers pulled out.

A dime and two pennies.

Going for the cut-rate dreams, I pitched my puny twelve cents into the fountain, vowing never to tell Nonna. I don't like to encourage her. Mind you, I really wanted to wish for nothing bad to happen to her at the hands of the Psycho-Chefs Club—really I did. But then I thought about wishing for the doomed Choo Choo Bacigalupo to trip on some little irregularity in the sidewalk as he beat it on down the street just ahead of me in my tennis shoes while I hurled my cheese grater at his bald head. In the end, though, as crazy as it sounds, I just wished for a nice lunch with Joe Beck—nice and not too business-y. Some laughs and longing looks from him that might have nothing to do with wishing for more mustard to mysteriously show up on his Michael Pollan wrap would also be welcome.

Inside the offices of Carson and Beck, I was

pleased to see a male receptionist. Strictly from a feminist angle, of course. The kid had the basics of grooming down, in that his pants covered his flesh, and whatever body art he may have had was staying coyly out of sight. I also appreciated his not sending anything flaming in my direction. In short, Milo Corwin (according to the nameplate on the kidney-shaped desk) looked like he most definitely did not fall out of CRIBS.

I set the cardboard multicup coffee holder and recyclable Sprouts bag on Milo's desk. Then, just as I was giving the lad my name, with my hands stuffed in my pockets, which for some reason was reminding me of some movie with Charlize Theron, Joe Beck emerged from the office of the same name. He's a compact kind of guy—about five foot nine inches' worth of trim and lean—with dark blond hair cut short but not so short every single hair didn't add to the total, beautifully shorn and golden effect.

He had blue eyes that really looked at you even when you wished they didn't. He had the shoulders of a Marine and the hips of a work by Michelangelo. He had a smile that made you think all was peachy in the world even though snow leopards were endangered. And let's not even address that dimple in the right cheek that rivaled all other facial sinkholes in all other humans. Just three weeks ago I had to stop my cousin, the kale-loving Kayla, when she wanted to share the details of her three-night fling with this man. Because if there's one thing I hate more than pepperoni pizza (a failure of imagination), it's experiencing glorious things only secondhand.

Today he was wearing a crisp white shirt and summer-weight gray pants. In the awkward silence when we stood there looking at each other with our hands in our respective (instead of each other's) pockets, Joe Beck said, "Angelotta," with a smile that was just a little bit wary. The dimple was only semideployed.

"Beck," I countered, thrusting the lunch at him.

"Hold my calls," he said to Milo, which felt thrilling to me in a Hollywood kind of way. Then he opened an arm toward his inner sanctum—Milo actually gave me a look that told me it was all right, not that I asked, thank you very much—and I swept in front of Beck Boy into the heart of his lawyer lair.

I took a seat in an armless black leather chair and set the coffee on a glass and teak desk that I judged to be the size of Delaware. My esteemed counsel set down the Sprouts bag and took a seat in the Aeron chair the commercials have been calling "true black" for the last two years, easy. In silence he dug out the sandwiches so slowly you'd think they were evidence in a homicide. "It's not evidence in a homicide," I said with a little eye roll as punctuation.

"It will be if you keep it up," he rejoined (I think that's the proper word).

For a moment I felt like the very annoying Brigid O'Shaughnessy from *The Maltese Falcon*. I uncrossed my legs. "Mine is the bagel."

He grunted and we ate for a while in silence, our eyes on fascinating spots on his glass desk, on which sat an iPad and iPhone and (unbelievably) an old-fashioned desk calendar. All I could read upside down was something as fascinating as "pick up dry cleaning" on June 27th. What a life. I dabbed a Starbucks unchlorinated paper napkin at my lips, after which I wondered if I still had some lipstick going on.

"The problem?" he prompted, halfway through his Michael Pollan. No longing looks were coming my way that had anything to do with either mustard or sex. So be it.

I wound up: "Maria Pia got an invitation from Belfiere." There. Enough said. Let him do what lawyers do: get restraining orders, file motions, put up billboards.

He waved his sandwich around in a dim but encouraging way. "Who is—?" said Joe Beck slowly.

"Belfiere," I repeated, licking at the goat cheese schmear. "To quote my nonna," I said, trying to be impartial, "the oldest all-female totally secret culinary society in the world."

Joe Beck in the crisp white whatever and summer-weight ya-ha picked up his bold and black Venti. So did I. Together—if that's what you can call it—we blew across the hot coffee and locked eyes. Was it a promise of things to come? Had I gotten all this on a mere twelve cents?

"And the problem is—?"

"Short story?" I said, trying to keep my mind on the problem.

"Yeah, whatever," said Joe Beck, ditto.

"Landon and I—"

"Landon?" He looked like this was a first.

"My cousin."

"Right, right, right." And then he added, in case I was in any doubt: "Landon!"

"I'm glad this is a business lunch."

"Totally."

"We make a good team."

He studied my lips. "If that's what you want to call it."

"Landon." I blurted, setting aside the rest of my Alice Waters bagel.

"All right, all right. Landon."

Be professional. This man doesn't like you, I reminded myself. Have some pride. Use some common sense. For the love of God, you've invested a buck. "Landon and I"—I launched into the facts, just for a change of pace—"did some research and discovered a post on a blog for the victims of cults by someone named Anna T. She had been a member of Belfiere."

"Go on." Joe Beck steepled his fingers. How could such short hair look so, well, disheveled?

I wiped my lips and fingers on a paper napkin and found myself wondering just how much weight a glass-top desk could withstand. "Anna T. described a poison-guessing 'game' they played that led to the collapse and death of one of the members."

Joe Beck Lawyer kicked in. "Well, the police will have a record—"

I shook my head, smiling what I hoped was a knowing and superior smile. "Ah, no," I countered. I actually raised my index finger. "The police," I said, raising my eyebrows at him, "were never called." I paused for dramatic effect. "Anna T. says nothing about the death ever appeared in the local newspapers."

Joe Beck glowered at me.

I swirled my coffee and looked steadily at him over the plastic rim. Marine shoulders. Michelangelo hips. Twelve cents, baby, twelve cents. Have I caught his interest? I wondered, breathless. "And they make you get a tattoo!" I blurted, like it was worse, even, than killing off their own members here and there. "On your wrist! A *B* for Belfiere!"

I watched it all sink in. It was like watching the moment when a four-beer buzz leaves, and what's left is called sobriety. Finally, Joe Beck sucked in air while he studied the ceiling, and he pushed himself out of his chair and came around to my side of the desk. "This is worrisome, Eve," he said softly, setting a hand on my shoulder. It needed to be lower for any real pleasure, but I murmured anyway, which I hoped he didn't hear. "I'll put Milo on it."

Then I told Joe Beck about my first class of Basic Cooking Skills at the Quaker Hills Career Center. His eyes were wide. Like listening to his dad tell him when he was eleven about the birds and the bees. Thrusting out my lips, I concluded the tale of matches, knives, and Death Eaters with, "Apprentice felons. Believe me, no squirrel is safe around these guys."

Joe Beck nodded. And nodded again. Leaning against the door to his office, Joe Beck suddenly switched subjects. His beautiful blue eyes were closed. "About Belfiere," he said, "since there's no known crime—yet—my advice is for you to stand back and let your grandmother make her own decisions."

I bristled. "Well, that's crummy advice."

"What do you want for a buck?"

"A buck and a sandwich," I protested, getting to my feet.

"I stand corrected." He moved toward me.

For some crazy reason, it sounded sexual, but maybe it was me.

At the same time, we both blurted, "I need more info."

He whirled and went to the outer office, apparently to put Milo on the case. I'm pretty sure there were snorts.

When he was gone, I pushed my thick auburn hair from my face and stalked around my lawyer's office. All in all, for a business lunch, I think it went pretty well. I think maybe he disliked me a little less. I think maybe Joe Beck and Eve Angelotta could be—

And then, with a little swagger, I stopped in front of his open calendar.

The entry for July 5 read: *National Trial Lawyers Association Dinner Dance. Philly Ritz Carlton. 8 p.m.*

Not in itself bad.

And then my eyes settled on the line below: *Kayla. 7 p.m.*

At which I went weak in the knees and I'm sorry to say it had nothing to do with any granting of wishes that cost me all of twelve cents.

4

So Wednesday June 18th was shaping up to be the Eve Angelotta contribution to Miracolo's Grief Week. What with the body blows from the miscreants in my Basic Cooking Skills class and the discovery that Joe Beck was taking the odious Kayla Angelotta to a swank dinner dance, I found myself wondering what framed photo of myself I could add to the Grief Week shrine on the bar. *Eve Angelotta: Run Over by the Lying Underhandedness and Crappy Romantic Choices of Others.*

Wretched didn't quite cover what I was feeling by the time I left the offices of Carson and Beck, Attorneys at Law. As I passed him, where he was talking to Milo, I just couldn't bring myself to call him out on dating my cousin—dating her and not coming clean about it—so I thanked him for his time, said I'd see him around, and got out of there as quickly as I could. He looked kind of quizzical at my speedy exit, but maybe he could apply Milo to that problem as well . . .

The only bright spot about Joe and Kayla's upcoming date was my knowledge that Flaky Farmer Girl couldn't dance. Let's put it this way: two left feet would have been a considerable improvement.

I drove slowly to the restaurant, stopping home briefly for my work clothes. And when I parked down the street from Miracolo, it looked like we were besieged with vendors, what with their vans double-parked outside. I liked Arne the table linens delivery guy, but creepy Sandor the carpet delivery guy was also on hand, waiting for me to make an entrance so he could make his Sandor versions of erotic remarks with an attitude that implied the only thing standing in our way was the rest of the staff. The good news was that the Kale and Kayla Organics van was also there, so maybe Sandor would find an easy Eve substitute. And I do mean easy. Kayla's van gave new meaning to the term hot wheels.

Slipping inside the restaurant, I was barraged with four times the usual energy level for an average Wednesday. I figured Choo Choo was around somewhere since *The Best of the Rolling Stones* was slinging itself around the dining room on the sound system. Giancarlo Crespi was inventorying the liquor; Sandor was spreading clean floor mats and ogling Vera Tyndall. Paulette was arguing with a delivery guy I had never seen who was trying to get her to accept—a day earlier than arranged— an order of scallops for Maria Pia's scallop fritter appetizer on Friday night. She was poking his chest and yelling something like *You think we're going to serve two-day-old scallops, hey?*

The Stones were rocking out to "You Can't Always Get What You Want," which, as I made my way through the throng of busy staff, I thought maybe I'd take on as my personal theme song. At a back table was Nonna, poring over her recipe books and acting surprisingly in control. I thought she must have had a couple of mojitos with her eggs over easy that morning.

"Nonna!" I yelled over Mick's insisting that sometimes you just might find you get what you need. Maria Pia looked up at me, pulling her red reading glasses off her nose. "The new help's coming at three p.m. today." I kept walking, but not so fast I didn't hear her *"Bene!"* sailing after me.

In the kitchen, the lean and lovely Jonathan was showing Landon the signs he had just brought from CopyMax. He was wearing jeans and a pale blue fitted shirt and as I angled in close for a good look at the handiwork, I got a heady whiff of CK Man, which should most definitely be charged with incitement to riot. Landon flashed me a wry, longing look: *I know, I know.* CK Man was his chief inhibition killer. I noticed he was actually sitting on his hands on Li Wei's stool.

Jonathan smiled and held up the first sign. It was a nice little workmanlike eleven-by-seventeen-inch piece of red cardboard with bold black lettering—pretty much your basic bordello colors—and although the font wasn't as appealing as Nonna's tattoo, it was plain and legible. *Miracolo Will Be Closed Friday, June 20, for a Private Party. We Regret Causing Any Inconvenience and Look Forward to Serving You the Finest in Food and Drink on Saturday. Mille Abrazzi, The Staff.*

I nodded encouragingly. Should I mention "inconvenience" was missing an entire syllable? Jonathan might know his wines, but he was not so great with the spelling. In a split second I decided the message was still plain—we're closed—and he had brought two Angelottas such pleasure already today with his CK Man, which was more important than correct spelling. I didn't mind being inconvienced in the least.

The second sign was a twin to the first and simply read, *Closed for a Private Party.* "This one will go up on Friday," said Jonathan, very sensibly.

Landon beamed as if his crush had just found a brand-new planet in a distant solar system.

"Good work," I said, clapping Jonathan on the back, which sent up an invisible little scent-cloud of the hypnotic cologne. Everyone was happy. Jonathan headed through the double doors to post the first sign on the front door.

My fingers sorted out some of the waves in his brown hair as I told Landon about the new help. "Dish," was all he said as he happily closed his eyes. I covered Corabeth Potts—which was more than I could say about her shorts—in a couple of sentences. The skeleton rubber bands, the scene from Harry Potter (sounds like *Order of the Phoenix*, Landon opined), the anxiety sweat, the natural grace. He didn't need to know too much about her since she'd be on Paulette's team out front. But I had hired Georgia Payne for Landon, so I went into some detail.

Georgia Payne looked to me to be in her late thirties—forty, tops—and was back in school, from what I could tell, as kind of a refresher course, having been out of the food industry for a while. No wedding band, no mention of kids. A petite blonde with dark roots. Conservative but stylish dresser what with her long sleeves and below-the-knee skirt on a summer day. A quiet personality. "She's here for Nonna's big Belfiere thing to make your life easier, Lan, okay?"

He liked the idea of personal help. "Understood." Then, taking in a big breath, he gave me a probing look. "As long as you can stand by her kitchen skills, dollink, because I don't want to have to teach."

I studied the ceiling. "Let's put it this way," I said judiciously, "when I announced we were going to be making polenta next time, Georgia Payne wanted to know where we keep the flat whisk." Only the initiated would know that a flat whisk keeps the cooking polenta off the sides of the pan, where it likes to hang out.

Landon gave me his flat, broad smile, contented. "She'll do," he said, tipping his chin at me. "Oh," he suddenly remembered, "*Numquam Nimis Multi Cultri?*"

I nodded. "The Belfiere motto?"

"I went online to the Latin Forum and posted it, asking for a translation."

I was interested. "And?"

"And," he preened, "I got a hit."

"So what is it? 'Protect Your Nonnas'?"

Landon gingerly slid off the stool, curling a forearm around my neck. In a low voice, he told me, "'Never Too Many Knives.'" We gave each other that look in the old movie when the snowbound weekend guests realize they're locked in with the killer.

At that moment Kayla shouldered her way through the back door, toting a yellow bin of produce from the back of her van. I crossed my arms, and, despite my best efforts, my nostrils flared. Someday I'd really have to learn a proper *malocchio* at my nonna's knee. Just as an insurance policy against the maddening worst of Kayla. Today she was wearing light denim shorts overalls and a pink floral tank top. Her tanned legs ended in steel-toed boots. It was, admittedly, kind of a cute look if what you were going for was Farmer Chic. A matching floral stretch headband was controlling her gobs of curly hair.

I found myself wondering what she was wearing to the dinner dance.

At the Philly Ritz Carlton.

As Joe Beck's date.

"You can just set the order down on the far counter, Kayla," I told her with a grim smile. I couldn't manage anything better than grim. She lifted an eyebrow and I swear she was trying to communicate that she was not communicating something. Did she really think she was putting one over on me about kicking up her steel-toed heels with Joe Beck? Two can play at that game, missy. "Things good in Kayla Land, cuz?"

She boosted the load with an assist from her hip, and once she had set it on the counter, she turned to me, with a hand on one hip. "Busy," she said with the kind of smile that made da Vinci slap oils on canvas.

Busy!

Busy!

I didn't need to post anything on an online forum to know that "busy" translates into *Poor little Eve, your lawyer and I are doing the electric slide, and, honey, it has nothing to do with a dance floor.*

"You?" she challenged.

I looked demure. "Also," was all I said, with a quick look at my fingernails.

"Ah." She grinned, heading for the back door for the rest of the order. She actually wrinkled her generous nose at me and said like a confiding girl-friend, "Sandor?" With a bleat, she dashed out.

So many things started happening at once that I didn't have time to contemplate a witty come-back. Sandor himself actually leered and toothlessly grinned his way through the laying of the carpet (better the carpet than me) at the back door, making some kind of gesture that I believe was meant to put me in mind of bedsheets. The depressed and Austrian Arne was stacking table linens in the store room and muttering to himself that no good could come of it. I figured he was referring either to Belfiere or to the Phillies/Yankees series starting that night.

Maria Pia started dashing in and out of the office, her skirts all in a swirl, proclaiming something about pantry pests and new shipments of semolina flour for the saltimbocca—throughout the raving, her hands had tugged her thick salt-and-pepper hair into the stratosphere.

At the fateful moment I spotted Choo Choo out in the dining room, the only voice I was hearing that made sense was Mick Jagger's going on about Jumping Jack Flash, which should tell you something. "Choo Choo!" I yelled, cursing myself for not remembering to put on my tennis shoes.

At that moment he was leaning on the podium—as maître d', his center of operations—chatting up James Beck, Joe's florist brother, who used to make my sore heart break out into four-part harmony until, well, he didn't anymore. James was the taller Beck brother, the married Beck brother, the Beck brother you want to turn to in an orchid emergency, and the one who leaves a trail of swooning males and females, if what you like is obvious good looks and you don't mind the total absence of dimples.

"Choo Choo!" I yelled again, unmindful of the swarming vendors with all their various produce and products. My big cousin, who had dropped another two pounds, looked at me blandly like he was tuning in to some distant sound that was only infinitesimally interesting.

Too bad the object of his affection, Vera Tyndall, was smiling at me and smoothing out the linen cloth across table 8. Shame to see the big guy scamper like a bunny. I headed toward him, my jaw working. This was the man who had talked me into babysitting the CRIBS crew, who were on the lookout for their first felony the way normal people scouted out prom dates.

"Hi, Eve," he said, turning back to working out an order with James Beck.

Apparently I wasn't transmitting my displeasure sufficiently.

He stood his ground.

Was my voice alone not fearsome enough?

I flung my arm up in a broad sweep in the Italian gesture that translates as *If your head were a bocce ball I would pitch it from here to kingdom come.* "What's the matter with you?" Turning to James, I smiled. "Would you excuse us, please, James?" With that I walked my monumental cousin out the front door, where I backed him up against the window. "Why are you trying to kill me, Chooch?"

He looked genuinely perplexed. "What are you talking about? Oh, say, how did your first class go?"

I gave him a little whoosh of a push, which was like taking a feather duster to Mount Rushmore. "Well, if the goal was Eve flambé, then I'd say it went pretty well."

The light dawned. "The CRIBS kids, right? Yeah"—he actually chuckled—"they can really push buttons, huh?"

"We're not talking merry pranksters, Choo Choo." I got in his face. "They tried to set me on fire. And now, thanks to you, I've got them for a month. In a classroom filled with knives and rolling pins and marble cutting boards and cast-iron skillets and—" With a yelp I pressed my lips together and whispered, "meat grinders." I shook my head, dazed. "It's like Supermarket Sweepstakes for delinquents."

Thoroughly entertained, Choo Choo waved dismissively. "They're just yanking your chain."

"After they've wrapped it around my neck!"

The big guy pulled me in for a hug—practicing for a shot at Vera, I thought—and reminded me how our job as humans is not just to provide good food but also—here he took a deep breath, signaling he was lobbing something profound at me—to *be* good food. I had a quick, disturbing image of myself trussed up in a roasting pan with Mitchell and Slash wearing oven mitts, but I pushed it from my mind as Choo Choo held me at arm's length. He gave me that look of boundless Choo Choo Bacigalupo faith (which usually entails the sacrifice of others) and cheesy love for Vera Tyndall.

"It'll settle down," he said magnanimously.

"You owe me," I hissed at him, my brown eyes locked on his own. For a brief moment I wished it had been Little Serena's brother who had taken off to live the dream at Disney World, leaving Little Serena here for me to enlist in the Kayla Wars.

My cousin opened his hands wide and said, totally reasonably, "Whatever I can do."

I told him I'd let him know.

When Georgia Payne arrived mid-afternoon with Corabeth Potts, I swept them into the office first to present them to Nonna, whose hair by that time was horizontal. She was so awash in paperwork, purchase orders, and diagrams of seating arrangements for the Psi Chi Kappa (the Psycho-Chefs Club) that the new help didn't register.

The petite Georgia Payne looked quite nice in a yellow blouse with long ruffled sleeves, a white linen skirt, and a cool silver necklace that held a tourmaline in what looked like a fine silver birdcage. Georgia said appropriate things, and Corabeth, still in her Michelin tube top and plaid short-shorts, flapped an arm in greeting and said nothing, which was a good choice.

In the kitchen, Landon, who was wrist deep in homemade pasta dough, hid his surprise at the new help pretty well. I figured the skeleton hair decorations were more a jolt than I had thought they would be. He said something funny and nice to Corabeth while he managed to check out the ensemble by pretending to look for his rolling pin, but to Georgia he seemed a bit tongue-tied, muttered a "hi" and turned back to what would become dough for tonight's mushroom-and-truffle ravioli.

Did the lovely and unsuspecting Jonathan suddenly have some competition?

And was it female?

When Vera and Paulette barreled into the kitchen to get the Target bag and my instructions for the nuclear makeover of Corabeth, I glanced at my pale Landon, who was kneading the dough the way he normally would, only his green eyes were staring straight ahead. Maybe when he came face-to-face with the new sous chef, he didn't like the idea after all, even though it meant a second set of capable hands. Off the makeover team went, with Corabeth trundling along behind them, but it wasn't until ten minutes later that Landon even realized they were gone.

I was cleaning and slicing mushrooms with the southpaw Georgia, who was slicing at the speed the Roadrunner beep-beeps his way out of the frame, despite the bandage on her hand, when Landon seemed to come out of his reverie. He looked around with a sudden jerk, and asked where the girl with the draggin' tattoo had gone. At which the reserved Georgia threw back her head and laughed, and I saw Landon warm up.

He complimented Georgia on her necklace, she told him she inherited it from her mother, and Landon asked whether she knew that men's underarm sweat produces the same sex pheromone found in truffles. She pretended she didn't, and Landon was pretending he didn't know she was pretending, but this little charade seemed to suit them both as they settled into new roles, so I figured they'd be all right.

Because slicing and dicing mushrooms is just about as much hilarity as I can stand for any twenty minutes you care to name, I started grilling the new sous chef on matters of interest. To me. "So, where are you from, Georgia?"

She smiled. "Here and there." She waggled her head like she was trying to remember. "Outside Philly."

"And your folks?"

She raised two carefully arched eyebrows at me.

I shrugged. "What do they do?"

"I was adopted."

I said "I see" when I didn't see anything except diced truffles.

Hunched over his floured bread board, Landon heaved a sigh.

Like a girlfriend, I said teasingly, "Any—significant others?" What a stupid term.

She glanced at the ceiling. Finally: "My cat Abbie."

Landon, who owned the splendid tabby Vaughn, nodded over his ravioli dough.

That silenced me for all of fifteen seconds, when I said to Georgia, "So . . . where have you been working?"

"Oh, I've knocked around for a while now." Then, with some spirit: "Most recently I was selling gloves at Bloomingdale's."

I tried to get into the swing. "Men's?"

She smiled, the expert knife work still going. "Women's."

And now we were having fun together. "Wool?"

"Calfskin," she countered, the little flirt.

"Were you living in"—let's see, where could she sell gloves at Bloomingdale's and afford to live?— "Brooklyn?"

"Queens," she said triumphantly. And added, "Ha!"

First we laughed, then we shifted the diced mushrooms and truffles into one bowl, and before I could even reach for the bottle, Georgia drizzled just the right amount of olive oil over it with a circling flourish. Out of the corner of my eye I caught Landon studying her.

"And before gloves?"

She smiled but it was paired with a steely look. "Oh, I knocked around—"

And together we finished, "Here and there."

Her hands paused midair. "Right," she said softly.

At that moment Li Wei showed up, plugged into his iPod, wearing gray ripstop cargo shorts and a black motorcycle jacket. When I introduced him to Georgia Payne, he lit up and sang a soulful few bars of "Georgia on My Mind," then finished with a bland look that makes you wonder whether you were imagining it.

We kept working, picking up the pace as I glanced at my watch, dealing with interruptions from Choo Choo, Jonathan, and Giancarlo, who wanted permission to play the soundtrack from the Plácido Domingo version of *Carmen*. (Personally, I prefer the Stones, but said fine.) I had all but forgotten the fact that three weeks ago my nonna's boyfriend turned up murdered on the very spot where I was presently chopping tomatoes for a *pomodoro* sauce.

Li Wei started emptying the industrial dishwasher from the night before, so the noise level increased, what with clattering pots and plates competing with dangerous tenors and scoffing sopranos. Then he started on the flatware. But there was a pause in the activity at the moment Maria Pia emerged from her office lair. I sensed her presence the way animals can tell the tsunami is on its way. "Tomorrow at one," she declared, "she's coming to check out the preparations for Friday night."

I pushed back my hair. "Who's coming, Nonna?"

"Fina Parisi."

At that moment a knife hit the beautiful black-and-white tiled floor.

Over the next couple of hours, once I could tell Georgia was fine on the prep work, I paid some bills, complimented our aged bartender, Giancarlo, on his new Clark Kent eyeglasses, and debated with our pianist, Mrs. Crawford—resplendent in a white cocktail dress embroidered with gold— whether chiffon has indeed had its day. Landon settled it unequivocally when he breezed by and flung "Never!" at us.

An hour before we opened on this third night of Grief Week, Paulette and Vera returned with Corabeth, who was actually, well, dressed. The shirt and pants from Target, as a quickie spin on the Miracolo look, fit her pretty well. But the biggest change was from the neck up. Her short, shrieking-red hair had been freed from the skull rubber bands, dyed ash blond, brushed, and swept behind her ears. With some bronzing, plucking, volumizing, and glossing, this CRIBS girl now looked kind of like Michelle Williams on steroids.

Our new sous chef, Georgia, hit it off with sommelier Jonathan, and they were discussing whether the merits of Barbaresco had indeed been overlooked when the mandolin and clarinet players showed up early to set up the framed photo shrine on the bar and meet Dana Cahill to go over the repertoire. The fact that they even had a repertoire was news to me, but I always enjoyed it when I saw all over again how Miracolo has a life of its own. All the friendships among the staff.

Leo, the mandolin player, offered that his hip had never been the same since he had a botched hip replacement five years ago. And Dana piped up that she had never been the same since Clinique stopped making Ruby Red lipstick five years ago, at which everyone else laughed, and she looked at them in wonderment. They all got more out of newbie Georgia Payne than I had success at finding out about women's calfskin gloves, but it was fine by me.

If the chemistry turned out to be as right as it seemed, maybe I would keep Georgia on after Friday night. Also Corabeth, who was looming over Paulette, with her big arms crossed, as my best server showed her the ropes. The big girl had shown

an interest in the framed photos, alternately cluck-
ing and tsking, which endeared her right away to
the band, and especially to Dana, when her glossy
lips quivered at the shot of poor little Booger.

Now that everybody was as nicely bonded as
pomodoro sauce to rigatoni, I donned my white
lightweight chef jacket and toque, schooled the
servers on the specials, and took my post at my
beloved Vulcan stove, the stove of the gods. Together we whipped up a northern Italian version
of Olympian fare on a daily basis.

Choo Choo opened the front doors at 5:30, and
in they came. Into our Miracolo, this Angelotta
sacred space with brick walls and black-painted
woodwork and gleaming plank flooring and hanging globe chandeliers and impeccable white table
linens and black votive candle holders. The first
rush was always the after-work crowd hankering
for drinks and antipasti. Then came the older din-
ers, who preferred a nice settled meal followed
by some nice settled digestion followed by a slow
drive home.

The last rush was the younger set, who dashed
from one place for happy hour to another spot for
tapas and finally to Miracolo for whatever I was
dishing up that day—plus the experience, later, of
whatever Dana Cahill and her band of Merry Men
were offering up as entertainment.

So there's a kind of predictability about business hours at Miracolo.

Which is why a murder just thirty-six hours later put an end to predictability—and to the life of one of our very own.

On Thursday, Maria Pia wore the apron she had hung up when I came on board, and she dominated the kitchen, prepping whatever she could in advance of serving her Belfiere sorority sisters a gorgeous meal of Scallop Fritters with Roasted Chioggia Beet Carpaccio, Sestri Salad with Grappa and Fig Vinaigrette, Saffron Risotto alla Milanese, Saltimbocca, Granita di Caffè con Panna, and Biscotti all'Anaci.

Nonna was the queen of multitasking that day, not just overseeing the preparations, but doing them herself. Maybe she had no choice, considering that Landon seemed slow and preoccupied, and Georgia Payne had called to say she had lost a filling, had to make an emergency appointment with her dentist, and would be at Miracolo by 3 p.m. Amazingly, Nonna took it all in stride. She seemed to welcome the opportunity to make everything "alla Maria Pia."

When the Belfiere "La Maga" (Italian, apparently, for Big Kahuna), Fina Parisi, showed up,

Earth did not actually grind to a halt in its orbit. While I brined the chicken for that evening's entrée special, Maria Pia showed La Maga the plans for the dinner the following evening, and I was introduced to her briefly. If Nonna wanted to remind me that this woman was the daughter of "that *strega*" Belladonna Russo, she resisted, settling instead for a meaningful look, which I always had a hard time telling apart from gas.

Fina Parisi was in her late forties, slim, average height, with chin-length wavy black hair, a heart-shaped face, the kind of lips that show up in Estée Lauder ads, and dark blue eyes. She was gracious, stylish, and if I had to decide in a split second, I'd say I liked her. But then, I liked Joe Beck, so don't go by me. Wearing a pale-blue summer linen sheath, the Belfiere *B* was visible on her right wrist. On her it looked like very cool jewelry.

Fina Parisi asked to see Nonna's tattoo—no longer hidden by a Darth Vader–style glove—and the two of them disappeared, chatting softly, into the office, where Nonna closed the door. To keep out all of us non-Belfiere troglodytes, apparently, the Oompa Loompas of Miracolo . . .

By the time Daughter of Strega had left, pleased, Maria Pia went home to change, and Georgia Payne showed up with a numb cheek and a watchful manner. But still pleasant. Landon, I noticed, had nothing more to report on either the Belfiere whistle-blower named Anna T. or Psi Chi Kappa itself. He left his assistant, Georgia, totally alone to figure out how she could, well, assist. He seemed not to notice when the beloved, Jonathan, showed up in new duds—still the Miracolo black-and-white look, but with something modest in the way of bling around his neck—although I overheard Landon murmur something about how jewelry shouldn't be allowed in the workplace. He had nothing more to say either about Corabeth Potts or the lasting contributions of Bob Fosse to Broadway theater.

When I touched his forehead to see if he was running a fever, he even flinched.

5

When asked later—by the authorities—about Thursday night, I was able to say honestly that it was normal. Even better than normal. The gender-mysterious Mrs. Crawford, a vision in a Pepto-Bismol-pink Vera Wang rip-off and a triple strand of black pearls, stepped up her jazz repertoire with witty asides. Choo Choo seemed unabashed by anything except his crush on Vera Tyndall, who nearly outdid Paulette in terms of sleek service. Before the regulars arrived to bring us all down with Grief Week, Corabeth harmonized with Dana Cahill on the old boogie-woogie number "Frankie and Johnny." Dana was even on key. Which tells you something about what a fine, rare evening June 19 was.

And the customers loved everything—the food,

the jazz, the rosato Jonathan recommended with the ravioli special, the opera memorabilia on the beautiful old brick walls of my Miracolo—everything. Two came back to the kitchen to compliment me (okay, so one of them was Leo, but his eyes glistened with love for the calamari appetizer, so, yes, I counted him as a customer). Georgia Payne and I exchanged a knowing look. In that moment I decided she was rock solid and we were lucky to have her.

The customers even ate it up when the regulars tuned up and the clarinet played the opening breathless notes to the *Titanic* tearjerker, "My Heart Will Go On." Pretty soon the customers were swaying back and forth, their arms across each other's shoulders, bellowing, "Near, far, whereEEHHHHver you are, I know that my heart will go on . . ." The musicians seemed particularly choked up, and Giancarlo wiped off his Clark Kent eyeglasses with a bar rag. Karaoke night, Grief Week, something for everybody.

The candles burned brighter.

Glasses clinked, but not too loudly.

There was nothing but laughter.

The perfect summer night.

The next morning, after a great night's sleep, I had a sweet, solitary breakfast in my blue butterfly chair out on my porch the size of a welcome mat. There I nibbled a chocolate croissant I had the foresight to pick up from Au Bon Pain the day before, and a mug of French-pressed espresso-roast coffee. While I sipped and chewed, I watched the sky, where clouds seemed to bunch and collide the way they do before it rains.

At that moment I could honestly say I didn't care so much as an anchovy about whether Joe Beck and Kayla Angelotta went to a fancy lawyers' dinner dance for fancy lawyers. At that moment—despite whatever funk my poor Landon was in—I knew I'd figure out what to do about the likes of Belfiere. As I picked every buttery flake of chocolate goodness off my chest, I somehow just knew that a bunch of old cooking drama queens didn't scare me.

But if Nonna wanted to join their silly club, I could at least be sure she gave them a dinner that would make them have to get some alterations in their midnight-blue satin costumes.

My plan was to arrive first at Miracolo that eventful day, the day when Maria Pia Angelotta was supposed to remind the fifty fuzzies of Belfiere exactly why they had drafted her, to eyeball the place after the lovely evening before. For Friday, June 20, Eve Angelotta was making herself Field Marshal for a Day, and Paulette could concentrate just on serving.

Lucky thing: I was in the shower when I suddenly realized, with horror, that we had forgotten to call the cleaning crew, Maid for You, to come last night after we closed. Of all the days! Of all the nights! I think I told Nonna that I'd take care of it, and then, what with being thrown a curveball in the form of the teaching gig at the Quaker Hills Career Center and Home for Sociopaths, I forgot.

So I threw a can of Pledge in my car—pretty sure there was an old Eureka upright vacuum cleaner in the storeroom—and took off for Market Square sooner than I ordinarily would have. Maria Pia wasn't the only Angelotta to leave early last evening in order to rest up for her big day— thanks to Georgia Payne, who offered to stay and lock up, Landon and Choo Choo and I took off an hour earlier than usual. Landon had disappeared without a kiss, and Choo Choo had trailed off after Vera, who didn't seem to realize it. But the stars had seemed especially steady, anyway, and I believed all of our problems were small.

So, late that Friday morning I parked my old Volvo up the street from Miracolo, grabbed my stuff, and decided to go through the front. The street was already busy, what with the Quaker Hills street-cleaning machine brushing its way up the south side of the commercial district and a couple of hungry brunchers two doors up at the outside seating at Sprouts. I waved to Akahana, who was jaywalking across to Providence Park, carrying a bag that claimed, *I'm Out of Estrogen and I Have a Gun.* She flung an arm at me, then cursed the guy in the VW Beetle, who narrowly missed her. Overhead the clouds collided, and it even smelled like rain.

I turned the key in the lock of Miracolo's front door—which had a linen curtain running the length of the glass—but the door wouldn't open. At least, not very far. I stepped back, then put my shoulder to it, without any luck. Something was blocking the door on the inside. I put my hand to the glass and tried to peer inside, but the curtain was in the way. Finally, I sighed and rolled my eyes. Just what I needed on a day I also had to be Eve Angelotta, Cleaner of Restaurants Before Grandmothers Show Up.

I pushed open the black wrought-iron gate and sprang up the side path to our courtyard and back patio, then let myself in the back. The kitchen looked spotless and the air seemed very still. More still, even, than outside, where everything waited quietly for a summer rain. Heading through the dark dining room—always strange to arrive first, when there's nothing that reminds you of life, not even the ticking of a clock—I didn't notice anything out of place.

But in that crazy way we have when we try to make sense of what's deeply unexplainable, I wondered if Kayla had left an order just inside the front door. But how? Had someone given my wayward cousin a key again? After using the back office for her three-night tryst with Joe Beck, she had lost her key privileges. My eyes were still adjusting to the low light, but I realized as I got closer to the foyer, where the inside door was half open, even Kayla wouldn't do that.

Pulling open the inside door, I nearly tripped on something.

And when I realized it was human, I fell back against the door frame. Peering at the shape— small, blond, and still in a chef jacket—I leaned over. "Georgia?" From the way she was lying, face-down, it looked to me like she had sunk to her knees and flopped over, her left hand flung out on the tiled floor of the foyer, her right hand jammed underneath her. Both ballet flats were half off her feet. Not quite her usual capable self.

Had she been here all night? Was she out cold? Dead drunk? Not what I had in mind for the biggest day of Nonna's year. Not quite noon and already I'd blown it twice. One, forgetting to call the cleaning service. Two, failing to vet Georgia Payne before signing her up based on the fact that in a Basic Cooking class for crazies-in-waiting, she seemed able to tell a saltimbocca from a salamander. Where could it go from here?

"Georgia?" I gave her a shake. Maybe I could sober her up, spread around some homilies about not drinking on the job, and get on with the day's work. When I didn't get as much as a groan out of her, I crouched next to her and gave her another shake. "Come on, Georgia," and I think I actually added "Rise and shine" as I eased her onto her back. I realized several things at once, the way you do if, say, your transmission has just fallen out on the railroad track and you wonder for a split second whether that train whistle you hear is coming or going. In my experience, it's always coming.

Georgia felt like rubber.

Her eyes were open and staring, and not the way mine are when I listen to Dana Cahill sing "Me and Bobby McGee." I sat back on my heels, pretty sure this meant Georgia wouldn't be plating Maria Pia's Sestri Salad with Grappa and Fig Vinaigrette anytime soon, when suddenly the front doorknob started to rattle.

"Hello? Hello? Why won't the door open?" It was Nonna, just four inches of wood and glass away from a nervous breakdown. I pictured the EMS, the fire truck, the crowd gathering outside, the Channel 12 news team blaring "Second Death in Three Weeks at Local Eating Establishment!"—

and that *strega* Belladonna Russo laughing in the background. My grandmother wouldn't survive the shame.

I quickly frog-walked myself between poor dead Georgia and the latest sorority pledge of Belfiere. My single thought was to prevent my grandmother from seeing the train wreck that was about to ruin her precious day. "Nonna?" I said like a strangled soprano that could still do a better job with "Bobby McGee" than Dana. "Hi, *bella*, it's me, Eve."

She pushed against the door. "The hell are you doing?"

"Just setting out the new mat so it's all nice and ready for"—here I went singsong, laying it on thick—"you-know-what." I looked desperately around me for something more convincing, but nothing was suggesting itself, and Georgia didn't have any better ideas.

It worked. So I had better also find time to get a mat. "Ah," said Nonna, musically. "My favorite granddaughter." At that moment, had I ever any doubt, I understood perfectly that my cousin Little Serena Bacigalupo had made the right career choice to decamp from Quaker Hills to run a ride at Disney World.

I pressed my lips together. *Georgia, Georgia*—I yelled at her silently, my hands spread wide—*what in the name of holy roasted nuts happened to you?*

There was no blood, no apparent wounds, no blue skin, no swollen tongue, no vomit (the worst of all words to utter in a fine Italian restaurant) . . .

Had the poor woman just up and died on us?

I heard Nonna take a step back from the front door. "You just do what you have to do, darling. I'll go around the back . . ."

And with that I literally sprang into action, popping up to my feet, bug-eyed, needing suddenly to put Georgia somewhere else before Miracolo hosted a second heart attack in twenty-four hours. Apologizing to her repeatedly, I grabbed poor Georgia under her white-jacketed arms and dragged her backward out of the foyer as fast as I could. If I could get Nonna into the back office, I could put Georgia . . . put Georgia . . . I whirled around, looking for a place out of view from what in very short order would be the entire staff of Miracolo.

Put Georgia where?

When I heard Nonna come through the back door—thanks to the squeaky hinges I still hadn't oiled—I watched my options sink to zero. "Eve?" she called, coming closer. With that, Georgia and I slid like crème brûlée on a greased plate to a safe haven behind the bar, where I gently set down her head half a second before Maria Pia Angelotta burst through the double kitchen doors, beaming all around in some nonexistent spotlight while I tried to catch my breath.

"Nonna!" I hailed her heartily, stepping over the hidden body and dashing out from behind the bar to catch her in a big hug. When out of the corner of my eye I noticed one of Georgia's ballet flats, I kicked it into the shadows, hoping my nonna didn't notice. I'd have a hard time explaining a third shoe. But her eyes were still adjusting to the low light. As my nonna and I rocked each other and she murmured the day's menu like it was sex talk, I said, "It's your big day!" all the while knowing that if I didn't get Georgia out of the way, it might also be her last day.

I managed to send us both through the doors back into the kitchen, telling Maria Pia she should check her timetable carefully before we begin. "Paulette will be bringing my blue Belfiere gown," Nonna nattered, having apparently appealed to the seamstress in Paulette to "run it up," as Nonna understated it, on her machine. Paulette sews like the future of the Free World depends on it, and I can picture her churning out parachutes for paratroopers and thinking a sweatshop is a beauty treatment.

"Well, you just better call Paulette to remind her." I gave her a gentle push toward the back office. "We don't want your big day to die"— here I winced mentally, thinking of Georgia—"in the details."

It is sometimes useful to know that my nonna responds quickly to alarm.

Off she dashed to the back office to call Paulette.

And off I dashed to the business side of Miracolo's beautiful mahogany bar, where Georgia was—alas—showing no more signs of life than before. Suddenly I heard another set of footsteps in the kitchen—my heart sank as the likelihood of keeping Georgia's untimely heart attack a secret dwindled fast—and I held my breath. "Nonna?" came the new voice.

Landon.

"Oh, Landon," I piped up, like I wanted him to join me for tea in the drawing room.

"Eve?"

"May I see you in here when you, oh, get a chance, please?"

My cousin appeared in the doorway, and although I was always happy to see him even when dead bodies weren't posing problems, I was especially glad to see Landon Angelotta at that moment. Although I could tell from his expression that he was still in whatever funk had reached up its slimy tentacles and drawn him in by the heels over the last couple of days. Landon's moods were fluid and usually had nothing to do with me, his beloved Eve. And they usually had nothing to do with matters of the heart—for a gay male in little old Quaker

Hills, Pennsylvania, Landon never found the field too small. He was just that romantic. No, usually his less effervescent moods had something to do with inferior strawberries for a signature cassata cake. Or wondering how many pairs of shoes Suri Cruise has in her $160,000 collection.

"Cuz?" He looked around, then caught sight of me motioning wildly to him to come around the bar. Landon brought his five feet ten inches of lithe grace over toward me, where I kept shushing him even thought he wasn't speaking. His brown hair was still wet from the shower and he was wearing black- and white-checked chef pants and a white-on-white collarless shirt with snaps. "Mice get into the bar towels? What?" As he turned the corner, I flung an arm out at the body at my feet and stared meaningfully at my (in all real things) personal Marine. Who had the good sense to gasp and cry out, "Whoa!"

So I shushed him some more.

He stepped back, I think either to get a better look or to put a little space between himself and whatever pestilence was afoot in our Miracolo. "Is it—Georgia?"

"Yes," I managed to get out.

He crouched down, touched her briefly, and I saw a mix of emotions on his beautiful face. Shock, followed by some kind of breathless understanding that didn't include me. Then he lifted his head. "What happened to her?" he whispered. "Not—?" And I could tell he was remembering our discovery of a murder just three weeks ago. Considering the guy had been konked but good with one of our marble mortars, it's not the kind of thing you want to stumble across on a stylish black-and-white-tiled floor—"even though," my cousin admitted to me, kind of shamefaced, later, "the red really made it pop."

"Murder? No." I went on with the kind of hasty catalog I used to confess my sins as a kid. "No bullet holes, stab wounds, bashing, throttling, swollen tongue, blue skin—" I took a breath. "Have I left anything out?"

Landon got it. "We've got to take poor Georgia out of here."

"In broad daylight?"

He squinted at the bottle of absinthe Giancarlo keeps tucked away. "Maybe in stages?"

"Yes," I said slowly, as though Landon had just floated the idea that Earth might not in fact be flat after all. "Stages."

"Otherwise," he said, swiping his hand across his forehead, "Nonna will die."

"Die. Absolutely." Which is not to say that option didn't have some appeal.

Landon, who could tell what I was thinking,

gave me a push, then chewed his lip. "Where is she?"

That at least I could answer. "In the back office calling Paulette."

Landon grabbed Georgia under her arms and, wincing, I lifted her by the calves. Together we carried our new and former sous chef—I sighed at all the failed promise—through the kitchen doors. All I knew for sure in that moment was that—even if we could keep it from Maria Pia— we had to keep Georgia Payne's short employment history with Miracolo strictly on a need-to-know basis—otherwise anything could happen.

I pictured Vera weeping into the Scallop Fritters with Roasted Chioggia Beet Carpaccio as she set them in front of a gowned Fina Parisi. I pictured a flattened Jonathan describing the differences between a Barolo and a Barbaresco like he was Hamlet describing the prep for a colonoscopy. I pictured Leo and the other regulars setting a framed picture of our stricken sous chef on the Grief Week shrine and then launching into their own rollicking dirge version of "The Night the Lights Went Out in Georgia."

And I knew I couldn't take it.

Grappling with Georgia's body, Landon and I paused momentarily in the middle of the kitchen, where, up until that moment, the only dead things we had ever handled had pretty much spent their lives either grazing or swimming. We could hear our nonna in the back office, chatting it up on the phone with Paulette. At which point Landon widened his green eyes at me: *Now what?* I mouthed at him what suddenly seemed to me to be the only possibility for Stage One of Georgia Removal: "The storeroom."

Landon sagged, like it didn't seem ideal, but caved, and we trundled our load toward the storeroom in what sounded like a demented shuffle. Once inside, I pushed up the wall switch with my shoulder, and we headed to the darkest, farthest corner, where we made a little bed out of twenty-five-pound bags of semolina flour and laid poor Georgia across it. Then we rearranged big cartons of extravirgin olive oil, boxes of various vinegars, crates of booze and mixers until we had built a screen around the flour sacks that would buy us some time.

But not much.

Landon and I haggled over a next step.

"I say we find some excuse to get Nonna away from Miracolo for maybe forty-five minutes until we're safely away with Georgia." That was me.

Landon cocked an eyebrow. He wasn't liking it. "And then what?" he asked, scratching the side of his face. "Where do we go with her?"

"Your place, my place," I held up fingers as I

rattled off a positive bevy of harebrained choices, "the ER, the urgent care—"

He held up his hands. "We're a little past urgent care."

"So, then, the ER."

"Where one of us has to wait with Georgia for two hours before we'll get any attention."

I gave him a stony look. "I think Georgia will be okay with it."

Landon rolled his eyes. "Do you have that kind of time today, Eve?" He spread a hand dramatically across his chest. "Do I?"

I paced, which was not satisfying because of the shelving and the boxes on the floor, and Landon tapped a foot. We finally agreed that it was surprisingly difficult to deal with someone dead of natural causes. "Who knew?" I said, hunching my shoulders. Murder, on the other hand? No problem. Cops like the Ted Guy and Sally Belts and Boots, who had helped us out three weeks ago, have a whole instruction manual for it.

Finally we started spitballing more sanity-challenged ideas for Stage Two of Georgia Removal. Driving her to New Brunswick, New Jersey, and depositing her on Belladonna Russo's doorstep and then just waiting to see what happens. Driving her in her own car back to wherever she lived—problem noted: that precise location was as yet unknown—and then just waiting to see what happens. Driving her to the Quaker Hills Volunteer Fire Department and then just waiting to see what happens. We thought we could see a theme emerging about waiting to see what happens and decided we liked that part of any plan, anyhow. It was progress.

In the end, waiting to see what happens became the entire plan.

I threw up my hands. "I got nothing else, here, Lan," I said.

"So we leave Georgia here for now," said Landon decisively, smoothing his hands across the air in front of him, the way I'd seen him "frame" an antipasto plate he was particularly proud of.

I held up a finger. "But we"—I gazed at canisters of almonds, looking for the precise word—*"do"*—it was the best I could come up with—"something final—"

"And responsible—" added Landon responsibly.

"And at the first opportunity."

"Agreed."

"And we're agreed our goal is to keep knowledge of Georgia's—" I groped for some great concept that just wasn't coming.

Landon jumped in, "Death."

I toggled my head like, well, it was the easy choice, but we were in definite straits. "Death,"

I acquiesced without any taste for it, "to keep Georgia's death from Nonna on her big day with the Crazy Club."

Landon dipped his head once. "Also agreed."

Then we did a quick shuffle of our human resources, trying to smooth over the sudden and inexplicable absence of Georgia Payne. We decided to pull Choo Choo off his usual post at the podium and put him with Landon and me in the kitchen. Paulette could handle the initial seating of all the Belfiere guests, who would more or less arrive at once, and then return to her default setting as server. Jonathan would need to stay as sommelier just for the full classy effect of what he does best. (Landon insisted. I caved.)

So Paulette, Vera, and Corabeth would serve. With a whiff of panic, we realized we needed two more servers, so Landon agreed to give the sixteen-year-old Li Wei a battlefield promotion and call him pronto so the kid could run out and furnish himself with the Miracolo look. We could only hope none of the Belfiere lady maniacs didn't also happen to be members of the state liquor control board. And I agreed to call L'Shondra Washington, from the nondelinquent half of my cooking class, probably the only one aside from poor dead Georgia who was actually interested in the restaurant business.

I shot Georgia a quick look, who not surprisingly seemed okay with the plan, and I was convinced all over again that the present dilemma was all the fault of Choo Choo Bacigalupo. But running down blame is a lot like tracing your roots, and I was able to get to the next level of blame genealogy. Had Choo Choo not fallen in love with Vera Tyndall, he never would have talked me into the cooking class gig as a way of—his—performing some community service. I narrowed my eyes. In a strange way, then, the fact that Landon and I were whispering in the storeroom next to a dead body was Vera Tyndall's fault.

So shouldn't Georgia Removal be Vera's problem? It was tempting.

No, even I could tell that wasn't fair. I didn't need Joe Beck smelling delectable and wringing his ringless hands and explaining annoying things like laws to me. Poor Georgia was my problem. I should have had her go for a physical as a condition of employment.

Suddenly I heard the inevitable outside the confines of our hidey-hole storeroom: Maria Pia emerging from the back office, calling my name, and other voices heading through the dining room. Landon and I gave each other a quick look, and I loped to the door. "Coming, Nonna," I called. Over my shoulder I caught a glimpse of Landon leaning over poor sprawled Georgia, where he moved her legs closer together over the semolina flour sacks and gently lifted the necklace by the tourmaline pendant and gazed inscrutably at the silver bird-cage that enclosed it. As I slithered through the door, the last thing I noticed was Landon sinking quietly onto the sacks, where he folded his hands in his lap and stared without comment at our dead sous chef.

6

To understand how we lost track of Georgia, you have to know something about the path of that violent little weather system known as a *derecho*. It's a fast-moving windstorm that topples towering trees like bowling pins and that's only slightly friendlier than a landfall hurricane. This also describes Chef Maria Pia Angelotta in a kitchen. She whirls, dashes, races, mystically creating a swath of culinary havoc in at least four separate locations all at once. I think there are even moments when her feet leave the floor.

Whenever I happened to be her sous chef, before she retired, and my pals would call from Manhattan, I'd have to get off the phone, telling them, "I'm putting out fires." Most people mean it as a kind of expression—the copy machine is jammed and the boss forgot to take her Xanax. Not me. If I wasn't actually putting out real fires, I was at least turning them down when Nonna's back was turned. If you close your eyes, all the bubbling and sizzling in a kitchen run by Maria Pia is like the soundtrack of Hell.

Still, one of her greatest gifts as a chef is that she's a wonderful tactician. She sets all the mini-tornadoes in motion and never loses sight of the big picture. Once I realized she was a force of nature in a commercial kitchen, I relaxed about helping her, chopping and grinding my way into a Zen state that let the culinary chaos swirl around me. I had to trust her. I had to trust that what was terrifying primordial chaos to me was just a fine welter of magical morsels to her. All the rest of us cooking Angelottas had cauldrons in the kitchen. For Maria Pia, though, the kitchen itself *was* the cauldron. She's just that great.

So, after Landon and I left Georgia Payne life-less in the storeroom (which we locked and hoped no one much noticed), the *derecho* began. Maria Pia appeared in the center of the Miracolo kitchen, wearing the loose boxy top and pants from the Mao era in the color I call Congestive Heart Failure Gray. I think when she invokes the gustatory gods she likes to appear before them as a blank slate—a blank slate with no taste of any kind. In clothes, food, home décor, or men. It clears her mind. It frees her of prejudices. She becomes one with the glorious universe, in which the firmament was created pretty early on just as a place to stick a stove.

And then it began. She marshaled the troops—Landon, Choo Choo, and me—and we knew she was getting in the Zone when she forgot all our names and just called us "you."

"You"—she pointed to Landon—"pound the veal."

"You"—she pointed to Choo Choo—"batter the scallops."

"You"—she pointed to me—"whip the cream."

Pound, batter, whip.

Like General Patton only without the warmth.

Then our nonna got that misty look she usually saves for when the garlic in her *bagna cauda*—garlic and anchovy—sauce is coming up short. "Where's what's her name? The new girl?"

And if Georgia were alive and standing next to me, she'd still be called "you."

Landon muttered she was under the weather. And I muttered she had heart trouble.

At that, Choo Choo lifted a whisk from the batter for the fritters and drew together his eyebrows, which pulled his whole bald scalp down over his eyes like an avalanche.

"Car trouble?" barked Nonna.

Landon and I gave each other a regretful look like, yeah, *car* trouble might have been the better lie, in the circumstances.

Over the next couple of hours, several things happened. Several things quite aside from cooking. James Beck arrived with the order of white calla lilies and bemoaning the shortage of clear glass marbles for the vases. This, by the way, pretty effectively killed whatever was left of my crush on James since I discovered I didn't have much taste for a man for whom a shortage of glass marbles was a serious problem on the level of, say, world hunger. Corabeth arrived looking slightly the worse for wear, bemoaning Georgia's failure to pick her up, so she had to steal a bike. (We laughed merrily, assuming it was a joke.)

Jonathan arrived, and announced he was having an anxiety attack about whether we had enough pinot noir on hand to pair with the veal, and as he headed for the storeroom, Landon and I both bellowed, "No!" And then added: "We'll check!" And Paulette finally arrived with Nonna's new midnight-blue satin "chef jacket" gown for her membership in the Psycho-Chefs Club, beautifully steamed and hung.

Bubble, sizzle, pop.

At one point I happened to glance out the back windows and saw a couple of familiar figures dashing through the deserted courtyard and scrambling over the back fence. This I would have chalked off to kids just passing through had it not been for the flopping mane of dirty, beaded dreadlocks on one of them. Mitchell Terranova! And the clean-cut miscreant with him must be his partner in crime, Slash Kipperman. Paying me a visit? Casing the joint? Too shy to hand me my polished apples in person? Even after one class with those two, I knew better. I set down the beater I was jamming into the hand mixer and hurried outside.

Gone.

I headed through the courtyard, eyeballing everything, looking for some evidence of—what, exactly? Theft, first. Scanning, scanning. Nope. Votive candles all there and intact. Hmm. Slipping on my delinquent hat, I even peered into the compost bin, just to see—ascertain, as Detective Sally Belts and Boots would say—whether they'd deposited some roadkill. Nope. Could it be Mitchell and Slash just wanted a peek at where I worked? Despite their tough talk, were they harboring a little crush on me? The psycho lambs . . .

On my way back inside, I spied a colorful can lying at the side of the building. I picked it up—an empty can of neon orange spray paint. Two feet away lay a half-full can of neon green spray paint. And then, of course, I looked up, and staggered backward to get the full effect of the graffiti on the beautiful old red brick of the restaurant. It was an orange, eight-foot-high, pretty fair likeness of my face in profile, downing, with great relish, a neon green cannoli, or what I could only assume was a cannoli. Also in green was my phone number.

As I walked back to the kitchen door with spray paint cans in my hands, and my eyes narrowed to slits, I pondered the situation. If I called the cops then, we'd have the same problem on Nonna's busiest day ever that we were already hoping to avoid by stashing poor Georgia for the time being. For now, I had no proof and no time, but plenty of conviction that the wall defilers were none other than Mitchell and Slash. Who didn't know I had seen them.

Ah.

A grim smile played about my lips.

This . . . this was a job for the fictitious Don Lolo Dinardo. And it could wait until later.

Right then, though, once I was back inside the kitchen, I called Adrian the bouncer at Jolly's Pub across the square, who owed me for a few free meals I'd given him. He was quickly enlisted to spray over the graffiti with as good a match to the brick as he could find at the local hardware store and to do it pronto. By me, Adrian and I were now square. Then I dropped the paint cans into a gallon-size ziplock bag and stashed it on the low shelf on Landon's

prep table, just in case they'd yield some incriminating fingerprints later. Lastly: I'd talk to Choo
Choo at the first opportunity about how—oh, yes,
how—he could make good on his colossally stupid
idea about teaching cooking to CRIBS kids.

Then I glanced at my watch and let out a little
yelp. Were we really just three hours away from the
arrival of the blue-haired psycho sorority? I threw
myself into the prep work with manic glee, just
to forget the billboard-size sketch of myself on the
side of our restaurant left for all of Quaker Hills to
see. And, with my luck, call me up.

In the couple of times I came up for air, I was
vaguely aware of a babbling flow of humanity,
whose questions I just waved away or ignored altogether. We were already up to our elbows in scallop
batter and scaloppine, yelling across the kitchen
to one another for time checks. But when Maria
Pia paused in the creation of delectable chaos long
enough to go back to the office with Paulette and
try on the official Belfiere gown—"Not that it
isn't perfect," murmured the confident Paulette—
Landon and I paused, shot each other a wide-eyed
look, and saw our opportunity. I cleaned off my
hands with a dish towel so fast you'd swear I was
wrestling a wildcat, then tossed the rag to Landon.
Our pants got the rest of the stuff off our hands as
we scampered off to the storeroom.

Looking around furtively as though we were busting into Tiffany's, we slunk into the lighted room, where I had a quick, bad moment trying to remember whether we had forgotten to turn off the light. We leaned breathlessly against the back of the door.

"I can't wait for this day to be over," I whispered.

Landon suddenly said something useful. "I parked in the alley at the back of the courtyard."

Bingo. We had a destination for Georgia.

"But we have to get rid of Choo Choo," I hissed.

Landon looked at me anxiously. "You do mean just get him out of the kitchen, don't you?"

My mouth hung open. "Of course that's what I—"

"I can't help myself, all right?" His words tumbled over each other. "Somehow I've got to make risotto and granita in three hours, okay? I didn't even shave this morning." He clawed his cheeks. "And I'm not sure I fed Vaughn."

So my cousin was definitely off his game.

"Listen," I said, my brain in overdrive, like I was telling my unit just how we were going to take out the enemy machine-gun nest. "I'll get Choo Choo out of the way, and then we get Georgia's arms over our shoulders so she looks like she's drunk—"

"In case we run into anybody."

The reality of that possibility made my heart

pound. How on earth were we ever going to pull this off? "Then we make a dash with poor Georgia out the back door—"

"To my car."

"Exactly. On three. One, two—"

"Three, already, three!" Landon couldn't take the suspense.

I stuck my head out of the storeroom and peered around until I caught a glimpse of Choo Choo. "Hey, Chooch," I called, "you better make sure the Closed for Private Party sign is up on the front door, okay?" When we heard an answering grunt, followed by some shift in the force we took for our monumental cousin's leaving the kitchen, Landon and I turned to each other and said, "Go!"

We bounded to the back of the Miracolo storeroom, where we had shielded Georgia from view with a half wall of stacked boxes and cartons. Frantically pushing up our sleeves like any sensible person would do in order to drag a dead body, we stepped around the boxes to the stacked bags of semolina flour, where we had set poor defunct Georgia.

Only, Georgia was gone.

It was definitely mysterious, I don't mind telling you.

And strangely terrifying.

Wordlessly, Landon and I scoured the storeroom looking for our fugitive corpse. We dug to the back of stocked shelves, wondering if she had somehow found a cozier crypt. Nothing. Nobody. Finally, tugging his hair into a state of emergency, Landon whirled on me. "Are you sure she was dead?"

It was actually a good question.

Was I?

Did I feel for a pulse?

Did I set a little mirror below her nostrils?

We stared at each other, paralyzed. "No, I'm not sure," I whispered. Aside from the corpse three weeks ago and Ronnie Rosa, my high school boyfriend, who made me realize there's actually quite a fine line between signs of life and a well-placed call to an undertaker, I've had no field experience with dead bodies. "Maybe Georgia was in a deeply meditative state." I widened my eyes at him, full of meaning. If I could make Landon buy it, I had a prayer of hanging on to my sanity.

"In the foyer of Miracolo?"

"A fair question." Was he going to be no help whatsoever?

"And where is she now? Why isn't she out there in the kitchen with the rest of us, pounding veal and battering scallops?"

"Again," I said primly, "a fair question. Maybe Georgia was . . . cataleptic."

"What's that?" Landon huddled toward me, all ears. Still open to possibilities of life.

"It looks like death. That's all I know."

"Well, how long does it last?"

"I don't know."

He chewed his lip, and I could tell he was thinking back to the Georgia Payne we had most recently experienced. "Does it include fixed and dilated pupils—"

"I don't know!" I whined. Picky, picky.

"— and a body temp heading toward the—shall we say—suspiciously Arctic?" We both blew out air and stared fatalistically at the ceiling. "No," said Landon darkly, "dead is as dead does."

At that moment we heard Choo Choo calling our names and Landon and I clutched each other the way we used to back when we were eight and nine years old and our grandfather Benigno used to regale us with stories about *l'uomo nero*—Italian for bogeyman—which usually ended in tears and wet pants. Still, we enjoyed the clutching. Even then, Landon Angelotta was the best girlfriend I've ever had. But right then in the storeroom it seemed like *l'uomo nero* was back and he looked a lot like Choo Choo Bacigalupo. Which surprised me. I always sort of thought it was really Maria Pia.

We babbled. "Quick, hide."

"Don't let him come in."

"Don't let him find—"

What, exactly?

And then the beauty of our situation struck us both. Georgia was gone. Beamed up, vaporized (we checked quickly for a little pile of ashes—nope), reanimated and gurgling around the courtyard, or had dropped down to Starbucks for a triple Venti espresso to counteract the whole sleepy thing—who knew?

Swamped in relief, Landon smoothed his hair and I tugged at my jacket, smoothing it down around my hips. We were good. For the time being. I shoved a sack of arborio rice at Landon and grabbed a bottle of vinaigrette. Smiling serenely, we stepped out of the storeroom and held them up to Choo Choo, who was giving us the look he gets when a customer asks if we deliver.

Maria Pia returned to the kitchen—which still didn't look quite like something FEMA would take an interest in, but give her an hour—cooing about her beautiful new gown. And when somebody—Paulette, probably, who thinks he's "still sexy," as she puts it, "albeit dead"—slipped a Frank Sinatra CD into the sound system, Landon gave me a baleful look. Cooking to Italian-American crooners relaxes our nonna. But to her, "relaxed" means owning the Zone, which in turn means the *derecho* has struck but good.

The problem of the disappearing Georgia Payne was forgotten for the next couple of hours. I peeked into the dining room as Vera was lighting the votives and Li Wei—slicked back and decked out—was moonwalking to Frankie Avalon's "Bobby Sox to Stockings"—a particular favorite of Maria Pia Angelotta—while Corabeth nibbled her nails in excitement. Paulette had L'Shondra Washington, who was thrilled to get the call, in a corner, where the two of them—with plenty of furtive glances—looked like they were planning the overthrow of the government. I gave Paulette the benefit of the doubt and figured she was bringing my student up to speed on what she likes to refer to as dining room "choreography."

Still, from the oddly murderous look on L'Shondra's face, I wasn't convinced she understood we were all on the same team. Jonathan was locked in an argument with Giancarlo about whether Umbria or Piemonte produces the better grape. Tonight the gleaming bar was shrine free, even though Grief Week still had three days to go, and Dana Cahill and the regulars knew we were closed to the public. (I still half expected to see Dana breeze in, since she never thinks the words "private" or "members only" exclude her.)

Mrs. Crawford, who I was pretty sure knew we weren't expecting Maria Pia's nonexistent mah-jongg club, was dressed in black. Black without yards of gold embroidery or silver chiffon or Swarovski crystal beads. Just . . . plain . . . black. Below the knee, nothing shiny, a neckline that started north of her cleavage. With her wiry hair pinned back, she was the picture of a church organist. What gives? Why the change? I had a bad moment, then, wondering whether Mrs. Crawford had stumbled onto the contents of the storeroom, and this was what she wears to a send-off for the formerly vertical.

Then I remembered Maria Pia had requested that the piano repertoire for the evening be all opera. But opera as elevator music. Just a bland background—"of notes," as my nonna had put it. At which Mrs. Crawford looked calculating, which worried me a bit.

When finally Nonna was satisfied that the meal was "respectable," which means the dazzling aromas of onions, Parmesan, and marsala were filling the kitchen, she disappeared into the office, slamming the door behind her, to get ready for her big night. Landon happened to go into the walk-in freezer to check on the *granita di caffè*, when I heard a squeak. "Eve! Eve could I get some help in here, please, with this—this—side of beef?" What was he doing moving sides of beef—here I glanced at my watch—just thirty minutes from the witching hour—otherwise known as half an hour before the Belfiere Bat Association showed up? Wait a minute. We don't even *have* sides of beef . . .

I walked stiff-legged to the freezer as Choo Choo sidestepped gracefully from the saltimbocca to the salad to the risotto, stirring, tweaking, humming. At the precise moment I stepped inside the Miracolo version of the Yukon in December, I found Landon grappling with Georgia Payne, who had about as much color in her cheeks as Morticia Addams, and Nonna chose that moment to clang out our names. "Eve! *Bella! Cara!* Landon! *Bellissimo!*" On Maria Pia's good-looks scorecard for her grandchildren, Landon was always at the top.

Our nonna was definitely on the prowl for us.

I joined Landon in grappling with Georgia. "How did she get in here?" I hissed at him.

"Well . . ." He gritted his teeth, trying to reposition his hands, which were groping her in places that was bringing pleasure to neither of them. "I'd say we can lay to rest the hypothesis that Georgia may not be"—he winced and bit his lip—"dead."

With that, her poor head lolled and her chin rapped me in the collarbone. And I could swear I pulled something in my back as I tried to lift her by the hips. Visions of a worker's comp claim danced like a skull and crossbones in my head. Although, for the life of me (sorry, Georgia), I couldn't figure out how to describe the nature of the work-related injury.

Muscle strain from grappling with coworker's corpse?

Effects of head-butt by deceased sous chef?

I was just deciding to pay another dollar for a face-to-face with Joe Beck on this matter, when someone jiggled the handle to the freezer door. The look Landon shot me was the one I remembered from our childhood when—thanks to our grandfather, who apparently couldn't tell squeals of delight from those of abject terror—*l'uomo nero* was just about to burst into the room. Landon danced the frosty Georgia over to a corner obscured by shelves of grass-fed, cage-free, antibiotic-free (but still dead) chicken breasts, where he propped her upright with his body. I heard a little whimper, and I'm pretty sure it wasn't Georgia.

Grabbing a small pack of something frozen hard as a rock, I swiped the sweat from my forehead and let myself out of the freezer, where I ran into Maria Pia, decked out in her midnight-blue satin Belfiere "chef jacket" gown. "Oh, there you are, *cara*!" she warbled, her arms outstretched, as she turned to give me the full effect. Gone was the cooking outfit from the Mao era. She looked like she was born to be a member of the Crazy Club, what with her dramatic good looks, her thick hair you've either got from birth, never mind the gray, or you don't, and her poise. I'd accept a plate of unrecognizable poison from her any day . . .

With my free hand I grabbed her wrist. "Gorgeous, Nonna," I said sincerely.

While she bent my ear about whether she should wear her hair up or down—which was my cue to tell her it's equally dazzling either way—and, if up, whether the diamond clips look better than the gold, I kept a smile plastered on my mug while I started to collapse a little inside just wondering how long Landon would last, pressed up against the uncomplaining Georgia in the Sub-Zero freezer before freezer burn held them together permanently. I gave Nonna a playful little shove. "Go try the diamond clips, Nonna, and I'd go with the charcoal-gray eyeliner, if I were you."

"But," she sputtered, "that's at home!"

"Precisely. But well worth the trip."

"But"—here she lowered her voice, her eyes darting sideways over the suddenly untrustworthy Choo Choo and Vera, who was dashing by us with rolls of toilet paper to restock the customer restrooms— "my, ah"—this she yelled because to Maria Pia screaming always carries a certain quality of convic-

tion—"mah-jongg club will be here in twenty minutes."

I wanted to fling her back into the office.
"Then just use what you've got and tart yourself
up right nice, missy, there you go!" Blinking at me,
and about to launch into something fake-anxious
about the evening's menu, she nevertheless turned
on her von Furstenberg heels and tripped back to
the office. At which I flung open the freezer door
and Landon fell into my arms, practically sobbing.
He waved behind him in a way that was meant to
convey that Georgia was just about as fine as she
was going to get, and we twirled ourselves out of
the frozen air and shut the door hard.

"How in the ding-dong doo-wop did she get in
there?" I whispered.

He widened his eyes at me. "Well, I'm just
guessing here, but I'm thinking someone else is on
to us."

We loped back to the kitchen, where Choo
Choo was stirring something—I no longer knew
exactly what—placidly. My money was on Choo
Choo. I narrowed my eyes at him. Did he really
think he could go moving our corpse without
our figuring it out? Between this macabre little
game he was playing and his responsibility for the
CRIBS mess I was in, well, the flicked match most
definitely stops here.

It was Landon, however, who came up with an alternative explanation. "I'm thinking," he said, scratching his chin, "that someone"—he lifted one eyebrow at me meaningfully—"happened to come across the poor unfortunate Georgia stretched out on the semolina in the storeroom and concluded—in much the same way we did, darling—that she just dropped dead on the sacks . . ."

I saw where he was going. "And then that someone moved her to the freezer—"

"Perhaps a spot less likely to be entered."

"—until he could get her out the door, right?"

We turned our heads slowly to our majestic Bacigalupo cousin, who was humming in a highly suspicious manner. "Someone who is also protecting Maria Pia."

I was about to jump on the hummer's back and beat him about the head and shoulders with what turned out to be a pack of frozen beef short ribs, when Paulette marched through the double doors, planted her feet, and gazed around the kitchen appraisingly. I could tell she was about to make an announcement on the order of either a new pope having been chosen or the Beatles having broken up. Our wooden spoons stopped mid-stir. "Maria Pia's"—her eyes glittered, the wily Paulette—"mah-jongg club is arriving." She added, "Battle stations," then headed in a stately manner down the short hall to the office to let the guest of honor know.

The Belfiere ladies wafted into Miracolo in groups, kind of like jellyfish. Where they all parked and how they all rustled in their cheesy get-ups down the south side of Market Square without drawing just the kind of attention we were hoping to avoid was beyond me. I overheard our sweet Vera, who was standing by the kitchen doors at the time, tell Jonathan that she never knew mah-jongg clubs could be so elegant.

I didn't recognize a single solitary one of the Belfiere members, except, of course, Fina Parisi. We were feeding an assortment, that was for sure, what with blue-satin-clad ladies running the gamut from spindly to squat. When Paulette and Jonathan seated them, they raised identical silver masks with handles that looked like tongue depressors to cover their faces, which was certainly an improvement. Meanwhile, Mrs. Crawford was inscrutable at the piano, and maybe it was me, but I could swear the middle of a famous aria from that tearjerker *La Bohème* morphed into "In Them Old Cotton Fields Back Home."

Nobody else seemed to notice.

As I stood at the window to the kitchen door, she caught my eye and winked.

Once Chef Maria Pia Angelotta, who had gone for the diamond bling in her hair, swept into the dining room, decked out in her Belfiere outfit, I stepped back, relaxing, but not before I saw Fina glide toward her with outstretched arms. What followed was a ceremony before Paulette, Vera, L'Shondra, and the irrepressible Corabeth served the first course. It consisted of the kind of choral hum you get in high schools where students have to choose between choir and woodshop.

From behind their raised masks they chanted something about keeping the flame alight, Maga, Maga, a sip before death, a taste before life, Maga, Maga, and then it seemed to veer off into promises of faithfulness to the alchemy of alimentary bliss. Which, for me, means avoiding hot peppers. How the wide-eyed Vera reconciled this stuff with mah-jongg, I'll never know. But in the background Mrs. Crawford's fingers were just moving across the piano keys from the spot *when them cotton balls get rotten you can't pick very much cotton* to Rodolfo's singing to Mimi that her hands are cold.

Each dinner guest then raised her free hand and the midnight-blue satin sleeves slipped down to reveal the Belfiere tattoo on fifty wrists. At which point, seated, they all thrust out their tattooed wrists toward the center of the table and waved them about—prompting Mrs. Crawford to slide

into a few bold bars of "The Hokey Pokey"—
and then their voices dropped as they took what
sounded like a pledge to chop till they drop.

But I reminded myself that it would be foolish to underestimate this group that looked like its
idea of activity was a rousing game of chair vol-
leyball. After all, there was still the little matter of
the mysterious death of one of their own that went
unreported. Of course, what with the contents of
our own walk-in freezer, I wasn't one to talk.

Finally, tattoos disappeared under flowing
sleeves once more, and then Fina Parisi—from
behind her silver mask—welcomed all to the culinary home of Chef Maria Pia Angelotta. Here
my nonna—the only one without a silver mask,
I guess because she was still uninitiated—bowed
and scraped and waved her arms in the manner she
usually reserves for the more passionate moments
in her nightly signature song, "Three Coins in a
Fountain."

Then Fina nodded to the servers, Maria Pia
joined Fina at her table, and the staff barreled
into the kitchen while we started furiously plating the appetizer. Corabeth wanted to know if
she should call Georgia, to which I could only
reply airily, "That ship has sailed" and Landon
added, "A dead issue." Despite the assembly line
of bodies either plating or power-walking with

armfuls of Scallop Fritters with Roasted Chioggia Beet Carpaccio, Li Wei chose this moment to do a spin kick that accidentally grazed the chin of the simmering L'Shondra, who told him in no uncertain terms to get his skinny little crackerhonkey ass out of her face. Only she said it like she was squaring off before a congregation of unbelievers. If it was a little too loud, we didn't have time to care.

Vera chose this moment, as I handed her three plates of Scallop Fritters and shooed her away, to announce that she was going to learn mah-jongg. As she turned, beaming, back to the dining room, to serve a beautiful appetizer that wasn't going to yield us so much as a cent, it struck me that this Belfiere gig was pretty much a way for members to get some free chow on a regular basis. So, I might have to reconsider my position on just how crazy they were.

Then it happened.

A break in the madness.

All the appetizers were being served, Maria Pia and her mah-jongg club were happily buzzing, Choo Choo must have wandered off to the john, and Landon and I had the Miracolo kitchen very much to ourselves. Our eyes shot to the back door: clear shot! With a now-or-never kind of desperation, we dashed to the freezer, steeling ourselves for dealing with both cold and corpse, and slipped inside. "Hurry! Hurry!" Landon pushed me.

"All right, all right!" I whirled and flapped at him.

The plan was simple.

There was no plan.

I kind of liked it, to tell you the truth.

Out the back door with Georgia, that was all we had.

Prop her up at the farthest table on the patio, maybe stick a drink in her hand.

Prop her up behind the compost bin, maybe stick a drink in her hand.

Prop her up in the front seat of Landon's BMW, maybe stick a drink in her hand.

I was feeling positively creative, and very nearly lighthearted. We were actually going to pull it off, postponing any dealing with death until after this meal for the Psycho Society. I was so happy envisioning just driving Georgia to the ER and explaining with so many Italian shrugs and hand gestures that she just up and *died*, that the roadway seemed strewn with more goodies than the Candy Land game board.

However, by the time Landon and I passed the chicken breasts, the short ribs, and the flank steaks, we found a hitch in any of the loose plans to prop up the problem somewhere for just an-

other two, three hours, max. One thing nice about
a commercial-grade walk-in freezer: it's frost free.
But at that moment in my life on Friday, June 20,
it was also Georgia free.

She was nowhere around.

Landon and I let out a wail.

7

Within five minutes Landon and I had eliminated all other hiding places—short of the Miracolo dining room, which was just too painful to consider—in this game we were apparently playing with the dead but nevertheless elusive Georgia Payne. We dashed by each other in the back hallway. Landon slowed just long enough to whisper, "Office is clear," and I shot back, "So's the storeroom." And off he went to check out the customer restrooms while I pushed open the door to the staff restroom, which was empty of Georgia but not of Choo Choo.

When Landon got back and shrugged his findings, we huddled by my Vulcan stove. "Look at it this way," I said with sudden insight, "this is actually good news."

He nibbled a nail. "Explain."

"She's nowhere inside the restaurant."

He tapped the tip of his nose while this idea sank in. "Someone else has achieved what we have failed to do."

"This is so."

"Still, I'm troubled."

"Is it your whole competitive thing?"

"No, no, no." He waved away the very idea. "Although I'm"—his voice dropped as he talked to my shoulder—"relieved that Georgia is not likely to be an obvious problem while Nonna's psycho sorority is here, I'm troubled that we've only eliminated hiding places inside the restaurant." His voice dropped even lower as he talked to the side of my neck. "If you catch my drift."

It was a reasonable point of view. "I see," I said gravely as Jonathan swanned into the kitchen to announce that the Scallop Fritters with Chioggia Beet Carpaccio was a big hit. Although this was excellent news, my knees clacked together kind of uncontrollably—truly, I believe, from the stress over the problem with the dead Georgia Payne's whereabouts.

But at that moment I mistook Jonathan for some kind of savior. All I wanted to do was hear his full report from the battlefield, but only after I flung myself sniveling into the poor lad's arms. I think Landon was wishing he had thought of it first. Tough. Jonathan pried me off his shoulders and smiled so sweetly, telling me it was all going just perfectly and I shouldn't worry. I was hoping he would add *your pretty little head*, but he didn't.

As I sank onto the stool with *Lee Way* stenciled on the back, and my whole face was trying to work up the energy to blubber, two things happened. Neither of which included Georgia Payne miraculously reappearing. One, the servers started trooping into the kitchen with appetizer plates, and two, the Sestri Salad with Grappa and Fig Vinaigrette was supposed to get plated.

While I blubbered softly, fingering one of Jonathan's shirt buttons, and he regaled me with stories about how the mah-jongg ladies were out there happily disagreeing about the last winner on *Top Chef Masters* . . . and Maria Pia consulted with Mrs. Crawford about whether a little "Three Coins in a Fountain" would be amiss, and learned that it would be . . . and Dana Cahill had pressed her nose up against the front window, but Paulette lowered the blind . . . the back door opened.

And in walked Joe Beck.

I pushed myself to my feet with as much dignity as any woman could whose face had recently been featured on the side of a building doing highly suspicious things with Italian pastry. I straightened my shoulders, I straightened my toque, I straightened my bra strap as I pushed my way through the obstruction called L'Shondra Washington (who was giving Joe a crocodilian smile) and over to my lawyer. Landon and Choo Choo, whose combined twenty fingers were furiously arranging sweet butter lettuce on gold-trimmed glass plates, called out a hi to the man who had been an old Angelotta family retainer for all of three weeks.

"Hello, Joe," I said, sounding all world-weary in a Lauren Bacall kind of way.

Joe smiled, like he'd forgotten all about my beating a hasty retreat at lunch the other day, and looked around, his blue eyes taking in the activity. I folded my arms and winced a smile back at him, because I for one had not forgotten his upcoming date supreme with my maddening cousin. He was wearing a lightweight blue-and-brown plaid shirt over his cargo pants, and his close-cropped blond hair caught the summer sunlight that irritated me no end by coming in the windows at just that angle. And truth be told, he smelled like citrus soap and all my very best dreams.

Behind me, Corabeth was chuffing and wheezing and I couldn't tell whether she was asthmatic or turned on. "Don't you have salads to serve?" I fluttered my eyelashes at her because, well, I couldn't flutter them at Joe and still respect myself in the morning.

Then she joined the fray, which Joe watched for about twenty seconds—just enough time to take in Choo Choo, Landon, Paulette, Vera, Jonathan, Li Wei, Corabeth, and L'Shondra—and then turned to me. "Controlled chaos?"

I placed a hand on my chest. A cheap tactic, agreed. "In Miracolo?" Aghast.

"No chaos in your restaurant."

"No," I had to own up, "no control."

He eyed me. "You're looking fine tonight."

I crossed my arms. "I bet you say that to all the clients."

"Only the ones who pay me top dollar."

I laughed a little and then we stood there in silence. I scuffed at nothing on the pristine floor. "Well . . ." *Shame about this man,* I thought.

Joe Beck jerked his head to the kitchen doors, which L'Shondra was shouldering open like she was doing a house-to-house check in Kandahar. In floated a new entertainment from Mrs. Crawford, whom nobody out there seemed to be paying attention to, and I recognized a combination of the "Toreador Song" from *Carmen* and "I'm a Little Teapot."

"Is that the Belfiere group out there?" he asked.

I nodded.

Then he gave me a little nudge. "See," he said, "they seem to be behaving themselves."

"They're eating."

"Well, they're not flinging the dishes."

"No, I think we can leave that to L'Shondra."

"So maybe you've got nothing to worry about."

If you don't include the odd corpse.

I made a noncommittal noise.

Joe went on: "Well, I'm here to pick up a couple of bottles of an Argentine Malbec that Jonathan special-ordered for Landon."

I gave him a cool, appraising look. I could have given him a hot, appraising look but I didn't want to confuse the issue. "Pricey stuff."

He grinned and tipped his head. "Strictly special occasion."

Here I muttered something, and I'm pretty sure I bit the tip of my tongue senseless so I couldn't utter the word *Kayla*, and I told him Jonathan had put the whole order in the back of Landon's BMW, out behind the courtyard. At which point I saw Landon's keys—he's used the same metal rainbow key ring for years now—on the counter by the back door. These I grabbed and handed to Joe Beck. Our fingers touched briefly.

Out of the corner of my eye I caught sight of Corabeth Potts starting to rubber-band her short hair into spiky little ponytails that reminded me for some reason of Shrek. Maybe the stress of the Miracolo dining room was getting to her. "No, no!" I called out. As I headed over to her—her shirttails were also flopping on the outside of her black pants—Joe told me he'd bring the keys right back.

When someone says "right back," you figure you'll see him again in . . . what? Fifteen minutes? Twenty, tops? As I was just starting to warm to my lecture to Corabeth about blah blah appropriate attire and blah blah personal grooming, Joe Beck slammed open the back door, where he teetered, backlit by the sunlight. Landon and Choo Choo were suddenly arguing about whether the strawberries in the Sestri Salad get sliced lengthwise or diagonally (Vera suggested crosswise and was met with murderous looks), so the reappearance of Joe Beck didn't grab them.

It did, however, grab me.

In fact, he grabbed me, by the shoulder, by the upper arm, by whatever his shaking hands landed on, which, I must say, I found sadly devoid of imagination. "Something?" I said. "What?" Somewhat impatiently. After a day that featured dangerous graffiti artists and dead sous chefs that make their own travel plans—not to mention the cabal of culinary cutthroats presently enjoying our signature Grappa and Fig Vinaigrette topped with a mangle of strawberries, I was really not in the mood for the latest from the Beck Dramatic Society.

"What, Joe?" I sighed. "See a little possum out back? You can outrun *him*—"

He gurgled at me. Finally, he managed, "Eve!"

Choo Choo was calling for me to referee the strawberry wars.

Joe Beck discovered some reserves of what I can only call manic determination. Looking back at the others several times, he planted firm hands on my back and arm and steered me right out the back door. "Hang on!" I yelled to Landon and Choo Choo. Then, thinking maybe my lawyer was impulsively taking me somewhere interesting and far away, "Diagonal!" I shouted my professional decision. Choo Choo blustered his strong disapproval, calling it a major culinary misstep and a crime against fresh fruit.

How Joe Beck managed to keep me so close to him while pushing me forward seemed quite a trick—reminding me of a memorable cast-party tango with my dance captain, Tony Treadwell, but that's another story—and I have to say I think he was pushing the lawyer-client privilege thing a little far. You'll note I made no objections.

He weaved us through the patio tables, skirted the compost bin by the back fence, and danced the two of us out the gate. The sun was low in the sky over the back alley and this was the best company I had had all day. "Joe?" Still Lauren Bacall but a little less world-weary. Fitting nicely up against a new guy is always cause for celebration.

Landon's black BMW was parked close to the fence just up the way. As alleys go, it's not traveled much except by the garbage truck once a week. The asphalt could use some repair, and weeds pushed up through the cracks. Joe angled me alongside the car, and when we got to the trunk, we stopped. He motioned to the trunk in a sweeping gesture— twice, wordlessly— that has no correspondence in Italian.

I set my hands on my hips and shot him a rueful look. "For a lawyer, you're not so much with the words."

He gritted his teeth, turned a key in the lock, his chest heaving. Then he shoved open the trunk like a ringmaster introducing the next act. So I was guessing there was a problem with the special-ordered Malbec and he was holding me responsible.

I looked over the side. "Georgia!" I cried.

While Joe staggered backward, away from the trunk, pulling me with him, certain things became clear. The choice of a car trunk I could definitely put down to Choo Choo Bacigalupo, who had a taste for wise-guy movies and moves. Choo Choo, who was afraid of spiders and allergic to most laundry detergents. Maybe he had moved poor dead Georgia Payne first to the freezer, as a kind of temporary spot, until he could sling her over his massive shoulders and tiptoe out the door. Or maybe somebody else was responsible for the interim move to the freezer, where Choo Choo discovered her.

"Eve!" Joe said urgently, his hand rubbing his chest like Li Wei had just landed a spin kick. " 'Georgia'?" He was quoting me. I nodded matter-of-factly. " *'Georgia?'* he said again.

Heaving a sigh that didn't even cover my opinion of Friday, June 20th, I explained how I had discovered poor Georgia dead in the foyer of the restaurant that very morning.

He grabbed my arms and pulled me close. Right in my face, he asked, "Who is she?" Barely daring to glance back at the trunk.

"That I can answer. Well, limitedly."

He waited, his eyes locked with mine, his fingers pointlessly tapping the air between us. "Go on," he said in a strangled sort of way.

I explained how Georgia Payne was our temporary sous chef, just to help us through these few days before Nonna's big Belfiere event. Oh, and she was one of my students in the Quaker Hills Career Center cooking class. "Had I known she had a serious heart condition," I added reasonably,

"I would have had to go in a different direction, but . . ."

Joe started grappling with Georgia's body, and he was coming across as a little more ham-fisted than I had hoped, should he ever be grappling with mine. Although, to be fair, she was a deadweight. With a grunt, he managed to get out, "Why didn't you call 911?" Then he toggled his head. "Although I'm sure you have a perfectly good Eve Angelotta reason—"

I reached into the trunk to give him a hand. I must say, I wasn't warming to his attitude. "In fact," I got out through clenched teeth, trying to get a grip on Georgia, "I do. Georgia may be a goner, but Maria Pia's biggest day of her entire cooking life is not. Landon and I decided just to, well, postpone doing something about—"

"Eve!" Joe Beck said, letting go of his half of Georgia and standing up straight. "What's the matter with you? You've got to put her back."

"Put her back?" I cried, thrusting my hands in the general direction of Miracolo, which sent Georgia tumbling back into the trunk. The bottles of Argentine Malbec rattled. "Joe, they haven't even got to the Saffron Risotto alla Milanese!"

"This woman died under suspicious circumstances. Can't you—"

"Suspicious circumstances?" I stuck my hands

on my hips. Both of us became aware of a police cruiser heading slowly down the alley, of all the timing. "She locked up, she keeled over, end of story." Together we prudently lowered the trunk door and raised our hands in greeting as the cruiser rolled by, taking the ruts with complaining squeaks from the shocks.

Joe Beck brought his face close to mine, which enabled me to appreciate a handsome scruff that was just beginning. "How do you know?" he asked softly.

Easy one. I ticked off on my fingers: "No blood, no obvious wounds, gunshot or otherwise, no—"

He gave me a squinty look as he reached back inside. "Oh, excuse me, you're such an authority on violent death. Come on, we're getting her out of here."

I crossed my arms. Every drop of sheer Angelotta stubbornness—not to mention Camarata bloody-mindedness—marinated me but good. "We are not putting her back until after the Granita di Caffè con Panna."

He asserted himself, which was not necessarily unattractive. "We're doing it now."

I gave him the Italian hand gesture—very close to what you may know as the touchdown signal—that translates as *Your head is the size of a Coleman cooler and is filled with three-day-old polenta.* "What am I supposed to do with fifty dangerous cooking ladies who haven't had their entrées yet?"

He was ignoring me, all busy with Georgia. With the zest he was showing, you'd think it was Kayla. "Send them out the back."

"Through the kitchen?" I planted my feet. "Are you out of your mind? Have you no sense of decorum?"

"Decorum? You stash a human being in a car trunk. What are you, Tony Soprano?"

I sucked in one shocked and lengthy breath, hard. Then I got indignant. "How dare you!"

"Oh, please." Georgia was putting up quite a fight.

"It's not like she couldn't breathe," I yelled. Perhaps a little too loudly.

"Let's hope not," he yelled back, "because she sure isn't now."

"For your information," I said, tugging at my cuffs, "Landon and I carried Georgia to the storeroom."

"Because that's better."

Sarcasm at that level was not a pretty sight. "It is!"

"Then how did she get here? Answer me that."

"I think Choo Choo."

"Oh, great. So it's a whole big Angelotta—"

"And Bacigalupo."

"—family activity. Like bocce." Then: "We're putting her back."

I got very quiet. "Not until after the Biscotti all'Anaci."

He whirled on me. "I thought you said the Granita something something."

"I changed my mind. Oh, wait," I said, getting in his face, "I changed it again. Not until after the last of the Crazy Club is out the door. And in case you're wondering," I added in an airy way, "the front door. This is all nonnegotiable, Beck."

He got airy, too. "Oh, really."

"Yes, really."

"Oh, *really.*"

"Yes"—I gave him a little push—"really." Why had I never insisted on *malocchio* lessons?

He seemed to chew up the inside of his mouth, then jerked his irritating head toward the rest of the BMW. "Get in the backseat." His lips were practically clamped shut, he was so angry.

I stepped back. "What?"

"You, me, Georgia." He strafed a hand through his hair.

What was he suggesting? "Oh, so you're all Captain America when it's bodies in a trunk, but when it comes to making out in the backseat of someone else's car, there's nothing wrong with an audience"—I got right in his face—"who can't tell you you're doing it wrong."

Considering the look he gave me, for a moment

I had a flicker of doubt that that had been his plan for the backseat, but then I couldn't take it back.

"For your information, Angelotta," said Joe Beck with quiet dignity, "in that scenario, the only corpse in the backseat would be you."

"Fine talk that is. Fine talk!" I was growing more Italian by the minute.

"Give me a hand."

Pressing my lips together hard, I got my hands under poor Georgia's hips, while Dudley Do-Right managed her shoulders and head, and we tugged her up and out of the trunk. In the middle of the operation, Joe gave her a quick once-over, then looked a little puzzled. He was having to entertain the idea that I might possibly be correct in the matter of Georgia Payne.

I got the rear door open and climbed in first, backward, tugging the hips of the dead, chef-coated Georgia after me. Joe crawled in slowly, balancing the rest of her. And there we were. And just in time. A gaggle of spandexed cyclists came wheeling down the alley toward us, yammering away about stopwatches and water bottles. Joe quickly pulled the rear door shut behind him, which left us a cramped little threesome in the back of Landon's Beemer.

"I could use a drink," he muttered.

Peering in as they spun past, a couple of cyclists

got a load of the situation and whistled at us. Joe gave them a wan smile then turned to me in horror. Georgia was lying in a jangled mess, what with her torso faceup, her hips shifted off the seat, her head and arms lolling, her ballet shoes long gone, her necklace gently swinging. In order to get her balanced back on the seat, Joe set Georgia's head in his lap—

"I'll bet that's the most action you've seen in a while."

"Forgetting Kayla?" He gave me a challenging grin.

—and lifted her arms. Left, right, folding one over the other on her chest.

Alas, poor Georgia.

We were huffing quietly then, more from fear and emotional strain, I think, than the exertion. As Joe settled down—and I kept pushing back my hair long after it needed the help—he straightened out Georgia's sleeves, just to be doing something before we started arguing again.

Which was when it happened.

He tilted his head, bringing her left arm closer to his face. Holding her fingers in one hand, he lightly pushed back her sleeve, then folded back the bandage I remember from when the southpaw Georgia and I were slicing mushrooms, which was hanging half off her wrist. "Take a look," he said softly, his troubled blue eyes on my face. With that, he held out her hand to me. I shot him a quick, questioning look and then brushed aside the tattered bandage.

What I saw was the shadowy evidence of tattoo removal. Only, what was left was almost as visible as what had once been there. And there was no mistaking it. My heart started pounding.

There, on Georgia's wrist, was a scar in the shape of a *B*.

I was just about as creeped out as I'd ever been. I sat back on the leather seat and slanted my eyes toward that ghost of a Belfiere *B* on my dead sous chef's left wrist. Suddenly this was no longer a problem on the order of, say, whether I could safely substitute tarragon for dill in a recipe. No, Georgia's old *B* meant that (a) she was a member of Belfiere, and that (b) she had gone to some trouble to hide that fact. But just from me? And if so, why?

No, it made about as much sense as Nonna's dating that coal miner half her age for three loco weeks around two years ago. It wasn't so much his youth, or complete lack of conversation, that made the rest of us Angelottas refer to this fling in her life as "that time," it was the fact that he packed himself the same thing in his lunch box every day: a cold

Vienna sausage sandwich on Wonder Bread with yellow mustard. After about a week of sleepovers at a sketchy roadside place (we followed them) close to Philly called Outen Inn, Nonna saw the light and skulked back home. Even Maria Pia Angelotta yields, finally, to what does or does not make sense.

But Georgia Payne, Belfiere member? All I remembered about her personal history was that she had breezily gotten out of a culinary career somewhere and pursued glove sales at Bloomingdale's. Was it all a lie? And then paranoia nibbled at the edges of my mind. Had she come, well, undercover to Miracolo? Had Georgia Payne found out that Eve Angelotta was teaching a cooking class at Quaker Hills Career Center and signed up, just hoping for an opportunity to weasel her way into our restaurant? To do what, exactly? Was she a spy for Belfiere? A mole? Was that it? Did they send in their agents to scope out the kitchen lives of their inductees, just to be sure they weren't using Stella d'Oro shortcuts in their tiramisus?

Maybe.

Paranoia can be extremely persuasive.

And I had been fooled. Fooled but good. Blond little Georgia had shown me just enough natural talent to hire her, but not so much that I'd question her modest report of her past work life. And then it struck me. If she had been a Belfiere member, and she was only in her late thirties, Georgia Payne was more than just a fine chef who had delivered excellent and imaginative cuisine down the long years of a stellar career—Georgia was a cooking prodigy. Someone extraordinary enough for the Cooking Crazies to induct her into their exclusive international society.

What was she doing at Miracolo? What—

When I heard a sharp intake of breath, I looked up. Joe Beck seemed to have shifted into high alert. He was holding Georgia's right hand about six inches from his face. "Eve," he said in a low, tight voice, "I thought you said she wasn't murdered." His lips were pressed together, hard.

My heart sank further and faster than my very first *panna cotta* after I had opened the oven door prematurely. No, no, no. "No blood, no obvious wounds, no—" I had to make him believe me. It was one thing to keep a corpse dead from natural causes from crashing the most important meal in my nonna's life. But it was quite another thing altogether to have a second murder within a month at the Angelotta family restaurant that had been in our family—and abiding all the laws of the state of Pennsylvania—for eighty years.

With a pained and disbelieving look, Joe Beck slowly rotated both of Georgia's hands toward me as we sat there, cramped in the backseat of Landon's car. At first, I didn't see it. But then, what was I looking for? Joe could tell. "The fingertips," was all he said. With my two thumbs, I pressed against the inside of Georgia's fingers, until the tips straightened up and I could see them clearly. They were much darker than the rest of her skin, that was for sure. Practically blackened. I leaned closer to the fingertips, squinting at them, then raised my eyes to Joe's. Had poor Georgia burned herself somehow? "They look charred."

And I could see from his expression that he was trying to figure out how to break it to me. "They are charred, Eve," said Joe quietly. Then: "This woman's been electrocuted."

8

Charred?

Electrocuted?

These are words that never play well when coupled with a human being.

I don't mind telling you that over the next couple of hours, all Eve Angelotta wanted was for some kind soul to bean her with a frying pan, just in the event the grappa she planned on drinking failed. During our final minutes in Landon's backseat, Joe Beck was offering neither. "So? It doesn't mean she was murdered!" I cried. "Say she just got hold of a live wire somehow."

He looked weary. "Or stuck her paring knife into a socket." I was frankly too worked up to take him to task for mocking me. Also because I wasn't sure he was. Besides, I thought fleetingly, if sticking her paring knife into electrical outlets was something Georgia Payne did, then the really big mystery was how she ever got invited to join Belfiere. Even if they were homicidal, they probably frowned majestically on any member who shows such scant regard for the tools of their trade. I was thinking of the three knives rampant on the field of the Belfiere "crest."

"Is there an outlet in the foyer of Miracolo?" He opened his hands wide and actually tried to think of some possibilities that could keep Georgia's demise securely in the Accident category.

I tried to picture the space. A space I'd crossed practically every day—which tells you just how pathetic my social life is—for the last four years. Was there an outlet? A dangerous outlet? Why would there be? The foyer was a small space. Nobody did anything in it except stamp their galoshes in the bad weather and then open the inner door to the special place that's Miracolo. "No," I told him. I managed a small shrug. "There's no outlet."

Joe actually reached across Georgia's body and brushed a hank of hair off the side of my face. "You know what you have to do."

"I have to put her back." I bit my lip. I refused to entertain any scenarios that included lugging Georgia through the dining room anytime over the next hour. Maria Pia's shock and humiliation . . . the flight of the Belfiere Bat Association . . . the cops, the coroner's van, the local paparazzi . . . I'd do whatever I had to—even if I enjoyed it—in order to keep Joe Beck from pressing that point.

If it wasn't an accident—here my shoulders sagged—if it wasn't, then more than fifty pairs of feet had crossed that foyer since Georgia died, which was certainly not the cops' first choice in terms of how to preserve valuable evidence. More than fifty pairs of feet. And a bevy of cops railing about the crime scene. An already crappy day was about to get so much worse that no amount of Landon's heavenly Granita di Caffè con Panna would help.

An hour and a half later, the guests had let down their masks and loosened the belts underneath their midnight-blue satin Belfiere gowns and were— from all reports coming back to the kitchen— gossiping in four different languages about who'd slept with what famous chef. It must have been the wine. I had lit a tiki light for Joe Beck and settled him at the table at the back of the Miracolo courtyard, where he was staring moodily into a dry vodka martini and biding his time.

Biding time, really, for the three of us—himself, Landon, and me, for whenever the last member of the Belfiere Bats departed, dragging her mask and hitching up her pants, making her unsteady way up the street to wherever the limos had been tucked, noodling over revelations about lovers shared.

Meanwhile, I shucked my chefwear long enough to do two things. Invade Giancarlo's domain and mix a drink—unlike 007, stirred not shaken—myself. Some of the cutthroat culinary sorority sisters looked me over wonderingly. I went for mysterious. Maria Pia didn't even catch sight of me, although Fina Parisi's eyes seemed to follow me like those creepy paintings you used to be able to buy on the boardwalk at Atlantic City.

She seemed friendly enough, just curious. I was in no mood for overtures. Of any sort. The second thing I did without drawing much attention was to sidle up to Mrs. Crawford where she sat inscrutable at the piano and was seamlessly playing a medley of Madame Butterfly's suicide aria and "My Mama Done Tol' Me."

"Mrs. C.," I whispered so lightly I wasn't sure she'd catch my words.

She elevated her right eyebrow, waiting.

"I need to see you for a minute." Then: "In the kitchen," I added.

With a flourish that sounded a lot like "Chopsticks," she rose silently and followed me into the kitchen, where I cornered her. "Dear?" was all she said. I was momentarily distracted by the little gray pearl studs in her earlobes, which were shaped like perfect little sand dollars. Who knew? Her wiry guess-my-color hair always covered what turned out to be her finest feature.

I grabbed her sleeves. "You've got to get them"— I jerked my head toward the dining room, to leave no doubt in her mind just which "them" I meant— "out of here, out of here, out of here." I had her interest, I could tell.

"It is going on rather long, isn't it?"

"Did they not *eat* Landon's *granita*?" said I, plaintively. "Surely there's enough sugar in it to match the annual production of Jamaica. Why aren't they twitching and sugar-high-fiving their weird little way on out of here?"

She smiled broadly. "You know how mah-jongg clubs can be."

"Can't you do something? I've got some"—here came the understatement—"terribly pressing business to take care of . . . out there . . . and I need to get rid of the . . . mah-jongg ladies."

The resourceful Mrs. Crawford studied the ceiling fan and lifted a hand toward Landon, who still didn't know what was in the trunk of his precious BMW, and Choo Choo, who probably did. Finally, she jutted her chin at me and wrinkled her nose. Some pancake makeup cracked. "I'll see what

I can do." At which she sashayed back out through the double doors to resume her place at the piano.

What followed was a lively medley of goodbye songs, beginning with "So Long, It's Been Good to Know Yuh." Not so much, I thought, but I could see what Mrs. C. was aiming for, and as the servers brought the last of the dishes into the kitchen, I shook my cell phone at them, saying something regretful about a rumor of a gas leak. Mrs. Crawford had moved on to an up-tempo version of "Good Night, Irene" by the time I agreed with all our servers that it had indeed been a magical evening, positively magical, and that they should all get some sleep safely away from what could blow sky-high at any moment.

With a high heart and no further explanations I started to herd Corabeth, Li Wei, L'Shondra, Vera—too bad, Choo Choo—and Jonathan out the door. Landon watched him go with the kind of bereft longing you see on the faces of mothers sending sonnies off to war. I caught Corabeth's butt in the back door as I closed it a little too soon. She laughed, saying something about how she doesn't need those two pounds, and scooted into the night. To find the stolen bike, most likely.

From the dining room came what I could only think were the hopeful sounds of the Crackpot Club rustling around, getting ready to depart. I heard many comments about the menu—everything from "understated elegance" to "masterful blend of innovation and tradition" to "yummy"—and several comments about looking forward to Maria Pia's formal induction into Belfiere on the 22nd.

Soon enough, the hundred feet that had already pretty much shot to hell the crime scene in the foyer of the restaurant went back the same way—and to that number you could add Giancarlo's, whose hat I plopped on his wispy-haired head with a kiss, and then shoved him along . . . and Maria Pia's, who seemed set on following her new-found knife-wielding sisters down the south side of Market Square. I was hoping she'd climb into some limo and disappear into the night along with the delegates from someplace, oh, two states away.

Mrs. Crawford was packing up some sheet music, and I flashed her a grateful glance.

She could find her own way out, and I'd lock the door later.

And then I remembered: I could probably leave that to the police. The mere thought made me sag.

Stepping back into the Miracolo kitchen, where Landon and Choo Choo and Paulette were rinsing and stacking dinnerware and blurting the occasional positive comment about Maria Pia's big night—"Did you see the size of the teeth on that gal from Maryland?" tells you something about the level of discourse—I clapped my hands. For want of anything better to do. Or smarter. Or more original.

All three of them turned. I clasped my hands in front of my waist and prepared myself to shock them. Well, all except Landon. And probably Choo Choo. So, at least Paulette Coniglio was in for a big surprise. "Georgia Payne has"—here I happened to glance at Landon frantically mouthing *died, died!* at me—"has died," I said with the kind of sepulchral voice you hear at funerals and in the locker rooms of the losers.

In unison Choo Choo and Paulette said, "I know."

Then we all gasped and looked at each other with our fists at our mouths. You would think Choo Choo had just spotted a spider. Practically doubled over with relief that the burden wasn't his and mine alone anymore, Landon yammered on about how I discovered poor Georgia this morning and together we moved her to the storeroom—

Paulette crossed her arms, nodding. "To the bags of semolina. Right. Get on with it."

"So that was you!" I blurted, moving in close to the others.

Paulette, never one to hog credit, held up a warning finger. "And Vera."

At that, Choo Choo beamed at his beloved's

prowess, then chuckled. "Okay, so then I found the stiff"—Landon, Paulette, and I cringed—"in the freezer and got her out to Landon's car—"

Landon shrieked, "You what!"

I was the only one who saw Joe Beck listening on the back threshold.

Choo Choo ruffled Landon's hair. "Not to worry, Lanners. I put her in the trunk. No one's the wiser. Especially not Nonna, eh." Very pleased with himself, Choo Choo Bacigalupo moved liquidly around the Miracolo kitchen, looking for tidbits I was pretty sure Weight Watchers wouldn't approve.

Paulette held up both hardworking mitts and collected herself, about to deliver the kind of speech a referee makes when someone challenges a call. "Which was exactly what we were all working for, am I right?" Like we had worked together all along.

"Yes, yes," I said, sighing, "Nonna in the dark. No mishaps on her big day."

At which point, Joe Beck piped up: "Well, not for Maria Pia, at any rate, although the rest of us are in for it."

Landon shot me an anxious look like *Should we really be talking about this in front of oe-Jay?* My cousin Landon can become very proprietorial when it comes to what he believes is Family Business.

Choo Choo was the first to cotton to it. He laughed—I think the actual word is guffawed—and as he flung back his great head, the track lighting gleamed on all that bald. "Beck, don't tell me—" My Bacigalupo bad boy slapped his knees like he had just heard the joke about the lizard walking into the bar, which always makes him laugh. "You found her?"

Paulette and Landon turned horrified faces to Joe.

Checking his watch, Joe explained, "That Argentine Malbec you ordered, Landon, got stowed in the trunk. I went out for my two bottles."

Several questions bombarded him at once. Paulette wanted to know if poor Georgia Payne was still in the trunk. Choo Choo wanted to know if anyone saw him. And Landon wanted to know if he had tasted the Malbec yet. To which my lawyer replied, "No, she isn't, no, I don't think so, and"— controlling the sarcasm—"I've been kind of busy."

"Right, right."

Paulette was unsatisfied. "What happened to her?" She said it with a critical edge, like dying in the foyer was some kind of great moral failing on the part of the late Georgia Payne.

When Joe shot me a look that included a tight little under-the-radar shake of his glorious head, I answered truthfully, "I thought it was her heart."

Ohhh, they all moaned. Heart. That explains it. Every untimely, inexplicable death since man started tearing apart fatty animals with his teeth must be due to heart. "Up to the coroner," said Joe casually, "but for now we're putting our shoulders into getting Georgia . . ." He looked at me quizzically.

"Payne."

"Payne, back inside where it occurred."

"It's only right," Paulette muttered to Choo Choo, who seemed to be considering other alternatives, none of which I wanted to hear. Then all five of us went wordlessly out the back and crossed the courtyard. It was a very clear night—one of the last nights poor mysterious glove-selling, Belfiere-hiding Georgia was still above ground—and the stars were just beginning to come out. The sound of our footsteps on the stone patio just added to the silence, and out the gate we went, then in single file behind Joe to Landon's BMW.

As he went to swing open the back door, all the rest of us jerked our heads up and down the alley, just to make sure the coast was clear, which had to be the first time in a long time—maybe since high school when I had snuck out of Uncle Dom's house to meet the thrilling Ronnie Rosa—that I had cared about clear coasts. Joe and I stepped aside and the three others crammed themselves into a tight little adoration group and peered inside. There were murmurs of "aw" and "tch," the "tch" coming no doubt from Paulette, who varied "tch" with "tsk." You would think they were viewing a new puppy.

It was Choo Choo who pushed up his sleeves and set about the removal of Georgia from the back of Landon's car. I was seriously hoping it was the last removal we'd have to deal with that night—other, of course, than whatever the cops then did. At any rate, the last removal we Angelottas (the others were honoraries) would have to engineer. Choo Choo easily slid her out, unperturbed by Paulette's backseat driving of the effort—"Watch out, you'll bump her head; watch out, you'll tear her dress"—and lifted her away just as her feet clopped to the asphalt.

At that moment, a set of headlights bounced up and down as a car turned in to the alley down at the far end. All of us—except Georgia—stood taller. One of us actually said, "Cheese it." Someone else snorted. Choo Choo and Joe rapidly set Georgia upright between them and I arranged her arms over their shoulders. Landon darted ahead to open the gate wide, and as the car made unusually fast progress across the potholes, Paulette and I blocked the headlights from spotlighting the five—wait, six—of us like the beginning of an old RKO movie.

"Nah, not the cops," opined Choo Choo, who seemed to slow long enough to crane his neck. "Lights too close together."

"Can we please keep going?" said Joe through gritted teeth.

"Hurry, hurry, you useless, pointless—" That was Paulette.

As we stumbled along in the starry summer night, carrying our burden, sharing our sins, I felt like one of those shapeless, snarling villagers pumping a pitchfork or torch in a Frankenstein movie. Not a pretty sight, but we made it through the gate without attracting any attention from the Smart car that hardly took up half the alley as it skittered past. I closed the gate tight, grateful for the fencing that was overgrown with trumpet vine, which was when I noticed I was shaking.

Landon sailed back into the restaurant ahead of us, scouting out the territory, and reappeared just long enough to declare Miracolo a Maria Pia–free zone. He held open the door, and as we all squeezed through, I saw his fingers catch hold of Georgia's necklace for just a couple of seconds, and then let it go.

"Where does she live?" someone whispered.

Paulette barked, "Well, we're not taking her there."

"Who's her next of kin?" I wondered, sad already for that person, who was probably right then having a lovely night watching Letterman or wait-ing for the Ambien to kick in. Landon gave me a strange look and dropped back while Joe and Choo Choo started across the pristine black-and-white-tiled Miracolo floor, trailing poor Georgia's shoe-less feet pretty much right over the spot where our last corpse had sprawled too recently for comfort.

"Where's her purse?" demanded Paulette, who sounded like she was accusing us of something worse than how we had already been spending the evening. Cart corpses, honey, to your heart's con-tent, but woe is you if you nab a handbag. That's our Paulette. Nobody answered, but it did set me to thinking. I remembered seeing Georgia's red purse the day before, for sure . . . but today? Was it anywhere around when I had tumbled to her body in the foyer of Miracolo? She was closing up—everything, including life, as it turned out. So, by all rights, her red purse should be in the restaurant . . . and finding it would answer questions about her home and next of kin.

"Allow me," said Choo Choo, with that kind of dignity the Bacigalupos are known for (except for the ones here and there in the last three generations who were institutionalized for one thing or the other). Joe let go just as Choo Choo swept up Georgia in his arms, her blond head lolling back, and her arm dan-gling—fortunately (I breathed a sigh) not the one with the ghostly mark of membership in the Crazy Club. Choo Choo shouldered his way through the double doors and into the dining room, empty now of our nonna, the resourceful Mrs. Crawford, and Georgia's former sorority sisters.

Or—here came the rampant paranoia again— her spymasters.

Choo Choo swung around toward me. "Where does she go?"

Joe rolled his eyes—just once, restraining himself.

I took a deep breath. As Landon stood in the shadows and Paulette grabbed a bar towel to wipe her hands, I opened the inner door and exposed the Miracolo foyer in all its death-dealing smallness. A quick look told me I was right: no outlet. Very gently, Choo Choo Bacigalupo went down on one knee and set the body of Georgia Payne on the venerable old tiles of the foyer. The rest of us stared at her as the streetlights seeped through the curtain on the door and noisy late-nighters laughed their boozy way across Market Square, just feet away from what might very well turn out to be a murder scene.

"How was she lying, Eve?" That was Joe Beck, who held his iPhone, ready to make the call to 911.

"Can't we just lay her out across a couple of tables?" I wheedled. "Or on the banquette at table nine?"

Landon and the others all looked at me with sympathetic eyes.

Joe said with meaning that I knew was meant for me alone, "They'll need to see exactly how you found her, Eve." His hand flopped up at me kind of apologetically.

It felt really hard. And because it felt really hard, I saw suddenly just how shaken up I really was by Georgia's death here at Miracolo—charred fingertips or not. Heart or—something else. I had been busy all day long, between moving the body, hunting for the body, and prepping scallop and veal, and I hadn't stopped to just feel something.

I allowed myself one quick sniff. That was public. Later I'd pour myself a reliable Laphroaig back at my place and shake and cry until I was damn done. That was private.

So, with a little nod, I crouched next to Georgia, trying to recall how I found her. I gently set a hand on her chef jacket, sad that she had apparently been so accomplished as a chef that she'd been tapped for Belfiere maybe twenty years sooner than others get the nod. Georgia's chef jacket could get stashed away somewhere—like my tap shoes, the ones I'd been wearing when I went clear off the stage of the New Amsterdam Theater, another example of wasted talent. I remember thinking she looked like she had collapsed to her knees and folded over, dead. So I turned her over onto her stomach, raised her hips, turned her head to the left, and stretched out her right arm.

"That's it," I said, finally, sitting back on my heels. Paulettte wanted to know if she had been lying on her left arm like that. Joe wanted me to be sure whether her head was turned to the left or the right. And Choo Choo, a man colossally uninterested in footwear, practically broke down at the loss of her shoes and started to grill me.

"When was the last time you saw them?"

"I think while she was in the storeroom. No, wait, maybe the freezer—"

Like he had caught me out, he said a little snidely, "Well, which was it?"

"I don't know, I'm telling you. I'm not sure."

"Go easy on her." That was Paulette.

I gave my Bacigalupo cousin a shove. "Go follow the footwear trail, Giuseppe. Call me crazy, but I'm guessing you'll find the little ballet shoes somewhere between the storeroom and the car trunk."

He pushed his big hands all over his face, then went in search of Georgia's flats.

"Well, then," said Joe, who raised his phone and looked from Paulette to me. "Are we ready?"

We nodded, he dialed—and in that moment I realized Landon Angelotta had slipped out of the shadows . . . and was nowhere in sight.

9

The universe, you may have noticed, is the original multitasker. Just as Joe Beck, who had waited under the streetlights out front, was escorting the Quaker Hills firefighter paramedics down the alley to the back door of Miracolo, I experienced some serious déjà vu. The front doorknob rattled. A few muttered imprecations in Italian left no doubt as to the identity of the rattler. "Nonna?" I yapped. Just when you thought it was safe to go back into the foyer. Clearly, none of her Belfiere Bat Association sisters had offered her a lift home . . .

"Eve? What's going on?"

Choo Choo barreled back into this tiniest of foyers, which meant I had Nonna ahead of me, the authorities closing in, and my wild-card cousin showing Georgia Payne something nice in a flat. Always unflappable, Choo Choo eyeballed the shoes and when I recalled that they had half slipped off her feet when I discovered her there this morning, he gently made the modifications.

I looked around helplessly. "Just a minute, Nonna!"

Where was Landon? Why had he just up and disappeared on us?

Now she was knocking hard on the door, her shadow blocking out the streetlights. "What's the fire department doing here?"

Paulette touched my shoulder. "We have to let her in, Eve," she said in a fierce whisper. "This is more serious than the cannoli we got to serve when she wasn't around to stop us."

From outside came "Who's that? Paulette?"

I sighed, then raised my voice. "Go around to the back, Nonna."

She got high-handed, always a bad sign. "I am not going around to the back of my own restaurant."

"You do it every day." Bingo.

"Well, I am not doing it when I don't know what's going on."

Ah, an Angelotta Illogic Thread was beginning. . .

"But the back door was the first one Grandpa Camarata installed when he built Miracolo, remember? That's what you told me."

It worked. "That's true," she admitted.

I pressed my point. "Isn't the first door really more the 'front' door than the front door?'" I rolled my eyes at Paulette, who was giving me a look that involved lifting half her face in unadulterated scorn.

On the other side of the door, Maria Pia struggled only a few seconds with the dominant gene of Camarata pride that pretty reliably trumped every other human emotion. Then: "Very well." Off she went, moving out of the light that played feebly over the corpse of our late, lamented sous chef.

Choo Choo oozed out of the foyer, followed by Paulette, and with that I knew the jig was most definitely up. "Eve?" Joe Beck was standing in the dining room, rubbing back his short golden hair with his forearm. I looked up at two strangers, a man and a woman in blue T-shirts and pants, carrying equipment. In the dim light I could hardly make out their faces. All I felt was gratitude that it wasn't Nonna's body I was crouching next to in the sweet old foyer of Miracolo. "Honey," said Joe Beck, taking a step toward me, "come on out of there."

The side of my face tingled. I stood up, feeling like I was abandoning Georgia to an unknown fate—although, truth be told, she would probably have fewer postdeath adventures now—and my arms hung at my sides. All of them waited while I stood there uncertainly. Joe added softly: "Just let them do their job."

With a huge huff, I did the thing I discovered as a kid would sometimes keep me from bursting into tears: I walked straight into Joe Beck's arms, my own arms pinned tightly against my chest. There I sobbed, and sobbed even louder when Maria Pia burst onto the scene, invoking half the saints and the spirits of her father, the poet Dante, and Frank Sinatra.

Someone handed me a tissue—I'm assuming Paulette, who among women is the "always prepared" Boy Scout, unless anyone she deems ablebodied asks for a hand across the street. Someone else patted my back. I twisted my face into some semblance of Eve Angelotta's public face.

Twisting my neck just enough to see what was coming down, I saw Maria Pia actually push the medics aside. Getting what she thought was the full picture of what we had in the foyer, she propped her hands on her midnight-blue satin Belfiere costume and started nodding some big nods. I could almost guess what was coming but didn't have the strength to step out of Joe's arms. "So, Georgette, you're—what?" she addressed the body, jerking her proud chin at her. "Ten hours late for work and this is the best you can do?"

* * *

All told, once it sank in, Maria Pia took the news of Georgia Payne's death well. New employee, bad heart, whaddya gonna do? Then, a little embarrassed at her mistake, she got all airy and philosophical, delivering the opinion that it's not easy to tell the difference between life and death in some people. Especially (here I cringed) if they're not Italian. At that, the medics—whose names, as luck would have it, were Kaplowitz and Mahoney—turned slowly to look at her. Paulette jumped in, offering to help the Philosopher of Quaker Hills out of her Belfiere gown, which offered maybe two minutes of distraction as Nonna relived the success of the evening.

The mood changed, though, as soon as I raised the bar on the truth.

Choo Choo, who from the look on my face could tell what I was about to do, headed straight for the kitchen for the bag of Cheetos he keeps stashed on a shelf behind the coffee grinder.

Paulette held the cast-off costume in a stony reverie.

Joe Beck smiled at me and opened his hands wide. *Your story, your show.*

You know the expression *All hell broke loose.* This sentence always conjures up the kind of chaos only a great artist or a terrible ruler can create. But the kind of hell that can break loose has a real measure of subtlety. The crack in the ice, the one drink too many, the casual fib. Hell starts small. The rest of us just can't keep it small. The news of the death of the person whom Nonna waffled between calling Georgina and Georgette was manageable. Hovering near the medics, Nonna said surprisingly few words, mostly about how she supported the referendum to build a new fire station in Quaker Hills.

But then all hell broke loose.

It started at 10:37 p.m. on Friday, June 20. And it may have had something to do with my stepping up and announcing, in the kind of clear and concerned voice you hear in commercials about erectile dysfunction, "I found Georgia Payne in that position, and in that spot, at 12:03 this afternoon."

Maria Pia looked like she had swallowed a cannoli, whole. She was unable to speak, which is not in itself a bad thing.

Paulette's stony reverie cracked a little, but she withstood it.

The kitchen emitted a quavering groan. In between Cheetos.

The medics gave me a keen look like they had possibly never seen such a fine example of a duck-billed platypus. "Go on," said one of them slowly.

I decided to keep the knowledge of Georgia's

Belfiere *B* to myself, at least for a little while. Doing so might buy me some time to figure out where Georgia's purse had gone, whether her death had anything to do with her history with Belfiere, and why the presently absent Landon Angelotta was looking very much like a man with secrets—not at all like my beloved pillow-talking cuz.

I lifted my chin. "And you might want to check out Georgia's fingertips."

Ice was cracking hard and swift, everywhere.

And any guard let down after that third tequila wasn't about to see you home unbedded.

The female medic checked out Georgia's fingertips, raised her arched eyebrows even higher, and showed her partner. When he frowned and let out an appreciative whistle, then held up his phone, muttering, "I'm calling it in," Maria Pia suddenly found her voice and started clamoring in Italian. But I'm pretty sure not even invoking the spirit of Old Blue Eyes to deliver her from her enemies in Quaker Hills—which was the first I'd heard of them—was going to alter what was rapidly becoming clear to us all: that Georgia Payne had met a violent death.

It was Sally Belts and Boots, the fashionista half of Quaker Hills' two police detectives, who showed up. Right off she sat the four of us down at our finest table—Paulette got busy with the cappuccino machine—and told us some interesting things. When she happened to mention that her last name was Fanella, Nonna eyed me like we were as good as sprung already. Georgia's death was going to be a case for the coroner, but until they hear otherwise, the cops were treating it like a homicide, and the CSI team would arrive shortly. Paulette wanted to know if they liked their cappuccino with or without foam. Sally Fanella chose foam.

We spent the next hour and a half stepping all over each other as we tried to piece together the events of the afternoon, which, of course, was the first Maria Pia had heard of Georgia's postdeath travel plans, all in service of keeping the news from her and her, uh, mah-jongg club. At which Paulette winked at me and I smiled brightly at Detective Sally, who was definitely not sporting her signature double belts and knee-high boots. In fact, she was wearing yoga pants and what looked like a ratty camisole under a lightweight tan jacket.

Maria Pia, unbelievably, was practically swooning with pride at our devotion. She ordered extra foam with her cappuccino, which she savored with sounds really better off left to the bedroom. I could tell Detective Sally was thinking the same thing as she tried to take notes about the dead Georgia's itinerary. My job at nearly midnight on that day was to convince this gal in the yoga pants—aided by the best I could provide in terms of Italian hand gestures—that I thought poor Georgia had keeled over with a heart attack or a blood clot.

The parts that involved the back half of Landon's BMW we handled gingerly, and I'm pretty sure the word *trunk* never found its way into the conversation.

By that time Sally was clicking her ballpoint pen kind of manically. Her lips were pressed tightly together, no doubt because she was calculating just how much evidence was lost in the fouling of the crime scene, what with the equivalent of two hundred feet trampling it, coupled with the kind of manhandling of the body you see pretty much only at strip joints.

When the Crime Scene crew showed up, carting their equipment and arguing over whether the Phillies could go all the way, Maria Pia lost some of her bounce, probably remembering just last month, when a murder shut down Miracolo—such a nuisance—and she was jailed. Now, at least, she had the sweet comfort of Belfiere. How could the mystifying electrocution of one of her employees dim that glorious success?

The question of Landon arose.

Joe Beck sounded lawyerly and reassuring. Back on the job.

Detective Sally Fanella asked us to tell him to pay her a visit down at the station—at his earliest convenience. In the hour and a half she'd spent with us trying to get the overview of what had happened in Miracolo that day, the woman looked like she'd aged ten years. Her soft, wavy blond hair seemed to have lost its luster. Her skin had sprouted fine lines. She looked like she suddenly needed a trip to the local drugstore for a pair of cheaters. Wearily, she finally mentioned that the restaurant was officially a crime scene and that it was closed until further notice.

Actually, none of us moaned, not even Maria Pia, who, this time, might have been contemplating her "time off" as an opportunity for another fling with a brawny miner. Apparently she had an alibi for the time of "Georgette's" death—she and Choo Choo had stayed up late watching *Babette's Feast*, whereupon they both feel asleep—and was feeling footloose and unlikely to be considered a suspect. Ditto Choo Choo, because the two of them had stayed up late watching the movie together.

At the first indication from Sally Fanella that we were free to go, but not too far, I slipped out, exhausted, while the rest of the staff divvied up tasks for the following day. None of which included opening at 5 p.m. for the dinner crowd. I drove exhausted all the way home in my Volvo, which my poor foot didn't have the strength to push to 35 mph. When I pulled into my little parking spot and walked under the starry night to my Tumbleweed Tiny House, where I'd left a battery-op candle lighted in the window, I walked on shaky legs up to my front door. Grateful for an end to the day. Grateful for solitude. I always say I like my privacy, but really, it's my solitude. I stopped just to take in the sweet sounds of the night, and I was so happy happy happy I couldn't tell whether what I was hearing out there in the woods was spring peepers or summer crickets.

All I knew for sure was, they had nothing to do with Georgia Payne's death.

Could I say the same for the rest of us?

I left my teeth unbrushed.

That's how dog tired I was.

I stripped at the bottom of the ladder up to my sleeping loft, and I left my clothes right where they fell. At the top I sank into my mattress, crawling over to the window to push it open, and flopped onto my back. The peepers or crickets—or maybe some third possibility I hadn't yet thought of— were audible. So I listened and drifted.

Who had a reason to kill Georgia Payne?

I shivered at the fleeting thought that Nonna had just attached herself to a group that Georgia seemed to want all the way out of her life. But how far did she go? Was removing the Belfiere tattoo just the first step? How far did Georgia have to go to . . . what? Feel safe? Was she hiding out? If so, what bad luck, what with the whole mah-jongg club coming to the very restaurant where she'd just gotten a job.

And then I remembered Georgia's red purse that had disappeared. Did that have something to do with her murder? Who would steal a purse? It was like a different kind of crime. The sort of thing that middle-aged culinary cutthroats, no matter how out of control, would never think to do. Stealing a purse was more along the lines of . . .

CRIBS kids.

Corabeth?

Really?

As I started to doze off, I vowed I'd get on the case, not to nab Corabeth, but hopefully to clear her. All my arms and legs were arranged in just the right way as I slipped off to sleep. I'm pretty sure I had a smile on my face that no one could see because in those delicious final minutes I could hear very clearly those words spoken by Joe Beck when he wanted me to get out of Miracolo's foyer and give the medics room next to Georgia's body: "Honey, come on out of there."

Honey.

* * *

Overnight a storm blew in and I woke up once just to pull the window shut. Lighting darted through my little house, and thunder boomed away, right overhead, it seemed. All I felt was that drowsy kind of happiness that only made me slink farther under my lightweight comforter as the downpour pounded my tin roof. How bad can anything be, really, if at its absolute worst it still sounds like music?

But by morning it was still raining, so I had my coffee in my window seat, one of my favorite places in my precious little space, leaning up against a raft of colorful throw pillows, courtesy of Pier One. You can tell by the spangles and embroidery. All I had was my phone for company, and between sips, every time I called Landon, it went straight to voice mail. I could fool myself into thinking he was still sawing wood in his bed the size of a football field over there south of town in his pricey condo. But Landon Angelotta was an early riser. At any rate, Vaughn Angelotta, his handsome tabby cat, was, and would knead and paw him into submission, when he'd get out of bed and come across with a can opener.

While I nibbled a two-day-old chocolate crois-sant (I think the chocolate keeps it from getting stale), Maria Pia called—sounding totally on her best game—and told me she had called the entire staff of Miracolo and told them we were on hiatus and that they would, of course, assist the police in their efforts to solve the mystery of Georgina's death. I waited for her to add what I knew she was thinking—namely, that the sooner any evildoers were put behind bars, the sooner we'd reopen— but she was admirably restrained. For Maria Pia.

When she mentioned that she was contemplating entering the Sisters of St. Margaret Retreat Center to, er, contemplate for a day, preparing for her induction into—here her voice dropped to a whisper like she was uttering a state secret— Belfiere, I told her she'd better let Detective Fanella know her whereabouts. She grunted at me and we hung up.

I decided right then and there that I loved the word *whereabouts*.

I declared to myself that I'd celebrate this discovery with a second croissant.

The rain came on steady, driving hard against my roof.

Without leaving the window seat, I went to work, calling each of the Miracolo staff to check whether any of them had "seen" (subtext: stolen) a red purse belonging to the late Georgia Georgette Georgina Payne. Since Nonna had already awakened them, I figured to cash in on their stumbling around their homes trying to figure out what in the name of holy roasted nuts was going on at their place of employment.

Jonathan remembered seeing a red purse when he was first introduced to Georgia, but that was it. Vera thought the purse had been yellow and hemp and really sort of crappy, right? That one, I told her, was mine. Oh, then, sorry (I could picture her looking sheepish), but no. Li Wei asked, "What purse?" I told him the red purse. Li Wei asked, "What red purse?" I told him Georgia's red purse. And "Who's Georgia?" pretty much ended our conversation.

L'Shondra remembered the red purse because it was the one Georgia had brought to our first Basic Cooking Skills class and she thought it was kickin', but she hadn't seen it at the restaurant, and oh, by the way, can she collect unemployment? Giancarlo rhapsodized about a red purse worn by a sexy spy for the Allies he once knew, but couldn't help with Georgia's.

That left Corabeth Potts.

And Choo Choo Bacigalupo. Who owed me. Big. I placed a call to the Callowhill Residential Institute for Behavioral Success, where I learned I was welcome to visit anytime today, and that the students in question were indeed in their cottages. Saturdays were chore days. Not, I was betting, that many got done. Still, I'd go. And my mind slipped from thoughts of Georgia's mysterious death and the disappearance— whereabouts—of her red purse, to thoughts about the familiar figures of my hit-and-run graffiti artists.

I placed my final call for the morning to my monumental cousin, Choo Choo. Who actually sounded like lugging bodies was a beauty treatment, he was so upbeat. I dampened his exuberance a bit when I forged right ahead and told him what I had in mind. It wasn't until a little while later, as the rain started to let up and the sky brightened, that I got a call while I was slipping on a pair of gray cropped pants and a pink camisole.

"Eve?"

For a split second I had to admit to myself that I was hoping it was Joe Beck, even though the caller ID was unidentified.

"Yes?"

"It's Mrs. Crawford."

Like the sky, I brightened up. "Did you hear from Maria Pia, Mrs. C.? We're closed, probably until Monday." Even as I said it, I realized I had to call Dana Cahill and the regulars. Grief Week was about to get cut short. Shucks.

Georgia had been cut short.

"I heard," she said. Then she went silent.

"Everything?" I probed. "All about the—death?"

Not only does Mrs. Crawford read between the lines, she reads between the pixels in the spaces between the lines. It was one of the things I especially liked about her.

"Yes."

"So . . ." I was a little at a loss.

Her voice came back with some energy. "Let's get together today, you and I."

Was she inviting me out for tea? What? "Okay." After my trip out to CRIBS, I'd have some time on my hands. "What's up?"

"Well, I've been thinking."

When other people say that, it's usually along the lines of whether they want pizza or burgers for dinner. When Mrs. Bryce Crawford says it, you can bank on her having figured out crop circles or what happened to Amelia Earhart. So, I slowly replied, "Yes?"

"There's no Georgia Payne."

"Well," I stated the obvious, "not anymore."

"Not ever." I could hear the smile in her voice. "So, Eve," said Miracolo's mysterious pianist, "meet me at Jolly's Pub at three o'clock and I'll tell you who she really was."

Try having a normal day when you hear words like that. It's like hearing (not that this happened) a neighborhood brat blurt that he saw you and Ronnie Rosa lose your respective virginities in Ronnie's brother Ricky's bright blue Camaro. It hangs there. (I'm talking about the words.) It weighs. But my celebratory croissant had given me enough of a pastry fix for the morning that I was able to attend to other matters. The unbrushed teeth. The bug on the window, the slant of the maple flooring, and whether I needed a few more throw pillows for the window seat.

By the time Choo Choo pulled up outside, I was outfitted in black pants and an electric-blue, drapey jersey top (must have been thoughts of Ricky Rosa's Camaro). I paired all that with a black Coach bag Maria Pia had passed on to me—never used—years ago and a pair of joke earrings I kept from a Halloween party thrown last year by Landon: dangling chains sporting little replicas of human bones.

I smudged on some eye shadow and stroked some red blush across my high cheekbones and slathered tomato-red lipstick across my lips. With a felt-tip pen I even added a couple of beauty marks, then I sprayed my hair into vampy place. This was just about as bad-ass as I get. Coach bag and stupid earrings. Fake beauty marks straight out of the 1940s.

I even wore heels.

Which I shined with black polish.

* * *

Then I locked my front door and ran down the two little steps to the wet grass. Choo Choo was leaning against a black limo he had borrowed from his seriously sketchy friend Junior Bevilacqua, who sat behind him in homeroom all throughout their school years. Junior now owned a "livery service," and I hesitate to consider what he transports for a hefty fee.

Choo Choo himself went mostly for the stereotype, decked out in his usual fine black suit he wears at Miracolo, but today he'd added a black shirt, white tie—here he varied the classic look with a bolo tie, secured with a skull carved out of bone—and a hat. Not a fedora, like any self-respecting gangster would wear. A beret. A black one. The look was strangely sinister, so I loved it. Points for Choo Choo Bacigalupo.

We silently high-fived.

Then Choo Choo Bacigalupo—aka Don Lolo Dinardo—climbed into the backseat of one of Junior Bevilacqua's limos. And I slipped into the driver's seat. We were off.

10

A slave to any GPS, I got us to the Callowhill Residential Institute for Behavioral Success without incident. Don Lolo sat reflectively in the back, legs crossed, eyes narrowed with musings. CRIBS was west of town by about a half hour, set—I had found out online—on twelve acres of woodland. The drive up to the main building, the kind of staunch red-and-white colonial that gives nothing away, ran through an arbor of towering black locusts. The public face of Callowhill, I was guessing. I parked in front of the main entrance, figuring that when your wheels are a limo, no one asks questions.

Leaving Don Lolo behind his privacy glass in his bulletproof (well, probably not) vehicle, I went inside the main administration building long enough to identify myself as Mitchell, Slash, and Cora-beth's teacher at the Quaker Hills Career Center. A short young receptionist with a slight tremble in her voice, hands, and head—understandable, from what I'd already seen of this crew—and large haunted eyes, had me sign in, which I did primly. More primly than my eye shadow and earrings warranted. I had a sudden bad moment wondering if (I stole a look at her name tag) Jenny Johnson was scared of me, not them. Should have taken off the earrings. She was too young to appreciate the Coach bag . . .

Choking out some vague directions to what she called "Cottages Three and Four," Jenny let me go, and I skipped down the steps and back into the limo. We drove halfway around the semicircle and turned an easy right onto Alvin and Marcia Higgenbotham Drive. Big donors, no doubt. Naming rights, and all that. I found myself wondering whether half the problem for these kids was having to tell your buds you live on Alvin and Marcia Higgenbotham Drive. Can you blame them? I'd be flicking lit matches, too.

Brick "cottages" Three and Four, which stood next to each other, eased into sight. I drove slowly, since slow carries its own brand of menace, if you ask me. I parked silently, since silence carries its own brand of menace, if you ask me. I spotted the three of them—the dreadlocked Mitchell, the suspiciously clean-cut Slash, and Corabeth, whose hair was screaming red again and rubber-banded back into its Shrek 'do. Apparently the lads were mocking her, which she thanked them for with a quick twist of Slash's arm and Mitchell's, well, private parts. I shot a look at Choo Choo, who seemed impressed the boys didn't howl.

"Stay put for now," I reminded him. To which he simply lowered his eyelids in assent.

Out of the limo I bounded over to Corabeth. The other two shrank back, but only a bit, since I was arriving so—so—unexpectedly. So full of energy. Maybe even a homework assignment. "Hey, how ya doin', Miz Angelino," quipped Slash, that wit. Mitchell elbowed him and they feinted at each other for no explainable reason.

"Fine, boys, just fine," I smiled benignly.

Slash ventured: "Lookin' some kind of fine"— and he added, with a leer that was supposed to make me tingle, I guess, "*Eve.*" This overstepping led to more horseplay from the merry pranksters.

I flashed them as much of a hundred-watt Mary Poppins manic grin as I dared, so as to lull them but not lose their interest. "Catch y'all in a minute, just gonna have a word with Corabeth here."

I motioned to Corabeth, who angled herself off the bench with a quizzical look on a great face that was way too unappreciated by herself and everybody else. She fell in beside me and we walked across the grass toward—nothing important. More colonial brick buildings. More Alvin and Marcia, no doubt. Her hands were stuffed boyishly into her pockets and she looked unhappy. Out of earshot of the Hardy Boys, I stopped in my tracks, and set a hand on her big arm.

"Georgia's dead, Corabeth."

Her face got even bigger. "Georgia from class? Georgia from the restaurant?"

I nodded. She didn't ask what happened. Either she knew, or—more likely—in her world she always assumed the worst. "Miracolo's closed while the police gather evidence."

Now it was her turn to nod. I guess she lived in a world where evidence got gathered on a fairly regular basis. Finally, she worked up the courage to say, "I really liked working for you."

"You were really, really good." I sounded every bit as enthusiastic as I felt. She shot me a look like I was pulling her leg, which was impossible either literally or figuratively, and I laughed a little. "You've got great hands and a wonderful manner, Corabeth. I want you to stay on." I figured we'd review the dress and grooming code later, but for the moment the big girl was shuffling around in a way that looked a lot like the Cha-cha Slide. I took it for joy.

When I asked her about Georgia's purse, she got a look of intense concentration on her face. "Red thing about yay big with a chain handle and a pearl clasp?"

Even I hadn't noticed that much about it. *Red* was just about as far as my powers of observation went. "That'd be the one," I guessed.

Whereupon Corabeth rounded on the dreadlocks and tongue stud back at the bench. "You shit heads stole Georgia's purse?" she bellowed. I think there was a chance anyone pumping gas at the Marathon station a mile away heard her. Corabeth whirled to face me. "They been fooling with a fancy date book and an iPod in a purple case for like the last day. Now I know where I seen that date book before—class on Wednesday, Miss Eve." I watched as she headed like a riled bear toward her fellow CRIBSmates. Over her shoulder, she yelled back to me, "Georgia had it out."

Slash and Mitchell decided to stand their ground, aided by a glint of something that emerged from the skanky pocket of one of them. My heart started racing. At that moment, the rear door to Junior Bevilacqua's limo opened wide, right in front of the boys, who got jumpy, trying to get the lay of the land that was rumbling under their sneakered feet.

Out slid Choo Choo. As I closed in on the little

group, I was dying at the thought that Corabeth, in her big friendly way, would call out something to him, another Miracolo staffer, and blow the whole plan. "Corabeth, Corabeth!" I hollered. She pulled up short—I swear I felt Earth slow in its rotation—and gave the little scene the once-over. Then she turned to me with a grin only I could see. We were good.

Choo Choo oozed silently over to Mitchell and Slash, who could only glower at him like five-year-olds ready to carry on because some bully kicked over their sand castle. "Who the hell are you, Fatso?" sputtered Slash. I didn't know whether to laugh or quake in my heels. Could the kid not read the situation? Had he never seen the tollbooth scene from *The Godfather*? In all of his experience was a horse's head always attached to the rest of the horse? Were these two purse-snatching graffiti-artist firebugs really that unacquainted with popular culture?

Without answering, Choo Choo flicked open his suit jacket, conveniently revealing a shoulder-holstered gun I knew he had bought at the same costume shop where I got my chains-and-bones earrings. We went to the same party. Slipping a hand inside his jacket, while the boys were still trying to find their swagga, Choo Choo pulled out a roll of Mentos. Mitchell and Slash were just starting to work up a look that said the limo guy was not only fat but downright silly, when Choo Choo's arm seemed to get in touch with its inner mongoose and he had Slash Kipperman off his twitchy feet in a neck grip.

My turn. I stepped up and tried channeling a little bit of a big-hair Jersey girl. All I needed was the gum. "Boys," I said broadly, "this is Don Lolo Dinardo." I waxed positively waxy. "Legitimate businessman. Part-owner of a landfill in the Pine Barrens. Security consultant for local businesses."

With a dexterity I never knew he had, my cousin Choo Choo let the little turd go and snagged the blade, folded it, and tossed it into the limo before any of us knew what was happening. But Slash didn't get far, maybe because he was trying to catch his breath, and Choo Choo hauled them both close to him by the bunched-up crew necks of their T-shirts.

Then he delivered as fine a Brando impression as you're likely to see, complete with the famous Corleone hoarse, nasal underbite. "I sense you are disrespecting me, boys," he uttered with half-lowered eyelids. They answered in a series of sputters and gags that went completely over the heads of the rest of us.

"Today is the Feast Day of Little Serena, the patron saint of Space Mountain. So I am willing to

overlook your disrespect"—this was met with more
sputters and gags, which Don Lolo shushed with
puckered lips—"your disrespect to me, but you
must never disrespect my *bellissima cugina* [most
beautiful cousin] Eve, or"—his eyes slew frac-
tionally to my left—"my goddaughter Corabeth.
This"—he affectionately ruffled Corabeth's Shrek
'do, and his voice got very faraway—"is a special
relationship. Do we understand each other?" He
looked them over with his most reptilian expression. "It pains me to think what I should have to
do if you try to set them, oh, on fire, or paint dis-
respectful portraits of them on the side of a restaurant where the saltimbocca is particularly good.
For these places," said he, sagely, "are hard to find.
Do we understand each other?"

Mitchell and Slash, wide-eyed, nodded dumbly.

I was hoping Don Lolo's point was sufficiently
clear, because at that moment the front door to
Cottage Three opened and a brawl spilled out. The
cheering squad was so mixed up with the fight-
ers that it was hard to tell what was going—until
one of the ones in blue jeans and a darker blue T-
shirt turned out to be a child-care worker trying to
break it all up.

Before this guy could decide any strangers
hanging with the likes of Mitchell Terranova and
Slash Kipperman warranted closer attention, Choo

Choo swiftly eased himself back into his limo throne and I took a quick opportunity to get in the face of my two least favorite students ever in all my days of teaching.

"Where's the red purse?"

"Swear to God we don't have it!"

"Don't make me tell on you to Don Lolo." *Tell on you?*

"No, really, Miz Angelotta—"

"And by the way," said the other one, his watery eyes skidding over to the inscrutable privacy glass of the limo, "really sorry about that whole spray paint . . . incident."

"We don't have it. We found it outside in the back behind the restaurant a couple of days ago when we were casing—"

Slash elbowed him with gritted teeth behind a quavery smile. "While we were hanging around trying to get a peek at you."

And they must think I was born—forget yester-day— just after breakfast. I grunted. "Where's the purse now?"

Mitchell waved his scrawny arms like he was trying to get airborne. "We ditched it."

"Word."

White boys just can't pull that off.

"After we dumped it out and kept the money."

"Where?"

Corabeth kicked Slash's shin. "That's Georgia's purse, you jackasses. Did you kill her for it?"

At that the boys grabbed each other. I would have preferred the righteous Ms. Potts to keep that piece of information to herself, but their reaction was totally worth blowing the element of surprise. Suddenly they were two little snotty, burpy, blankie-toting kids who were as scared of *l'uomo nero* as Landon and I had been. "*Killed?*" Mitchell choked out.

The brawl was breaking up but threats were still getting lobbed pretty freely. A couple of them started to walk it off— and in our direction. Time's up. "Listen, *Terrarium*, and you, too, *Kippers*"— I was just in the mood to make up really stupid nicknames, knowing I had the full force of Don Lolo Dinardo sprawling with some Cheetos out of view behind me—"I want that red purse, and I want it by"—I pretended to consult my wristwatch, then had a brainstorm—"six o'clock tonight." They started falling all over themselves, protesting that they couldn't possibly—and here it got murky because one said they dumped it in a Dumpster behind Kroger's and the other said they shoved it down a storm sewer.

Corabeth rolled her eyes. "Guaranteed it's under the bed of one of them."

I held up a finger. "By midnight tonight, or

your new BFF Don Lolo Dinardo will hear how
you stole the money out of the purse"—here I
power-walked around the hood of the limo—"of
his dead lady friend." Poor old Georgia: dead *and*
connected. I winked at Corabeth and climbed behind the wheel, slamming the door, stitching Choo
Choo and me back into the cocoon of Junior's
limo, away for the next half hour from the brawls
and lies and charred fingers and bruised hearts of
the outside world.

"Are we good, *cara*?" asked Don Lolo when I got
out back at my place. He was leaning against the
driver's door, brushing Cheetos off his sinister
black shirt. Little billows of mist were lifting from
the acreage behind my sweet little house on wheels.

"We're good, Chooch." We gave each other a
rib-crushing hug, then he chuckled and climbed
behind the wheel. I shut the door as the window
noiselessly slid down. I asked him if he'd seen
Landon, but he shook his head no. Patting the
flawless black paint job on the limo's door frame, I
said, "Tell Junior I said hey."

Choo Choo, the world's worst matchmaker,
piped up. "You know he loves you," he reminded
me, his voice full of reproof. It seemed to slip my
cousin's mind that Junior Bevilacqua had sired five

children in five different states and had every intention of paying child support—*word*, as Slash the K would say—but he just had "all these friggin' expenses." Like getting the limo fleet detailed with disturbing frequency and like child support was something different from expenses.

"I don't need his love," I said with a laugh. "Just his car."

"I might not want to tell him that."

"You might not."

I swung by Miracolo, sighing at the sight of the yellow crime-scene tape, not to mention a small crowd that included someone I recognized as a reporter for the Philly *Inquirer*. For one split second it made me crave a real Don Lolo who could, oh, discourage with an airy wave of a bejeweled hand (holding an automatic) any unwanted attention from the press. Just how long could I avoid the reporters?

And pressing her nose against the glass of the front door, there was complicated little Akahana, who pondered consciousness as she dug daily through Quaker Hills trash cans for treasures both edible and otherwise. And when I realized that standing next to her was the unsinkable Dana Cahill, I gunned the Volvo and practically did a wheelie turning onto Callowhill Street. The presence of Dana was bad news since I didn't put it past her to hand the reporter a line of the most fictitious stuff about the death of Georgia Payne.

More at loose ends than I'd felt since four years ago when my leg cast came off and I was clearly going to have to come up with a plausible Plan B, what with a dance career that was nowhere in sight, I drove south out of town. At Innerlight Estates, the swank condo complex where my beloved cousin Landon lived, made possible by the dough inherited from his dad, my uncle Dominic, I parked right in front of his unit, got out of the car, and looked around. Towering locusts, ornamental pear and cherry trees, urns of blooms so unusual I couldn't even name them—even the grass knew better than to go rogue and sprout weedy aberrations. Rain still glistened on all of it, and the sun wasn't strong enough to dry it up.

My eyes glanced up at what I knew was Landon's window on the second floor. It was open but, behind the screen, dark even in the daylight. It was the window to the master bedroom. I performed my foolproof—and Landon proof—test. "Vaughn!" I called up to the window. If his handsome tabby self didn't appear at the window, Landon was home and providing enough wet food and games of fetch that Vaughn could ignore me. But if he popped into view and meowed, he was perishing of want of some sort because the human was off being irresponsible somewhere, working his job, say, and mine was a voice he recognized as someone being adept with a can opener.

"Vaughn!" I called again. Then I waited. When no Vaughn appeared in the window, I knew Landon was home. Home, and out of touch. And probably within earshot of my hollering for Vaughn. For a couple of minutes, all I could do was sigh and stare. What was going on with him? Then I pulled out my phone and called him. It went straight to voice mail.

It was one thing if Landon Angelotta needed a break from the world.

It was another thing altogether if he needed a break from me.

In the Miracolo world of June 21, Choo Choo Bacigalupo was a goodfella, Landon Angelotta was MIA, Joe Beck was calling me "honey," Maria Pia was heading for a retreat center, and I was threatening my students in more eye makeup than I'd worn since leaving the Broadway cast of *Mary Poppins*. None of these sudden changes in my known world compared to what greeted me when I walked into Jolly's Pub across the street from Miracolo just shy of 3 p.m.

Behind the bar was Giancarlo Crespi, our devoted elderly bartender.

I had to do a double take. I'm not sure I'd ever seen him out of the Miracolo "uniform" of white shirt and black pants, over which he chose to wear a red-and-black embroidered vest. But standing there behind Reginald Jolly's bar he was wearing a black shirt, silver tie, and gray pants. And in the space of half a day he had gotten an earlobe pierced. Maybe Maria Pia's *B* tattoo had inspired him to think outside the pine box.

All thoughts of Mrs. Crawford fled my mind as I stalked right up to the bar. "Giancarlo," I said, riveting him with my best incredulous look, "what in the name of Vieux Pontarlier"—his favorite absinthe, that herb and anise liqueur with the 130 proof—"are you doing here?"

Our dear old Giancarlo, who may or may not have seduced Maria Pia a century ago, pulled himself up tall at five foot six. "I am supplementing my Social Security."

I blustered, "But you supplement your Social Security with us!"

A steady hand smoothed his thin comb-over. "That may be as it is"—he inclined his Genovese head at me a fraction—"but we are closed, and my expenses . . ." Here he made the vague Italian one-handed gesture that has something to do with both the incomprehensibility of man's place in the scheme of things, and indigestion.

"Are what?" At the sound of my bark, I reminded myself of Paulette.

He got prissy. "Are not inconsiderable."

I was quietly shocked at myself that I never wondered about Giancarlo's life outside Miracolo. He always just showed up for work on time, did a fine job, didn't aggravate me—in fact, I decided to make him Employee of the Month. Just as soon as we start up the program. Did this old man's life really consist of something more than renting a third-floor room somewhere in Quaker Hills, taking the bus, watching PBS on his forty-two-inch flat-screen TV, and eating leftovers from the Miracolo kitchen? Shame on me.

"Well," I said kind of anxiously, "you'll be coming back when we reopen in a day or two, right?" He actually seemed to be thinking it over. Like a resounding "Yes" wasn't automatic. My voice got higher. "Right, Giancarlo?"

Finally, he answered, "If she wants me."

She? Could only be Maria Pia. "Of course she wants you!" Then I realized how that sounded. "Back!" Then I realized it wasn't entirely an improvement. "To tend bar!"

Giancarlo straightened his two thins arms and leaned against the bar. "The human heart," he shook his head sadly, "can only take just so much, then . . ." And mild little Giancarlo Crespi made a quick strangling gesture with both his hands and a sound like something juicy was getting way too squeezed. Either he was telling me in so many words what he'd like to do to my nonna's throat, or he was demonstrating what happens to the human heart pushed beyond its limits. On the record, I was hoping for the latter.

"Giancarlo," I said, wide-eyed, "we need you."

"Reginaldo pays me better."

Poker face, poker face, Angelotta. "I'm sure we can work something out."

He looked me straight in the eye—at that moment I discovered Giancarlo had his very own poker face—the man was full of surprises— and then said, "What can I get you?"

Glumly, I ordered a seltzer with a lime twist. While he spritzed the seltzer into a glass, I bent to get a closer look. "Are you wearing a fake in that ear?"

He glanced up. "It's a sticker," he explained, adding, "I didn't want to commit."

With great dignity, I told him, "I will take that as a positive sign." Then I took my drink and shuffled over to one of the café tables in the empty pub.

11

When Mrs. Crawford walked in, it was like a scene from a moody, backlit movie. She stood in the doorway, her eyes adjusting to the indoors, her hand floating up to her wide-brimmed picture hat. As she started across the room to my table, I saw she was back to her hot-pink cocktail dress, matching shoes, and chapeau adorned with a row of well-behaved tea roses. A day off from piano duties at Miracolo seemed to bring the blushing tea roses straight on down to her cheeks. Was she wearing bright blue contact lenses? Apparently murder brings out the experimental in otherwise dependable people . . .

"Eve," she intoned in her deep, soft voice.

"Mrs. Crawford," I acknowledged her. I gestured to the other chair and lifted my chin at her. "May I buy you a drink?"

We narrowed our eyes at each other. Mine were narrow because I was hoping to hell she didn't think this was a date. Hers were narrow because she was hoping to hell I didn't think this was a date. So, we were good. "Anyhow," I continued. "Something?"

She agreed to what I myself had ordered, and after I mooned over the slipping-away Giancarlo as he made the drink, I sat back down. A quick check showed me "Reginaldo" was nowhere around. Shame. I'd be interested in seeing what happened in Jolly's Pub when Reginald and Mrs. Crawford met each other.

Overhead—in the silence created by Mrs. Crawford and me, twizzling our sticks reflectively—the piped-in music was finally heard. Just then Linda Ronstadt was wondering when she would be loved. Get behind me, Linda. I twizzled my stick even harder, rapping it noisily against the side of the glass. Finally, I looked at our pianist, who wasn't wearing stick-on earrings. "So, Mrs. C., what have you got?" Her teaser had something to do with who Georgia Payne really was, that much I remembered. Had Georgia sold her some fake calfskin gloves at Bloomingdale's? What?

Mrs. Crawford kept her eyes on me while she slipped one hand into her summer straw purse big enough to take watermelons to market and drew out a little jar of . . . Bag Balm. A moisturizer for

farmers with hands made rough by repeated contact with cow udders. Mrs. C. unscrewed the jar
and started to rub some of the goop into her elbows. I kept a neutral expression on my puss while
she painstakingly moisturized. Finally, she spoke.
"In my field," she said kind of expansively, "you
take all sorts of gigs."

I nodded to indicate I was with her so far.

"Weddings, department stores, trade shows,
restaurants." She slowly closed the jar of Bag Balm
and wiped her hands on a cocktail napkin. "About
four years ago, I got hired to play at the Fabulous
Fare for Foodies at the convention center in Philly.
Two days of demonstrations, samples, freebies,
wine and beer tastings, door prizes. You get the
picture."

Again, I nodded. Linda was up to the part where
she was telling us she'd been made blue and lied to.

"I was one of the musicians playing while the
crowd wandered into the demos . . ." She spread
her hands and one hot-pink spaghetti strap slipped
off her broad shoulder. "You know the scene." I did.
"Celebrity chef cooks it up for an adoring crowd,
plugs his new cookbook, cracks a few jokes, drops
a few hints to make time in the kitchen easier for
us mere mortals."

I murmured. Took the opportunity to glower at
Giancarlo the Faithless. He seemed unconcerned.

"Which was when I saw her."

I felt so drugged by the thick air and empty pub, I was having a hard time following her. "Georgia Payne?"

She smiled cryptically. "The artist formerly known as Georgia Payne."

"The dead artist."

"So sad."

Having commiserated with the Miracolo pianist—I wondered whether our Georgia had made the Miracolo Grief Week cut and could join the shrine next year—I pushed on. "What was she doing there?" I asked. What *could* the glove-selling Georgia be doing at a Fabulous Fare for Foodies exposition? "Selling latex gloves for food handling?"

She actually curled her lip at me like I had taken complete leave of whatever senses I had left. "Eve," she said, drawing out my name like it had many more syllables than I had ever been aware of, "she was the headliner."

I was confused. "Headliner?" Why was I thinking Las Vegas? I flashed to an image of Georgia Payne in sequins and feathers.

"The main chef. The draw. The hot ticket."

"Georgia Payne?" The fortyish gal who showed up at Quaker Hills Career Center for my Basic Cooking Skills class? The pretty blonde petite enough to be schlepped from the foyer to the

semolina bags to the walk-in freezer to the trunk of Landon's BMW? That Georgia Payne?

And then I remembered the Belfiere *B*.

The shadowy remains of a wrist tattoo after it had been removed.

"Well, that woman, certainly," said Mrs. Crawford, waggling her head under her broad-brimmed chapeau as though she was about to make a comment on one of Jonathan's recommended wines. "But she wasn't called Georgia Payne."

I think my heart rate slowed. The way it does when the world is about to be revealed as something way different from what you had always thought it had been. One, knowable. Two, friendly. My voice, when it came, sounded smaller than small. Wee, even. "She wasn't?"

Slowly, Mrs. Crawford shook her head, and all I wanted in the seconds before she told me all, was to crawl under the sheltering brim of her hat, where I'd never have to bother with unanswerables ever again. "No, Eve, she wasn't."

"So who was she?"

"Back then," said Mrs. Crawford, her green eyes glittering, "her name was Anna Tremayne."

Georgia Payne.
    Anna Tremayne.

Why, oh why, was that name ringing a bell?

I jabbed at the pesto and dropped a speck on my tongue—weirdly sweet for an appetizer. As I eyed the empty carton of rice milk, I continued to ponder. So it had to be Anna Tremayne who was inducted into Maria Pia's culinary cutthroat club. But what had happened? Why had she quit? Or was something else going on? And why had she changed her name and taken up a below-the-radar career as a glove salesperson at Bloomingdale's? True change of heart? Sick of all things culinary? It happens. There were days when I myself was close. Days when selling gloves was more appealing than I could possibly say . . .

I had to wonder whether Mrs. Crawford got it wrong, but then, I had questioned her closely. The headliner chef she had known back then— Anna Tremayne—had longer hair, pulled back, and bangs, very cute. And—here Mrs. C. had narrowed her eyes as her memory worked hard— Georgia/Anna's eyes were different. We speculated like a couple of gossiping friends whether she had possibly had "work done." An eye job. Possibly a nose nip. But the walk and manner couldn't be altered when the identity shifted. It was the same woman. And now she was calling herself Georgia.

When I asked our Miracolo pianist why she hadn't mentioned to us earlier—say, while Georgia was alive—that she had recognized her from the Fabulous Fare for Foodies gig four years ago, Mrs. Crawford hit me with a slight and elegant shrug. Woman wants to hire on as a sous chef and call herself sweet potato pie, wasn't her business. *After all, identity is such a personal thing, as shifting as the Sahara, wouldn't you say, Eve?* At which we smiled at each other in a conspiratorial way.

Actually, I didn't know what she was talking about since my own personal identity had been as clear to me from the age of five as the silver bell Uncle Dom made for me while he was still doing some silversmithing as a hobby. He'd strike the little bell, which was about the size of a golf ball, hanging in a beautiful burl maple stand he had also made, and say, "This is the sound of you, Eve."

It was the first I ever knew I had a sound, and it was always the same, and I liked that. "This is the sound of you in the world." As I grew, I learned my sound was called "A," and I learned I was surrounded by other notes, and whenever I was sick I struck the little bell, and whenever I was heartbroken, I struck the little bell. By the time I was grown, whenever I struck the silver bell I thought only sometimes of Eve in the world, but mostly I thought of Uncle Dom's love.

So, when Mrs. Crawford smiled at me like we shared a common understanding about how shifting identities can be, I only knew it secondhand. And when I asked her whether Georgia had recognized her as the pianist from the food show, all Mrs. Crawford could do was smile mysteriously, those eyes as crinkled with secret fun as they could get. *Oh, my dear,* she had warbled in her deep, nasal voice, *I was very different back then.*

While my hands brushed the strewn basil into a neat little pile, my phone trilled. Twice. A voice mail from Maria Pia told me she was on her way to the Sisters of St. Margaret Retreat Center for a day of R&R, courtesy of Choo Choo, who had borrowed a lovely limousine to transport her, and yes, in case I was wondering, she left a contact number with Detective Sally Fanella, such a *bella ragazza.* A voice mail from Choo Choo told me Junior Bevilacqua sends me his love. I looked wryly at my dessert pesto—whatever love he can spare after scattering it like chicken feed. Did I have to start worrying about unwanted attentions from the sketchy Junior?

Ahead of me was the meeting with what I was sincerely hoping were two frightened CRIBS boys, Mitchell and Slash, who had jolly well better be presenting me with the cashless but otherwise intact red purse of Georgia Payne. Or, since I had no reason to doubt Mrs. Crawford, "Anna Tremayne." Anna Tremayne. If she was such a hotshot, why hadn't I heard of her? I wondered.

As I shook the contents of the blender into a storage container like I expected it to give up state secrets, the answer came to me: because I wasn't in food four years ago. Four years ago I was still happily dancing in New York and wondering whether those brief extra little touches from my dance captain and neighborhood tomcat, Tony Treadwell, "meant" something. Who knew food? Who knew the food world? Not me. I had a freezer full of Stouffer's Salisbury steaks. My idea of fine Italian cuisine was white pizza.

Anna Tremayne.

When I went to stash the mutant pile of sweet green ooze in my little fridge, the freezer door swung open. Peering inside, I took a step back. I had stuffed the freezer with tray upon tray of what I can only call pestosicles. Toothpick handles stuck up every which way. For a moment, I stared into what was feeling like evidence of the most irresponsible behavior toward perfectly nice basil, then I firmly shut the freezer door, followed by the fridge door, followed by whatever pocket in my brain was grooving to culinary aberration.

I sensibly decided to give Maria Pia a quick call to see if she recognized the name Anna Tremayne. As luck would have it, the one time I actually hoped to get Nonna on the phone, she was incommunicado. Landon. Landon, despite his knowledge of fine wine and fine art, was a secret pop culture hag and watched the cable TV cooking shows the way other people watch football or Judge Judy.

When I couldn't get Landon, either—now what?

I wasn't much one for metaphors, but this pesto outbreak was beginning to feel a lot like my confusion about the murder of the sous chef formerly known as Georgia Payne. How did she die? Why did she die? I peeked into the freezer. The sweet pestosicles were still there. They looked so—so— un-Italian, so very far from anything you'd find on the menu at Miracolo, that I felt strangely pleased. I'd just borrow a cooler and drop one off to everyone I know. The weather was perfect for it. Something "off the menu" in honor of Anna T., who certainly deserved better than a car trunk, even if a BMW's.

In the waft of freezer air, my head suddenly cleared.

Anna T.

What had Landon told me about someone called Anna T.?

He showed me a blog post. That's right. A blog for . . . victims of cults.

Then I remembered: *Belfiere*. And I got a chill straight up my arms that had nothing to do with Joe Beck.

I remembered that the post seemed hysterical. She had witnessed something, something about a deadly poison game and a collapsing member, something that never got reported to the authorities. And Anna T. had been scared for her life, and run out. Only she hadn't felt safe, had she? Is that when she had started a new life, a life as Georgia Payne? And then I remembered something that made me sit right down on my kitchen floor. Sit before I passed out. I saw it all again, the day Maria Pia had walked into the kitchen at Miracolo, on Georgia's first day, and announced that Fina Parisi was coming the next afternoon to check out the preparations. What could have gone through Georgia's mind when she heard that?

Then she had called in sick with a toothache the next day. To avoid the visit by Fina.

What must that have been like for Anna Tremayne, wanting the shot at a job at Miracolo, maybe hoping to get back into cooking, only below the radar, this time—wanting the job, but suddenly finding herself up against the thing she dreaded—Belfiere?

When had Fina spotted her?

I pulled myself up and hugged the counter top. How could so much go on right under our noses without our knowing? All that anger and fear. All that hiding out, all that careful plotting. Behind the hard, bright smiles. It made me shudder. Making the rounds with my pestosicles would just have to wait. I quickly cleaned up the kitchen and washed my hands. As I dried them, I realized I was about to do something possibly more stupid than sweetening and freezing an industrial-size batch of pesto. I was going to go behind the hard, bright smile.

I was going to confront Fina Parisi about the matter of Anna Tremayne.

Right after I rendezvoused with the bad boys of Quaker Hills. Well, two of them.

Who, as it turned out, were waiting for me outside the back gate in the alley behind Miracolo. First I checked my watch, then I pulled to a stop in exactly the spot where Joe Beck and I had spent quality time in the backseat with the dead Georgia. And now I was going to take the hand-off of Georgia's red purse from the knuckleheads who had swiped it. Did that make me a receiver of stolen goods? Nah. Not possibly. I was her employer and I was receiving her stolen purse—no, had to reframe that—retrieving vital evidence I planned to turn over to Quaker Hills' finest. Even if that was the first it had occurred to me . . .

Still, I thought as I got out of the car, and

looked around, this spot was becoming a bit of a magnet for sketchy—okay, criminal—behavior. Tumbling electrocuted corpses into car trunks. Handing off key property of murder victims. I was going to have to give some serious thought to why Eve Angelotta happened to turn up at all of those events, but it might have to wait until my next batch of pestosicles.

Mitchell Terranova had tied his dreadlocks back at the nape of his neck, which really made clear how much he resembled a ferret with acne. Slash was wearing a clean black-and-white T-shirt that said in small lowercase letters, *ask me about my complete lack of interest.* He had dressed for the occasion. Jiggling like they had put off a trip to the john just a killer five minutes too long, they were eyeing the weeds along the fence line. I strolled right up to them, then planted my feet. "You're early," I noted.

"'Ey, we got places to go," said Mitchell.

"It just worked out this way," added Slash, defensively.

In that moment I realized that in their weird little world it was hard to know which was worse—being late, or being early. Either way, they run the risk of disrespect. I felt a pang of pity for the little creeps. "Got the purse?" I crossed my arms and waited.

Slash gave me a luxurious eye roll and brought it out from behind his concave back. I held out my hand, at which he slapped it into my palm. A little too hard, but I didn't break eye contact. Mitchell, on the other hand, winced. I took my sweet time opening Georgia's purse and thumbing through the contents. A pair of drugstore cheaters in a Vera Bradley case. A Clinique lipstick. Travel hairbrush. Tube of Advil. Wet Ones. A Jeffery Deaver paperback. Receipts for a latte, some dry cleaning, and the Jeffery Deaver paperback.

Pay dirt came in the shapes of an iPhone, a set of keys, and an Etienne Aigner wallet with a Pennsylvania driver's license. The wallet, aside from a collection of cards that let Georgia Payne borrow books, buy on credit, see a doctor, get money from a machine, work out at a gym, and visit her local wholesale club, was empty—as promised—of cash. Since I'd never be able to prove how much Georgia had had on her when she died, it was a waste of time pressing the thieves for either the answer—or the cash.

The best I could do was make a mildly displeased face at them. I left it to them to figure out what it was referring to—their thievery, my indigestion. All things were possible. And it was in my best interest to keep them just jumpy enough to fear my connection to Don Lolo Dinardo. From these two I wanted no more flicked matches, no more questionable graffiti, no more—

"So," said Slash in what I could only call a ne-gotiating manner, "you can see we're righteous dudes."

Righteous dudes? Where do these two get their street language? I kept my sigh small, waiting to see where this opening salvo was going. If they were smart, they'd (a) dash on down the alley out of sight, and (b) pee on somebody else's weeds. "Well," I equivocated, "dudes."

"So we're wondering about . . ." The righteous dudes eyed each other encouragingly.

"Don Lolo," breathed Mitchell, like he was ut-tering a prayer.

Ah. I pulled myself up straighter. "Don't worry, fellas, I won't tell him you stole his, er, lady friend's—"

At which Slash flung an impatient hand at me. My head jerked back. "What are you talking?" he snarled.

"Yah," chimed in Mitchell, "what we're askin' is—" Having gotten that far, he went all inarticu-late. Slash shot him a fond but somewhat homi-cidal look.

Then the boy in the *ask me about my complete lack of interest* T-shirt got in my face. "You tell Don Lolo we're righteous, so maybe"—he slung a shifty-eyed look up and down the alley like he couldn't trust the trumpet vine or the crows on the telephone wire—"he'll take us . . ." What, for a ride? For the knuckleheads you are? Then Slash Kipperman jerked his thumb to Mitchell and then back to himself, like I was in any doubt. "Into the business."

12

Falling off the stage at the New Amsterdam Theater four years ago was looking like a blip on the screen of my life. Maybe I had bailed too soon. So what, my leg broke in two places and it had been a slow recovery. I was just thirty-two and I could sell my Tumbleweed Tiny House and boogie back on down the road into Manhattan and buy myself some righteous—curse those two benighted CRIBS kids—private dance rehab.

What was I thinking, playing a mob babe as performance art for the benefit of two troublesome students? What was I thinking, trying to keep the unpleasantness in the Miracolo foyer from the consciousness of my tough-as-nails nonna? She should jolly well be trying to keep it from *me*!

My judgment was beginning to look about as

emulsified as my blended basil. Was I honestly preparing to go seek out Fina Parisi, daughter of that *strega* Belladonna Russo, head of that Belfiere band of culinary cutthroats, the one the frightened Georgia Payne had avoided that day? What exactly was my plan with Fina? Hurl accusations over caramel macchiatos? *Where were you on the night Anna Tremayne got electrocuted? And oh, by the way, would you mind explaining to me how you managed it?*

No, on the subject of the beautiful Fina Parisi, I needed to be smart.

And being smart certainly did not include any solo trips up to her front door on Gallows Hill Drive. Snooping around her House of Edible Terrors would have to wait until I could find a foolproof way of sneaking around the premises looking for . . . well, suspicious things. This was a plan. A plan about as well formed as aimlessly stuffing my freezer full of pestosicles. In the meantime, I could pose a delicate question or two to Fina under some pretext or other. For now, I had Georgia/Anna's address off her driver's license, and as I zipped south of town toward a modest apartment complex, I was pretty sure I was one step ahead of Detective Sally.

Parking out front, I tried three of her keys until I found the one that opened the door to the building. A fragile-looking older woman with thin white hair and oversize blue-framed glasses passed me with an anxious glance. Behind me came a buff thirty-something guy in a seen-better-days peacoat with a springy little Chihuahua on a rhinestone-studded pink leash. After we sorted ourselves out in the doorway, I plunged into the lobby, where I scanned the building directory for Payne: number 302. Up the carpeted stairs I went three flights, then followed a hardware-store, black-and-silver arrow that pointed the way to units 301–306.

The dimly lit hallway was empty. Of people, for sure. Of the smell of boiled cabbage, not so much.

But as I tried the keys in the lock, I heard a small sound coming from inside Georgia Payne's apartment. When a key fit, and I thrust open the door, the source of the sound became clear. A little black cat with bold yellow-green eyes was quick to rub herself against my legs. The audio portion of the welcome consisted of some meows that seemed to convey that the absence of the human for almost two foodless days is actionable. And then I remembered what Georgia had said about her "significant other" that day we were prepping together at Miracolo.

"You must be Abbie," I said, crouching to pet her sleek fur and run a hand up her short but quite sensible tail. She bounded ahead of me to Georgia's kitchen, rightly pegging me for one not unacquainted with cat food, where I searched the

cupboards until I happened on a likely can of tender chicken morsels in gravy. As I dished it up, I
put the little cat's new, ownerless plight from my
mind. She dug in.

On a day when murder blew in with the rain,
and bad boys wanted to become worse boys, and
I had no beautiful garlic cloves to sauté in my
Miracolo kitchen for even the most modest of *pomodoro* sauces, feeding Georgia's Abbie made me
happy. It was, finally, something useful I could do.
Something real. And it made me nearly as happy
as hearing Joe Beck call me honey (I assume before
he could stop himself).

And then I snooped.

Although "snoop" sounds kind of leisurely, rif-
fling through mail, probing desk drawers without
too much fear of discovery. Abbie seemed to trust
me, posing no questions whatsoever about the
absent Georgia and content to wash up. But since I
had sudden visions of neighboring cabbage-boilers
pounding on Georgia's front door and demanding
an explanation for my presence—not to mention
suddenly coming face-to-face with Detective Sally
Fanella, who might have a reasonable question or
two to ask of me—I tugged on a pair of thin latex
gloves and worked fast. My hands felt twitchy
and my eyes bug-eyed as I went through Georgia/
Anna's stuff.

So to be strictly accurate, I wasn't snooping, I was tearing around in some crackpot manner that to any outside observer might appear worrisome. Lucky thing the apartment didn't contain a whole lot of crap from years past. "Storage unit?" I asked Abbie, who blinked and went back to the important matter at hand, namely, face washing. The bedroom yielded zero, which pretty much summed up my usual bedroom yield in other ways. But the scratched kneehole desk that looked to me like Georgia Payne had scored off Craigslist was a treasure trove. There, in the lowest drawer, I found a file folder secured with an elastic band on which she had scrawled the word *BELFIERI!* Somehow she restrained herself to a single exclamation point. Ah, reading material for my loft, later, Petzl headlamp strapped to my forehead, alone again in the empty bed. While I quickly thumbed through the Belfiere file, I found myself thinking maybe I should downsize to a twin-size mattress in the Tumbleweed loft—get rid of the queen—after all, I could use the extra space for important things like sweatpants and bargain cookbooks.

Belfiere could wait until later.

The only evidence of a significant other was a cat carrier and a litter box, which I took a minute to clean. Abbie declared it acceptable.

Georgia's laptop was a nonstarter since I didn't

have the password. And I couldn't find a helpful little pile of stapled Post-it notes with scribbled passwords. Clearly, she had a system that in no way resembled my own.

Her dresser-top jewelry box had a few nice pieces, but nothing with any telltale engraving like *Love you forever until you ditch me and I have to electrocute you*, signed *Bob 212-932-0406*.

I couldn't find a checkbook or bank statements. So Georgia was an online denizen, comfortable with all things digital.

And the walls didn't hold anything of her life as the illustrious Anna Tremayne. Just the sort of generic metal-framed things you can pick up at Bed Bath & Beyond when you buy a kitchen trash can. But I scored a file of some pieces clipped from magazines. Anna Tremayne as the "sizzling" newcomer to the culinary world. Anna Tremayne writing as a restaurant critic. (Motive for murder there?) Anna Tremayne in the lineup of the "sizzling" new *Top Chef*. It made me sad how none of these saved glory notices would have any meaning for anyone else, now that Anna T. was dead. Even if she had a family—and nothing I had come across in that apartment led me to that conclusion—how many relatives hang on to clippings from a life not their own?

Feeling about as 007 as I could stand without requiring an Aston Martin with front-firing rockets, I took pictures of everything with my phone. The most interesting things on Belfiere. The biggest ouchies in the way of her restaurant reviews. Her birth certificate. A couple of love letters. I was just replacing the last of the Belfiere originals back in their file folder when I happened to look out the window—and jumped back out of sight. Two Quaker Hills PD patrol cars had just pulled up out front. My legs tingled, probably in an attempt to get me to run.

Since legs are usually correct in these things, I did a quick dash to check my trail—happy to report no-trace snooping—and then I saw Abbie sitting in that composed way cats have when they believe their world is just one big fat sublime routine. She shot me a cross-eyed look that seemed a little flirtatious. Were the cops just going to leave her there until some nonexistent family member grudgingly takes her? Or would they just cart her off in chains to . . . the shelter?

I blustered at her in a state of terrible indecision. For a moment.

Then I stuck the litter box in Georgia's empty laundry basket, topped it with an astonished Abbie I had grabbed and unloaded into her carrying case, all of which I covered loosely with a couple of sheets pulled from the linen closet. Slapping my sunglasses onto my face, and thinking fondly of

Corabeth Potts, I rubber-banded some hanks of hair into a Shrek 'do on the top of my head. Then I hefted the laundry basket and dashed for the door.

I just made it into the hall when I heard the cops make it to the third-floor landing, chatting it up. One of them was the Ted guy, Sally Fanella's partner, I was sure of it, I recognized the voice, so I turned on my heel, affected a walk that would have looked better on any of the T-Birds from *Grease,* and headed unhurriedly—despite the low growling coming from the laundry basket— toward the rear stairs as they came down the hall behind me.

As I made it through the door to the stairs, my heart beating wildly, I peeked back through the narrow window. The Ted guy and a uniformed cop were knocking at Georgia Payne's door. I made it down the three flights of stairs and out the back door to my Volvo, all on a single breath. Once inside, I swiped the sheets off the laundry basket and peered into the carrying case at Abbie, whose yellow-green eyes were the size of quarters. I made reassuring noises, but I was wondering two things.

What had I gotten myself into?

And could I blame it on Choo Choo?

"Hey, Beck." I had just exploded back into my Tumbleweed and let the cat out of the carrying case when I decided a call to my lawyer was in order. I figured if Georgia/Anna had died accidentally, I could certainly make a case for going through her stuff—notifying next of kin, very appropriate—and probably even making off with her cat. Wouldn't the cat rescue people do the same? But if hot-wiring Georgia had been someone else's idea, then the cops might take a dim view of my pawing through her stuff on the sly. It could look, well, suspicious.

"Angelotta," he replied, obviously forgetting his "honey" slip of the day before. In much the same way as I had forgotten throwing myself sniveling into his arms at the re-creation of my discovery of Georgia Payne's body. Perhaps these revealing things—I thought, sniffing nobly— are better left undiscussed and unrepeated.

Right away I knew I couldn't support that point of view.

"Joe," I went on, wondering about the background sounds of machinery on his end, "I've got some new information about Georgia Payne." Was he weed-whacking? Ah, the secret life of Joe Beck.

"Hold on," he said to me, then laughed with somebody. I heard a lame joke about pole beans, countered by a lamer joke about big zucchini.

"Where are you?" I yelled.

He came back on. "Home," he said. "Almost done here. Want to say hello to somebody?"

If there's one thing I hate, it's when the person you call puts you on the phone with someone else. It should be apparent that if I had wanted to talk to—

"Hi, cuz," said the bane of my existence, and I don't mean Choo Choo.

—Kayla, I would have called Kayla. I felt deeply and infantilely offended. She was using that tone that's meant to make you think you share dirty secrets. It was my life's work not to have so much as a cheap cup of coffee with my cousin Kayla, let alone a dirty secret.

In my best pious saint's voice I had learned at my nonna's knee, I came back, "Hello, Kayla." What was the *strega* doing at Joe Beck's? A split second later, I silently screamed, *Do you really have to ask that?* It was a summer Saturday morning and love and pestilential cousins were in the air. I kept my eyes on Abbie as she slunk around, low to the ground, anxiously checking out her new, temporary digs. "Okay, then, cuz," I sounded all sorts of merry, "could you please put Joe back on?"

"Okey-dokey, back to work."

Making zucchini grow big, apparently.

"Hey," came Joe Beck.

Be positive. "What's Kayla helping you with?"

"It's a surprise."

Surprise? "For whom?"

"You'll see."

Aren't lawyers supposed to be more, oh, effusive? Gabby, if you will?

To the business at hand. "Can we meet? I've got information about Georgia Payne, Joe."

"Then call the cops."

The man was forever trying to get me to call the cops. What's the point of having a lawyer? That's what I want to know. I took a deep and patient breath. Abbie was checking out the litter box I had set in the bathroom, cramping the tiny three-by-six-foot space. "It requires finesse."

I guess Kayla was cheek to jowl (the jowl being hers) with Joe because it was her voice that came on and said in that conspiratorial way that leads to the overthrow of bedsheets, "Most things do, babe." Then they laughed together. She always finds her own "jokes" uproarious and declares other people's "lame, lame, lame."

"Kayla," I spoke quietly into the phone, "I'll see you on Monday with the day's order. Put Joe back on." I felt overly dignified in a dramatic sort of way. Like Scarlett O'Hara in the moment she pulls up a rotten turnip and vows she'll never go hungry again. Only in my scenario, I was brandishing some part of Joe Beck's anatomy.

When I heard his voice, I asked him if he thought he could hold the four-ounce phone without Kayla's assistance, and when he said he thought he could, I brought him up-to-date. The dead and possibly murdered Georgia Payne was really Anna Tremayne, hotshot chef until she fell off the radar two years ago, and Anna Tremayne was "Anna T.," the hysterical blogger who—

I finally had his attention. "—who blew the whistle on your grandmother's club."

"Belfiere, right."

He let out a long whistle. "So naturally you're thinking there's a Belfiere explanation for Georgia's death."

"What with the tattoo removal, the cosmetic surgery, the name change, the career change . . ." I paced my tiny "great room." "Joe, I'm convinced she was hiding out from the Crazy Cooks Club. She ran out of that meeting, remember? She had the goods on a suspicious death of one of their fifty who keeled over that night."

"A death that didn't get reported."

"Right. And I've got my hands on a file she kept on Belfiere—" Oops.

"What? And how did you do that, might I ask?" And we had been doing so well.

I was mad. No, I was already mad. Now I just sputtered, "Oh, Kayla can do naked handsprings all around your yard, but me, I do just a little re-search—using my employee's own key—to help solve the crime and you're all over me." I held the phone about a foot from my face and yelled into it. "And not in a good way."

"Okay, listen—"

"I need some help here!" Does a one-dollar retainer not mean anything these days?

His voice dropped, and I have to admit, it sounded good. "For your information, she's not doing naked handsprings."

"Cartwheels, then." I felt belligerent.

"She's making a garden. And if she was doing naked handsprings, it would only get my attention—"

"See! See!"

"In kind of an appalled way, to tell you the truth."

"Huh."

"I'm coming over," he said suddenly and decisively. "I'm not going to have this conversation with you over the phone. Is there anything you want?" Then: "Wine? Beer? Lunch?"

I felt my eyes slip very far away. As he waited, I thought how a thrill is really a subtle thing, not a spectacle, not even a great racket of nerve endings. It's the second the sun peeps above the horizon and all the light everywhere suddenly looks different. And you just missed it, even though you hadn't looked away, not for a second, and missing it coursed through you as a thrill. Out the open window I could almost see myself doing naked handsprings across the yard. When I spoke, my voice sounded soft to me. "Cat food," was all I said.

Twenty minutes later I had set up my blue butterfly chair and a tray table in the grass about ten feet away from my front door. Next to them I had set up a yellow butterfly chair. A place for Joe Beck. For whatever he had to say. Probably something legal and disapproving. On the table before me I had spread printouts of some of the most intriguing photos I had taken of Georgia's stuff on Belfiere and her life as Anna Tremayne. The table also held two red-wine spritzers with mint sprigs, although, depending on what Joe had to say, I was prepared to drink them both myself. If, for instance, he so much as mentioned the name *Kayla*. I considered bringing out some pestosicles, then decided the wine spritzers were a safer bet. I have never known basil to dull pain.

There I waited, barefoot and cross-legged in my butterfly chair.

A black Subaru turned in to the gravel path I call a drive. It came to a stop well before my beloved Volvo. A pang. Maybe he wasn't planning on staying very long. Just because naked handsprings by Kayla might appall him didn't exactly mean Kayla herself appalled him. On that score, he and I could be extremely different. Maybe he just didn't like acrobatics. Maybe he liked her just fine, just fine indeed, and all he wanted to tell me was to treat their relationship (here I choked on the mint sprig) with respect, thank you very much.

So I watched him get out of the car and stand stock-still just looking at me for a moment, dressed in jeans and a faded, charcoal-gray T-shirt that had no right looking that good. I found myself hoping it didn't mean anything that a cloud drifted in front of the sun. As he started over, something made me get out of the chair. The closer he got, the more decisive he seemed, and with my arms folded tight across my chest, I met him halfway.

Two feet away from me, Joe stopped, and pushed at the back of his golden hair, which was too short to go anywhere. I waited while he looked at the sky, the little house, the hedge one hundred feet away. Finally, he spoke. "You've got to stop thinking I've got something going with Kayla."

I shifted my weight. "You did," I pointed out.

Joe stuck his hands on his hips, an effective move that made me consider his hips. "Not one of my better moves." Oh, talking about Kayla. "Let's get past it, okay?"

I shifted my weight again, not sure where this was going. "Why should we?"

"Because it just keeps getting in the way."

I looked at the grass. "You've been a pretty good lawyer so far." Oh, Eve.

He shook his head. "That's not what I'm talking about. But you should get yourself another lawyer."

Suddenly we were both stepping closer and scowling at each other. The kind of scowl that can take off in interesting directions. I think there was a scowl before the firmament popped up and gases cooled into planets.

"I don't want another lawyer," I said, pressing my lips together. "I want you." I was pretty sure I was the only one of the two of us who knew I was really talking about two different things. Although the blush jumping right off my face might have sold me out.

And then Joe Beck slowly leaned in closer as we stood there with our hands on our hips in the gentle June sunlight. In the second before he kissed me, our eyes locked and we grinned at each other. I had a bad moment wondering if that's as far as we were going to get, nuzzling a nose, feeling the warm breath, that close, then stepping away. After all, it was Eve and Joe, and anything could *not* happen. We had a history of no history.

Then a car with a blown muffler roared by.

Kids with sticks went yelling through neighboring weeds. A black-and-gold dragonfly buzzed us. When it came, it felt light and playful and sure and earnest, that kiss. Forget distant galaxies and ocean depths and subatomic whatnot. Everything I wanted to know lay in that point of intersection. That kiss. And my hand flew up to the side of his face.

"No more fake kisses," he said softly, remembering, I guess, a month ago when we faked our way through a clinch in a tough spot when a patrol car cruised by.

Time for the truth. "They never were," I told him.

His fingers found the small of my back—too soon to tell him how delicious that was—and pulled me just a little bit closer. "Good to know."

"Good to know."

"So's this." We were standing so close maybe the dragonfly could have found a path between us, but nothing bigger.

All ten of my fingertips tapped his chest. "You called me honey." Oh, sure, Angelotta, throw that in his face.

His hands cupped my elbows, and then the man got serious. "I was holding back."

"Never hold back."

An eyebrow shot up. "I got the cat food," he

said suddenly, and sure enough, in those seconds before we kissed again, he dangled a brown paper bag, which thumped lightly against my back as his arms went around me.

"I got the cat," I said, my voice husky, and I wondered what we were talking about, as I held him tight. The bag fell to the ground. I like a man who's got his priorities straight.

Banking kisses for that rainy day, Joe ended up asking me to that fancy lawyers' fancy dinner dance on July 5th. I, of course, blurted, "But I thought you were taking Kayla!" After we cleared up that she was coming over earlier that evening just to drop off his weekly share of produce, I accepted the invitation and we got down to work, turning to red-wine spritzers and hard-copy info that could conceivably hold clues to Anna Tremayne's death.

Joe lingered over the Belfiere material. Georgia/Anna had made a list of members' names, when she knew them, maybe half of the total fifty in the society. Maria Pia might recognize more of them—pretty soon, a little too up close and personal, unless I could persuade her to stay out of their clutches. Studying the list hard, I cottoned on to a startling omission: Belladonna Russo herself, mother of Fina Parisi, and—if you want to believe Maria Pia Angelotta—biggest *strega* in the Tri-State Area. I hadn't seen her at Miracolo the other night, and Georgia/Anna hadn't jotted down her name. Joe declared the list "a start," in case the evidence pointed conclusively in that direction.

Then there was the rest of Georgia/Anna's material on Belfiere. Jottings by the names of the members she was able to identify. *She talks about the difference between chanterelle mushrooms and false chanterelles like she's experimented! How?? Worse yet, who??* Another: *Something about "harvesting" botulinum toxin. Sick, sick, sick.* Another: *Overheard her speculating whether the glycoalkaloid poison in potato leaves and stems could be introduced in large enough amounts to kill.* And on and on.

Then there were pages of notes . . . for an exposé on Belfiere. Notes of early questions for herself. *Should I go for a few shorter articles blowing this club of ghouls wide open? Or is it more effective to do a book-length thing? Can I fool them enough to get into a position of more power—could give me access to files, photos, stories??* The word *Pursue* was underlined twice. And then, underlined three times: *What's the danger?*

Also in the file were letters from a couple of big publishers. Joe and I raised our eyebrows at each other. Anna had already been going semipublic, with what looked like a book proposal. Both publishers expressed interest in seeing more on her exposé titled *Be Careful What You Eat: The Criminal Life of a Secret Society of Chefs.* "Dear Ms. Tremayne," went one, "Your account of the possibly criminal history and practices of Belfiere, a secret cooking society, is compelling. As a Belfiere insider, you are certainly in a position of authority. However, we would need to see a table of contents and sample chapters in order to get a better feel for . . ."

I held the letters in my hand and stared at them.

I recalled a line from my nonna's invitation to join Belfiere. *In all things pertaining to Belfiere you must observe* omertà.

Omertà. The code of silence.

Had Fina Parisi and Belfiere known about Anna T.'s book proposal, an exposé that was "blowing this club of ghouls wide open"? Anna Tremayne had violated *omertà* in even giving the publishers a brief taste of the sorts of accusations she was making against Belfiere, let alone spilling it all over the course of three hundred shocking pages, which could lead to who knew how many criminal investigations? Oh, Anna.

Was this why she was killed?

13

Munching mint sprigs and contentedly sipping the rest of our spritzers, we studied the couple of restaurant reviews Georgia had written as Anna. Anything there? Possibly. One, Diavolo, in Short Hills, New Jersey, I remember hearing flopped maybe a couple of years ago—thanks to Anna's acerbic review? Another, Magritte, in midtown Manhattan, shrank to nothing and closed its doors around the same time—thanks to Anna's tepid review?

Joe suggested trying to find connections between Belfiere members—female superchefs—and restaurants doomed by Anna Tremayne. This would take some plodding, but I agreed it made sense. We split up Georgia/Anna's list of Belfiere members, so we each had a dozen names to try to tie to any of the restaurants Anna had dissed in print.

The problem with discovering a motive for Anna Tremayne's murder was that it became kind of a wonder she had survived as long as she had, between exposés and damaging restaurant reviews.

We were just starting to pass the hard copies from Georgia's personal file back and forth when my phone rang. It was Detective Sally Fanella, who told me the CSI folks would be out of Miracolo late Sunday, when the crime-scene tape would come down. We could reopen for the dinner business on Monday. All good news. Joe looked at me quizzically, and I gave him a thumbs-up. But maybe I was too hasty.

"Your cousin," went on Sally Fanella, "Landon Angelotta."

Landon . . . "I called and left him a message about checking in with you at the station."

"Right. Well, you may have done what you were supposed to"—she took a big authoritative breath—"but he has not."

"Oh," I said kind of faintly, "I'm sure he—"

"Which," she overrode me, "beyond a certain point, makes him a person of interest."

Joe Beck took off to start trying to make connections between Belfiere members and failed restaurants. Me, I brooded about Landon. "A person of interest." I didn't like the sound of that at all. How could my beloved cousin be at all implicated in this woman's death? Although, to be fair, he had been acting weird ever since he clapped eyes on her the day she started at Miracolo.

Jealous because she seemed that good in the kitchen? Aggravated that I hadn't consulted him on the new hire? Just plain cramped by another sous chef on site, even if temporarily? No, no, no. I knew Landon almost as well as I knew myself, and he was never jealous about anybody else's kitchen skills, and he pretty much stayed aloof from the actual running of Miracolo.

But there was something.

And I just couldn't get to the bottom of it.

In the meantime, I was twenty-four hours away from what I could only think of as the point of no return—Maria Pia's induction into Belfiere. Was Nonna more likely to become like them, these dangerously secretive poisoners . . . or to become the vulnerable new Anna Tremayne, someone appalled by Belfiere, someone committed to bringing it down? I climbed out of my blue butterfly chair and gazed at the weak sunlight far across the yard, glimmering through the trees. About my nonna, I couldn't feel what was true, but I knew she was at risk, either way.

So that gave me twenty-four hours to figure out

how I was going to infiltrate her induction into the mah-jongg club at Fina Parisi's home on Gallows Hill Drive.

Certain things I knew for sure.

Notwithstanding the lovely kisses, Joe Beck was not going to approve of the plan. So I wasn't going to give him the opportunity.

Landon would be a great undercover agent but I couldn't smoke him out.

Choo Choo was never inconspicuous, so that let him out of the evening's agenda.

Aside from Paulette Coniglio, there was no one else I trusted. I might get to that point with Mrs. Crawford, but we weren't there yet. So I called Paulette, who was in the middle of getting her roots done, and laid out the plan for her, which she approved in principle. It wasn't a question of getting her to come along with me—on that score, I had decided it was wise to travel light—no, I needed her to do an emergency sewing job: running up a second Belfiere gown in midnight-blue satin . . . this time, for me. She declared the assignment "easy peasy," and thrilled to the challenge of fashioning the "extraordinarily silly" silver mask.

Over the next twenty-four hours, Joe called to report that Milo, his assistant, had made a tentative link between one of the Belfiere members—an Elodie Tichinoff—and Magritte, the failed Manhattan eatery. Apparently, Elodie's son Dimitri was head chef there, although he didn't own a piece of it. I made encouraging noises at Joe—the kind that lead in the direction of more research, not the bedroom—and told him I was, well, ordering a new outfit (true). Keeping me terrific company during this time was Abbie, who was exploring the few surfaces in my little Tumbleweed, settling on the window seat as the choice place for general lounging and luxuriating.

Choo Choo checked in with me to let me know he had picked up Nonna from her one-day getaway at the Sisters of St. Margaret Retreat Center, and would drop her off later at Fina Parisi's place for the Belfiere induction. Just far enough up the road that she could appear to be arriving on foot and alone. Count on Choo Choo Bacigalupo to figure the angles.

Maria Pia herself called me, high on whole grains and meditation, just to touch base. When she mentioned something vague about being interested in trying a "cleanse" after the induction was behind her, I came close to telling her the induction itself might produce the same effect. But I told myself, I'd be her own personal "special ops," on hand to keep an undercover eye on her so she wouldn't fall afoul of any of the highly suspicious

Belfiere activities that were afoot. Afoul and afoot. Even my language was changing . . .

I oohed and ahhed at everything Nonna told me, so as not to tickle her flawless antennae for grandchild crap. Nothing new to exchange about the police investigation into Georgia Payne's death. Yes, yes, business as usual as of Monday morning, when Miracolo could reopen. After such a momentous evening at Fina Parisi's, Maria Pia was planning on arriving at Miracolo a couple of hours later than usual (I mouthed "Yes!" at Abbie, who blinked with perfect feline understanding).

And then I remembered. "Nonna, before you go, Georgia Payne wasn't her real name."

"Who?" she barked. So much for whole grains and meditation. Nonna was back.

"Georgia. The dead woman. The victim."

"Yes?" she said in a clipped, get-on-with-it way. "Yes?"

"Georgia's real name was Anna Tremayne." Start her out small. "I understand she was a chef."

"Well, I wouldn't know about that," she replied. My nonna was a woman who believed—maddeningly—that if she didn't know something already, then it wasn't worth knowing, that it was inconsequential and possibly subject to review by a team of experts. "But the name . . ." she said in a high, vague way. "What did you say it was again?"

"Anna Tremayne."

She hummed. "Rings a bell, Eve. I've heard it before, but I can't remember where." Then, she tried it out again: "Tremayne."

Just then I heard an insistent rap at the front door. But Maria Pia's comment was interesting to me. If she didn't recognize the name Anna Tremayne from the culinary world—where, then? Georgia Payne she didn't know. But Anna Tremayne—maybe she did. And not from their lives as chefs.

At the same time, we both said, "Gotta go," and hung up.

Paulette Coniglio brushed past me into my tiny home, muttering something Paulette-ish, like, "Good thing you're not claustrophic." In her arms she carried a dark, shimmering garment that could only be my disguise. She chucked her purse into my one club chair and did a quick survey of the premises, remarking, "You got a cat."

"It's Georgia's."

"Ah." Her face was burnished with the June sun, and the color job on her hair looked expensive and expert. Why things had never worked out between her and my deadbeat dad—other than the fact that he was my deadbeat dad—I'll never know. I'd swear she was still carrying a torch for the guy, long after I, the daughter, the only child, had personally given up on him, but she always pushed off my comments on this score. And pushing off the comments usually entailed thwacking me playfully with a white linen napkin from Miracolo.

Paulette worked out religiously and dropped a pretty penny on personal grooming just, I think, to keep from looking not a day older than the last time she'd seen the wayward Jock Angelotta, seventeen years ago. Just to be prepared for that inevitable moment when he'd walk back into the restaurant, fall to his knees, and beg for her forgiveness.

Where he'd stand on *my* forgiveness was not, I think, part of her fantasy. She was that kind of faithful woman that beggars common sense, a woman who keeps the home fires burning long, long after the worthless man has stopped thinking about the home, the fires, or the woman herself. "So," she asked, shaking out the voluminous robe she had "run up" on her machine, "are you going to try this on? I haven't got all day."

I slipped into the Belfiere robe, tried retracting my tattoo-less wrist up inside the long sleeves— success!—and twirled the stick she had glued to the right side of the "extraordinarily silly" silver masks we had seen times fifty just the other night at Maria Pia's dinner. Paulette had fashioned a great fake, what with silver spray paint and glitter. I held it up to my face. "How do I look?"

"As flat-out creepy as all the others."

I lowered the mask. "Then I'll fit in just fine."

Paulette turned me in pushy little half-circles, eyeballing her work. Then she cast a quick look of concern at me. "All you can hope for tonight at Fina Parisi's House of Belfiere Horrors," she said, her broad, pretty lips stretched out thin, "is that no one's counting heads"—she gave me a tight hug— "and that their crazy mugs are hidden the whole time by their masks. She held me at arm's length and fixed me with a hard, bright smile, "Otherwise, darling, you're up the Amazon without a fly swatter."

You know the scene toward the end of *The Wizard of Oz* when the Scarecrow, the Tin Man, and the Cowardly Lion—Toto, too, I think—fall in behind the Wicked Witch's soldiers as they march across the footbridge and into her castle? That's precisely how I felt when I drifted into a loose cluster of robed Belfiereans converging on the home of Fina Parisi. From my reconnaissance point about one hundred feet down Gallows Hill Drive I had watched Choo Choo pull up—still driving Junior Bevilacqua's limo—and dispense our nonna, who batted away his attempt at kisses and headed up the long driveway.

I waited until she was far enough ahead of me and Choo Choo had eased on down the road to lock up the Volvo, slip the key into a tiny waist pack strapped underneath the gown, and follow the robed Maria Pia into what I could only think of as potential hell but with a fabulous menu, if you overlook the alleged poisons.

But at 9:55, just after nightfall, what kind of late-night goodies or diabolical food games was Fina planning? Why did my mind keep skulking around the words *human sacrifice*? Maybe Maria Pia Angelotta wasn't really here so much to be inducted as offered up to the Fates, Clotho and the other two Weird Sisters mentioned on the invitation.

Fighting off the trembling, I marched up the driveway and fell in behind a small group of robed Belfiereans, masks raised, voices low and sporadic. The moon wasn't up yet, but there were solar-powered lamps lighting the way. I thought I spotted Nonna up ahead, her thick salt-and-pepper hair bouncing with each unsuspecting step. Behind us a souped-up car blasted by, windows down, music with a pounding bass line disturbing the night. Right about then, though, I would have preferred to take my chances with Mr. Metallica instead of whatever lay ahead of me. When an old, wavery voice back on the sidewalk started encouraging something called Fritzie to "Make!" I felt uplifted. I could be back on Market Square in Quaker Hills, it suddenly felt so familiar.

Fina Parisi's house was what I could only call alight. Awash in light. Alight, awash, afoul, afoot. Sheer terror had flung me straight back to the nineteenth century, apparently. It was a two-story brick house with what looked like multiple chimneys and porticoes—for all those horse-drawn carriages, or hearses, that come to call at the Parisi homestead. I would call it sprawling but that would come off as a little too disorganized for this, well, edifice. For the temporary home of a two-hundred-year-old secret cooking society, it was brilliantly lit. Disturbing, considering I had been hoping for whole zones of shadows where I could retreat, unobserved.

The double doors stood wide open and in we all sailed, I with my silver mask high, murmuring something positive to the frumpy sorority sister next to me, who chose that moment to complain about her girdle. This was news to me—I didn't know such things still existed, let alone that they didn't fit any better than I heard they ever did— but I quickly dismissed it as irrelevant to the case of Anna Tremayne. In Fina Parisi's "foyer" you could park half a dozen of my little Tumbleweeds—you might cramp the sweeping central staircase that looked like it had been snitched from Tara, but you could do it.

Now that I was inside enemy HQ, my plan, aside from keeping an eye on Nonna, was to slink off into the shadows to snoop around Fina's digs. Had I but known that Fina's digs were the size of Uzbekistan, I would have brought a sleeping bag. And some pesto. As the others headed into the parlor the size of a hotel lobby, joining their sisters, I slipped to the side of the arched doorway and made a quick scan.

Hanging from the high rafters was, much to my relief, not a member who had violated *omertà*, but an eight-foot banner bearing the Belfiere "coat of arms." There in the upper-right quadrant of the funnel-shaped shield were the three silver knives with ebony handles, and the carmine-colored slash ran diagonally to the black mortar and pestle in the lower-left quadrant. And on the scroll below the shield was the Latin for Never Too Many Knives. Just seeing this creep-show banner reminded me that this was a group I couldn't let down my guard for, even if they do incorporate the Hokey-Pokey into their club pledge and then swoon over Scallop Fritters with Roasted Chioggia Beet Carpaccio. After all, even Lucrezia Borgia had to eat . . .

In front of the cavernous stone fireplace, a long table had been covered in a gold cloth and decked out in chafing dishes, demitasse cups, beakers, and what looked like an apparatus from a high school chemistry class. Was something being distilled? A handful of members wearing gold cowls seemed to be organizing the induction ceremony. Their masks were gold, smaller than the handheld silver "general membership" masks, and clapped to their mugs with elastic, leaving them hands-free for dishing out whatever was kept warm in the chafing dishes.

I was so busy sizing up the situation that I realized with a pang that I had lost sight of Nonna, who had disappeared into the crowd. I thought I picked her out, sitting to the left of the long table, on one of Fina Parisi's several love seats that had been pushed aside to make room for folding chairs. Finally, breaking into the subdued conversations came the voice of "La Maga" herself, Fina Parisi, who took her place behind the table and clapped her hands to settle the crowd.

Not surprisingly, she had a gold mask and cowl, not to mention a stage presence that stilled the room quickly. When I noticed that members were handling what looked like a two-page program of the evening's agenda, I found myself wishing I had managed to grab one. Then I caught sight of a basket on a table just inside the doorway—programs! But it was a dilemma. If I entered the parlor to get one, I could get stuck there and lose my opportunity to snoop. But if I didn't get one, I had no idea when the most worrisome parts of the ceremony were scheduled.

Well, it was a night of no guarantees. Either way.

And I needed to snoop.

While Fina chanted in Latin, her voice lifting above the silent crowd, I had two thoughts. One, now was the time to slip away into the other parts of her house. Two, she'd make a great replacement for Dana Cahill should we actually ever hammer together enough of a backbone to let Dana go. A few voices joined in with the chant in a strange counterpoint that sounded kind of plaintive. Maybe they were complaining about the maddening popularity of spaghetti and meatballs.

I backed away from where I had been lurking to the side of the doorway, out of sight of the others, and fled on tiptoe across the marble foyer. A quick peek into the room across the way from the induction ceremony showed me an empty formal dining room with the kind of heavy wooden table that looked like it had seen plenty of mead and roast pig in its day. Two beautiful crystal-and-silver candelabras lent an air of normalcy to the table that looked like it had been "distressed" by more than its share of maces and mauls.

But the room didn't look at all like a center of operations, so I pressed on down a stone-arched corridor, wondering how Fina Parisi kept up with this place. Looked like she hadn't even taken on temp staff for the evening—although, given the secrecy of the Crackpot Cooking Society, maybe that was no surprise.

Just as well I didn't have the time to ogle her kitchen, which was larger than what we had at Miracolo, and I passed an atrium that seemed to double as a breakfast room, and a powder room that actually held an Oriental rug. Me, I put down a shaggy oval with a rubberized back I picked up for $19.99 at Target.

And then I found it. Fina Parisi's study. Behind an ornately carved heavy wooden door.

The monster's lair.

I made myself shiver.

Shaking it off, I slipped inside, then fumbled under the folds of my fake Belfiere gown to slide a flashlight out of my pants pocket, since I didn't want to chance turning on the lights. I swung the beam across walls of books, two filing cabinets, a trophy case, shelves of objets d'art, and—La Maga's desk. Definitely sister furniture to the dining room table. A narrow tapestry runner stretched along the back of the desk, and a green-shaded library desk lamp seemed to keep everything in place.

Including an eighteen-inch gilt reproduction of Michelangelo's *David,* sporting only a fig leaf, which kind of spoiled the effect.

I dashed to the front of the desk and spread my hands at it inquiringly. Now that I was there, I hadn't a clue how to set about getting a . . . clue. I glared at a MacBook Air that was closed up and offering me nothing in the way of information without a password. So I'd just have to move on to other possibilities. Then I dimly heard a chorus of member voices swelling in a song from the Great Belfiere Songbook, apparently, although it bore a strong resemblance to "A Bicycle Built for Two." Easing open the center drawer, I cast the beam from the flash over the papers inside. Anna Tremayne, Anna Tremayne, please let there be something incriminating about Anna Tremayne . . .

The papers appeared, annoyingly, to be recent correspondence from Holy Sepulchre Cemetery in East Orange, NJ, thanking her for her donation, Sarah Lawrence College Alumnae Association, thanking her for her donation—we went to the same school?—State Farm Insurance, upping her premiums, and a few far-flung Belfiere members— from Hong Kong, São Paulo, and Alexandria— sorrowing over the fact that they couldn't make it to the induction ceremony of Maria Pia Angelotta. Tearing off a Post-it note from Fina's pad in another drawer, I scribbled the names and contact info of these members.

My fingers sifted through the stuff in the desk organizer. Keys, paper clips, coins, ChapStick, rolls of postage stamps, and . . . flash drives. Two. Well, well. I had just scooped them up, stuffed them into my pants pocket, and shut the desk drawer and started toward the filing cabinets, when all of a sudden I heard a sound out in the hallway and, with a trembling hand, I flipped my silver mask back into place against my face.

My only wee thought had something to do with hiding behind the door, should it open. It wouldn't win any awards for originality, but it might keep my fanny out of the *pasta fazool*. On my way there I snagged the gilt statue of *David* from the desk corner, and drew my arm behind my back.

But I never made it to the hiding place.

The overhead lights went on and I felt like I had been caught gazing directly at an eclipse. My breath caught in my throat.

"Who are you?" came the voice.

"Just looking for the bathroom," I tried, with a Southern accent that came out of nowhere, blinking at the figure in the doorway.

"No, you're not. So I'll ask you again," she said, her voice steady, "who are you?"

My eyes adjusted. It was Fina herself, her mask

pushed up to her hairline. Maybe I could lull her with a chorus of the school song from our alma mater, Sarah Lawrence. Mind you, I had never troubled myself to learn it, but given the musical tastes of this Belfiere crowd, I figured I could wing it. And if it turned out that college had not been a happy period in her life, and she rushed at me screeching in Italian, well, I always had David. I didn't think I could stall her any longer. My fingers tightened around the fig leaf as I considered how to handle Fina Parisi, the woman whose desk I had just been rifling.

Which was when I noticed the gun.

14

"Gum paste?" I asked.

She waved the gun. "Nougat." With that, she raised the little brown Derringer to her mouth and bit off the tip of the barrel. "Guns only interest me as a novelty treat," she said through narrowed lips as she chewed prettily. "Knives are more my line."

Too late I remembered the Belfiere motto, Never Too Many Knives, as Fina Parisi drew her other hand out from the folds of her midnight-blue satin gown. An ebony-handled knife gleamed, bearing a strong resemblance to the ones on the Belfiere shield. Unless I'm trimming the chicken breasts for the evening's special at Miracolo, I hate it when knives gleam. "How did you find me?" My voice came out about an octave too high to be taken seriously.

She jutted her shapely chin at me. "Zipper."

"Zipper?" I said belligerently, like it was the stupidest word in all creation.

"True Belfiere gowns are fastened with buttons."

I drew in a sharp breath. Busted. Oh, Paulette, Paulette, how could you have known? She must have finished off Maria Pia's gown with regulation buttons, and forgot when it came to mine. Right then I tried calculating the odds of her knife reaching me before my statuesque blunt object reached her, but when the business in my head started to sound like a word problem from an old algebra class, I gave it up. "You," I said with some indignation, "are going to come off really terrible in *Sarah Lawrence Magazine.*" And then I swung David out from behind my back.

And flung Paulette's sweet little mask to the floor. Go for the drama every time.

It was strangely satisfying to me when Fina Parisi blurted, "You!"

"I hope your specials show more originality." I sounded queenly.

She twirled the knife in her hand. Which gave me a chance to see her wrist: no *B* for Belfiere tattoo. So, not her dominant hand. So, maybe she'd miss me by a mile. I felt a brief surge of hope. Or . . . maybe she'd hurt me a whole lot worse than she intended. In what seemed a single motion, Fina Parisi tossed what was left of the nougat Derringer onto a bookshelf next to her and slipped the knife into her now candy-free right hand.

I didn't feel exactly sunk. More like semi-screwed.

"What year?" barked La Maga.

Our eyes locked.

I twirled David. "2004." Then, but not because I was interested: "You?"

"1989."

"I was a dance major."

"I didn't ask. Although it might interest you to know," she went on, "I was a darts champion."

I sneered at her. "Twenty-five years ago."

"Would you like a demonstration?" Her violet eyes turned cold. "You're trespassing."

I had no answer for that. I thought I was sleuthing. And protecting my nonna.

Fina Parisi added, "And I have forty-nine allies out there."

I was definitely getting in touch with my inner bitch. "You'll be out cold before you can summon them, Shorty." For good measure, I brandished David, then slapped him into my other palm like he was a tire iron.

Her eyes slid off my face for half a second while she seemed to ponder this declaration. I thought it was information, pure and simple, but it pleased me that the elegant and violet-eyed Fina Parisi seemed to consider it a threat. "What are you doing here?" She lowered her knife hand.

After a quick calculation—one that did not involve any sort of algebra—I straightened up. "Protecting my nonna from Belfiere." When you're in the monster's lair, it seemed that the best plan was either to lie outright or tell only partial truths. I decided to go for a mix of innocent but misguided Nonna-fear, the culinary equivalent of a *fritto misto*, fried mixed stuff.

"Protecting Maria Pia from Belfiere?" She seemed bewildered. "Why would you do that?"

Her bewilderment seemed, well, disingenuous to me. Which I discovered pushed a couple of Eve Angelotta hot buttons I never knew I had. I threw my own plan about Truth *alla fritto misto* out the window faster than I could possibly clobber Fina Parisi with a gilt statuette. I stepped closer to the woman, overlooking the fact that I was bringing the dartboard closer to the dart. "Because," I said, my voice dripping, "two years ago this, this cooking society"—I jabbed David in the direction of the dim chorus out in the parlor—"poisoned one of its own members—just a little criminal activity that went unreported—and, oh, did I mention the victim was never heard from again?" But I couldn't stop there. "And"—I stepped even closer—"the body was never found?"

Fina Parisi's eyes narrowed. "Where did you hear that?" she said softly.

Was she testing me? Seeing how good my source was? Seeing how good my proof was?

She was about to hear it all. In spades. Whatever that means.

"From Anna Tremayne."

She actually gasped.

I widened my eyes at the head of Belfiere. "Drama major?" I asked.

She ignored me. But not entirely. "How do you know Anna Tremayne?"

"Anna Tremayne," I said slowly, figuring it out as I went, "was my employee." Shouldn't Fina Parisi know that? After all, what did she think Georgia/Anna was doing in an empty Miracolo at midnight on the night she killed her for violating the Belfiere code of silence? "As you well know," I said pointedly.

At which La Maga shrugged.

At which there came a knock at the study door. I pictured all forty-nine cutthroat chefs out in the hall. For one bemused moment I wondered if Maria Pia Angelotta would take their side when they overpowered me. If, when it came right down to it, blood was thicker than, well, blood of another sort. Either way, bad times for Angelottas (which included Bacigalupos) lay ahead . . .

"Yes, what is it?"

A melodious voice piped up. "Maga? Are you okay? We've got about another five minutes of singing, and then there's the pledge, but then—"

"I'm fine, Elodie. Just five more minutes." She glanced at me, turned with a rustle to the bookcase, and with her ebony-handled Belfiere knife, cut the candy Derringer in half. "Listen," she opened the door a crack, "bring me two glasses from the flagon, will you, please?"

"Two?"

"Right."

"All right." And the voice started to move away. Fina Parisi's head fell back as something occurred to her. "Wait. Wait." Then she opened the door wider, motioning for the unseen Elodie to come into the study. All I thought was: *Two against one. Might as well be all fifty.*

Another gowned Belfierean rustled through the door. Once Fina was sure the door wouldn't close on the gown, she shut it quietly, then crossed her arms. The other woman, whose silver mask dangled from long fingers, was medium height with thick, dark hair, a trim figure under the yards of blue satin, and just a light application of makeup on her olive-skinned face. Fina Parisi introduced her as Elodie Tichinoff, and as soon as I heard the name, I remembered her as someone whose restaurant—or was it her son's?—was trashed in a review by Anna Tremayne.

Who had more motive for Anna T.'s death—Fina or Elodie?

Fina made a large sweeping gesture, saying, "Elodie, tell Eve here whether you've ever had anything unusual happen to you during a Belfiere meeting." Then she folded her arms Mandarin-style, her hands disappearing into the cavernous sleeves. At first, Elodie Tichinoff looked at us both blankly, then she remembered something, and an eyebrow lifted wryly. She went on to describe the night around two years ago at that induction when she passed out at the long table when she was sampling the "poisons."

"Who was the inductee that night, Elodie?"

"Well, it was that blond chef, that diva." Elodie twiddled her fingers like she was playing a scale. "Tremayne."

Fina Parisi looked at me. "Go on," she prompted. "Tell Eve about the poisons."

Elodie laughed and shrugged, then explained that ten members, on a rotating basis, provide tinctures of herbs and spices for the meeting—not every meeting, mind you, maybe every third time the society meets—and by a lottery system two

Belfiereans sample each tincture and try to tease
out the ingredients. The "poison" is an addition
that does not fit the other flavors, a kind of culinary "what's wrong with this picture?" That addition really complicates the game, which is already
pretty competitive, because at the end of the ten
trials, whoever identifies fewer samples is placed on
probation.

I think the proper word is *glowered*. I glowered
at Elodie Tichinoff, trying to get to the bottom of
this strange little Belfiere competition. "So what
does probation mean?"

Both women made airy gestures. "No newslet-
ter for one year," Fina put in.

"Suspension from three meetings," chimed in
Elodie.

"And," added Fina, "you're cut off from any recipe exchange." Both of them nodded solemnly, as if
not being privy to somebody's recipe for a low-fat
béchamel sauce, say, was a fate worse than death.

Elodie chuckled softly. "At the level of Belfiere,
you need to be able to identify ingredients."

Fina pushed back a lock of raven hair. "It's absolutely *de rigueur*." And she pronounced *de rigueur*
as though she actually knew what it meant.

I still didn't have the whole picture. "What happened at Anna Tremayne's induction?"

And Elodie Tichinoff went on to describe how

she had been busy at her son Dimitri's Manhattan restaurant, Magritte, that day, all day, before the ten-o'clock induction, trying to keep that losing proposition afloat, what with Dimitri's mediocre food and poor business practices. And, as luck would have it, she was one of the two sisters who drew the short straw, so she had to take the "poison" test.

She had not eaten all day, too busy, and she's hypoglycemic, which, before that evening, she had failed to mention to anyone else. What with the lights, the heat (it was late June), and not eating, she passed right out. This happenstance she punctuated with a gesture that looked like an ump declaring someone "Safe!" at home plate. Kind of like passing right out was the coolest thing ever.

Here Fina Parisi took up the story, recounting how naturally alarming Elodie's fainting was to some of the members. Nobody quite knew what was going on, really, and Elodie wasn't coming out of it quickly. But Anna Tremayne got hysterical—

"Which," added Elodie with a smile, "pretty much seemed to be her baseline, if you ask me, although I'd never met her until the night of her induction—"

"And she took off."

"Ran right out of the meeting."

I set figgy David back down on Fina's desk. "What did you do?"

An elegant shrug was the answer from La Maga. "Nothing. I followed her to the door and watched her run down the drive to her car. She sideswiped Gwen Henning's Honda as she tore out of here in a squeal of tires."

Something made me ask, "What time was this?"

Fina and Elodie looked at each other. "Well," said Fina thoughtfully, "we had already been through the induction, so Anna was technically a member, and it takes a while to set up the competition—"

Elodie put in, "It's very ceremonial, you have to understand. It's where we put the 'secret' in 'secret society.' We like to ramp up the suspense. Otherwise—"

Fina widened her eyes at me. "Otherwise it's really just a silly parlor game." She leaned against her desk. "As for the time, I'd say maybe around eleven thirty."

"I'm no help," laughed Elodie, adjusting her stylish black reading glasses. "I was out like a cod."

I tilted my head at them. "About Anna Tremayne's review of Magritte . . ." I said, looking squarely at Elodie.

The woman snorted and waved it off. "Best thing that could have happened. That review singlehandedly closed Dimitri's doors probably half a year sooner than they would have—which saved us investors a lot of money. The bloodletting stopped there. I was grateful to her, frankly. Anna Tremayne was a fabulous chef and a solid restaurant reviewer, but"—Elodie lifted her shoulders—"she sure seemed kind of emotionally unstable."

I wanted to argue the point, but didn't have much to add, considering I'd only known Georgia/Anna myself for about two days. "What happened after that night, after she drove off?"

"So fast I thought I heard a sonic boom," Fina quipped.

"We never heard from her again."

"So we moved her to Inactive status in Belfiere."

"Well, permanently Inactive now," I said, "considering she was murdered two nights ago. At Miracolo." Since they seemed genuinely flabbergasted at the news, although they had heard that a sous chef named Georgia had died at Maria Pia's place—I bristled a little at the "Maria Pia's place" line—I filled them in quickly. My brain by that point was running on two tracks, what with trying to integrate a whole new way of looking at the Crazy Cooking Club and now trying to cast about for a new suspect in the murder . . .

Fina gave Elodie a little push in the direction of the meeting. "Please tell them I'll be right in, okay? And, if you would, send someone back with two glasses from the flagon?"

The flagon with the dragon has the brew that is true.

Lines from old Danny Kaye movies come to me in my hours of greatest need.

Fina Parisi was going to offer me a drink, apparently. Truth be told, I might be better off with it than a sip of Giancarlo's absinthe. After Elodie disappeared, she turned and shot me a rueful look. "I can't let you stay, Eve. You understand. It's against the rules." Fina leaned toward me conspiratorially. "Half the rules," she confided, looking around, "are downright stupid, but it's a bear to change the by-laws and I've got just one more year to go in my tenure as"—she sketched air quotes—"'Maga.'" Here she touched my arm. "But we can have a drink together." Her violet eyes twinkled.

I turned to Fina Parisi. "Two questions," I said, sounding ever so official.

"Anything."

"What about *omertà*? Anna Tremayne violated *omertà*."

"She did?" Fina sounded genuinely unconcerned. Uninterested, even.

"She blogged about that meeting right after it happened. She called it homicidal."

"Wow. Really? I never saw it." Then: "Probably nobody else did, either. I've never heard any blowback."

"Well, what about her exposé of Belfiere?"

Fina's look was one of disbelief. "Exposé?"

"She had written to publishers about writing an exposé of that two-hundred-year-old secret cooking society, Belfiere. As a Belfiere insider."

"And she got some traction with that?"

Letters from just two publishers, when I really thought about it. "Well, preliminary."

Fina opened her arms at me. "What's there to expose? We sing songs? We take a pledge? We share recipes? What?"

It did sound absurd. "One more question."

A soft knock at the door was followed by Elodie Tichinoff herself, holding two stemless pewter cups. Without a word, she smiled, handed them to us, and flowed back out. "Go on," said Fina, her eyes locked on mine over the rim of her cup.

"Belladonna Russo," I announced, biting off at the very last minute my powerful inclination to add "that *strega*," the way my nonna always does. *That witch Belladonna Russo.*

"My mama," admitted Fina, circling the cup gently in her hands.

"Why isn't she a member of Belfiere?" A loving daughter protecting her own?

For the first time, Fina Parisi laughed out loud and the contents of the cup sloshed close to the rim. "For the simplest reason ever, Eve." She actually wiped away a tear with her index finger. I waited for the punch line. "She isn't good enough! Lordy, that woman uses Stella d'Oro ladyfingers in her tiramisu, and then lies about it." We sipped at the same time. "We aren't close," she added almost as an aside. "Here," said Fina, stepping over to the bookcase, where she'd left the two pieces of the brown nougat Derringer. "Your half," she smiled, offering me the butt of the candy gun. She nibbled on the rest of the barrel.

"Thanks," I muttered, then took another sip of the mysterious potion. Considering I hadn't dropped in my tracks, I was pretty much thinking I'd be turning up back at my Tumbleweed, none the worse for wear from my visit to Gallows Hill Drive in Pendragon, Pennsylvania. Oddly enough, I was feeling just a little bit let down.

Fina kept her eyes on me while we sipped the mysterious potion. "Like it?" she asked finally. I smacked my lips. "We make it right on the premises. Strictly for Belfiere consumption. From a recipe as old as Belfiere itself. It's one of our, oh"— she waved her cup around—"core activities, Eve. Very secret. Very central to the original idea behind the group. If there had been such things as Vision Statements back in 1810 when it began, this recipe would be in it." She lifted the cup high. "So what do you think?" Her eyes twinkled.

I took a long swig, let it roll around inside my mouth, then swallowed. And then the truth—but not about the murder of Anna Tremayne, a smaller truth than that—hit me. "It's—moonshine," I declared, staring into what was left in my cup.

Fina wrinkled her nose at me. "Welcome to Belfiere, Eve," she said softly.

For the very first time in my life, I was jealous of Maria Pia Angelotta.

We gabbed for about two minutes about our Sarah Lawrence days, but it fell a little flat. Chatter about college days long after those college days have ended is something you always think is going to take longer and be more fascinating than it really is. After you cover how nonsensical some traditions are—which was why you blew them off—and how you didn't have any of the same professors, you've pretty much exhausted the topic.

And Fina was just about ready to head back to the moonshiners' convention out in her parlor when she happened to gaze out the front-facing window while she adjusted her Belfiere gown. She let out a yelp of surprise, craning her neck for a better look, which was when I hurried over.

There's no mistaking the flashing lights atop a police cruiser. In the darkness all we could see was a shadow darker than the surrounding trees, swerve, dip, and move slowly toward us along the drive, red and blue lights strobing. "The moonshine?" I whispered.

"I don't know." Her lips were clamped tight.

"Is it illegal in Pennsylvania?"

Fina moved quickly around the desk, toward the door. At this rate, it might be some time before my nonna was inducted into Moonshiners Anonymous. "Only if we sell it."

There was no way I wanted to get hauled into the police station to explain my presence there, so I decided not to take a chance on the possibility that maybe the cops just wanted to hit up the wealthy Fina Parisi for a donation to the Police Athletic League. At this time of night. So I wiped my prints off the pewter cup and set it down on the desk.

Fina and I hit the hallway at the same time, but when she turned left to head back to the parlor and deal with whatever was about to come through the front door, I turned right, unzipping my gown. "See you, Fina, thanks," I called hoarsely after her, stepping out of the yards of Belfiere costume, snatching it up, and darting to whatever back door to this spread that I could find. Nonna was most definitely on her own. The image of what would be her queenly outrage at the intrusion of the local cops brought me almost as much pleasure as kissing Joe Beck. If Quaker Hills had anything close to resembling a paddy wagon, Maria Pia Angelotta would at least have a lot of company.

Without all the satin fabric crowding my legs, I made better time eluding the cops, who at that moment rang a bell that launched into some ambitious chiming like it thought it was in a bell tower at a cathedral. I slipped out the back through what turned out to be the kitchen door—after a quick ogle at her hanging Calphalon pots and pans—and was honestly able to say: I slipped into the night. As I felt myself melt into the woods at the back of 7199 Gallows Hill Drive, I had one nagging thought about the cops: *Who tipped them off?*

By the time I drove home, locked up, turned on my ceiling fan, and fell into my loft bed, it was close to 1 a.m. I lay there spread-eagle and worked my way through my impressions of the time at Fina Parisi's. There was plenty of information that, while interesting on some level—for instance, the excellence of nougat in the making of candy guns—seemed unrelated to the murder of Georgia Payne/Anna Tremayne. Below me, some plaintive meows in the dark drifted up from Abbie, who was trying to figure a way up to the loft.

"Get some stealth, Abbers," I called to her. "You got the black thing going on nicely."

When I sorted through everything illuminating I'd learned from Fina, I felt truly chagrined at having to let go of my pet theory that the murderous Belfiere was behind every foul deed since Hi-C discontinued the Ecto Cooler juice boxes. To Belfiere's ambiguous motto, Never Too Many Knives, I could pretty much add: And Not Enough Hooch.

If that's the club activity that put the secret in secret society, well, Detective Sally Fanella was going to lose interest fast. Unless, of course, La gun-munching Maga was wrong about the moonshine line in the sand being whether or not money changed hands. And if the club members wanted to play competitive Name That Tincture, no one, including me, was going to call the cops.

As for Anna Tremayne, I couldn't get past the possibility that—notwithstanding a nice cat and a way with a utility knife—she just plain sounded as hysterical as her blog post. Once the coroner handed down an official time of death, I'd check with Fina about her alibi for murder. Despite the fact that I could see going out for lattes with the head of the Crazy Cooking Club—I have to admit I liked Fina's style, not letting her own mother into the society—she still wasn't necessarily off the hook in the matter of Anna Tremayne. Somebody wired Anna for something more than sound . . .

Tomorrow I'd have to step back into the kitchen classroom at Quaker Hills Career Center and I had to face the fact that I did not have an asbestos suit in my tiny closet. Would Mitchell and Slash hit me with something new? Or did they now truly have the fear of Don Lolo Dinardo in them? Considering their interest in sketchy employment with the "organization," I wasn't so sure. The list of things I was unsure of was lengthening.

How Anna Tremayne died.

Whether Joe Beck was playing me.

Who tipped off the cops to the Belfiere moonshine.

Whether my loft bed was off-limits to Abbie— wait: a soft landing followed by triumphant purring and padding told me it wasn't.

And finally . . . where, in any of the places I had ever known or imagined, was Landon Angelotta?

15

On Monday morning, after I landed the materials I had removed from Anna Tremayne's apartment on the passenger seat, hoping for some time to fine-tooth comb them, I fielded three calls on the way to my Basic Cooking Skills class. It was like heading for a 10 a.m. appointment in a Tenth Circle of Hell that even Dante didn't know about. One call was from Choo Choo, who told me Maria Pia got inducted into Belfiere, finally, after a visit from the sheriff's department delayed the ceremony for about half an hour.

While he drove her home afterward, she practiced the Belfiere pledge the whole way—oh, and he thought she'd been knocking back some whiskey. Then my monumental cousin Choo Choo added, "And Landon's called in sick." I got queasy suddenly, which I didn't for a second chalk up to the cheese Danish I had left out on the counter overnight and still ate, and told him to move around the personnel and put himself back in the kitchen as sous chef. Choo Choo grumbled but hung up quasi-willing to make the calls.

The second call, as I hit the country road that led straight to the Quaker Hills Career Center, was from Joe Beck. Considering how all-business he sounded, I suddenly found myself wondering whether any of the delicious making out yesterday had actually happened. Too much too soon? Too little too late? Second thoughts? Since I was about a mile away from the battleground I was headed to and had made the probably fatal mistake of bringing only my invisible armor, I didn't have the stuffing just then for figuring any of it out.

"Got the results of the postmortem, Eve." He sounded like I was a line item on his Monday morning punch list. "I used to date one of the morgue assistants."

Ah, Mondays. Always reassuring. "And . . . ?"

"She died around midnight."

"The morgue assistant?" Why was this so confusing?

A beat. "Georgia Payne."

"Okay." I'd need some serious alone time to toss that fact into my mental hopper and see who or what it kicked out.

"And—just as we thought—she was electrocuted."

Not what *we* thought—I thought Georgia had dropped dead with no help whatsoever.

I noisily blew out some air. I'd like to think it had nothing to do with the fact that he was right. I felt my eyes widen as I wondered whether death was instantaneous—or whether in those final moments she had known her killer, or wondered what would become of Abbie.

To tell you the truth, I felt kind of stricken. All over again.

"Eve?"

"Here," I said. "Thanks, Joe. I'm just about to turn in at Quaker Hills." I flicked down my turn signal. "Where I'm teaching them how to make a simple white sauce that I'm pretty sure will end up either down my back or dumped on my car seat." Then I actually babbled something to him about having a nice day. He said something kind of quick—it might have been as complicated as "Wait!"—and I thumbed the phone off.

As I wheeled a little too fast into the parking lot— were those my tires screeching?—I got the third call.

"Eve?"

"Fina?"

"Maria Pia gave me your number."

While she started to tell me about what hap-

pened at Maria Pia's induction after I left last night,
I turned off my ignition and watched a blue-and-
white minibus emblazoned with *Callowhill Residential Institute for Behavioral Success* pull right up
to the front door of QHCC's main building. Out
jumped Corabeth Potts, Mitchell Terranova, Slash
the K, and Renay Bassett, who somehow managed
to get inside the building while they punched,
tripped, mocked, and otherwise reviled each other.
Ah, the groves of academe.

But in a matter of seconds, Fina Parisi had my
complete attention.

The cops who came to 7199 Gallows Hill
Drive around 11:30 the night before, explained
Fina, were from the county sheriff's department.
Fina imparted this tidbit as though the difference
between town cops and county sheriffs was the key
to everything worth knowing. These worthies had
just received an anonymous call about the death of
Anna Tremayne, who had died violently at Miracolo Italian restaurant, a popular eatery in Quaker
Hills. (At that I cringed, hoping the word *eatery*
never made it to my nonna's ears, although the
word *popular* might soften the blow.) "So . . ." I followed up slowly, "it wasn't about the special Belfiere
brew, after all?"

"Not at all," she replied. "It was all about the
suspicious death of your sous chef."

No time like the present. "Who died around midnight. How's your alibi, Fina?" I reached for my stash of pico de gallo chips. For this conversation, I needed serious damage control.

"I had company all night." She sounded matter-of-fact.

"The kind of company that wasn't asleep in the east wing?" Did that sound a little sarcastic? I munched. Checked my watch: 9:57. Three minutes until my descent into madness.

"It was the kind of company," she drawled, "who, if he's asleep in the east wing, you've got to wonder what he's doing there in the first place. So, no, Eve." Then she added by way of explaining the guy's creds: "He's both a judge and an insomniac, so he can vouch for me at the key times."

Nice for her—nice in so many ways I decided just to let them roll on by me. She gets the judge. I get the likes of Junior Bevilacqua. Fina Parisi went on to describe how the sheriff questioned her about that hotshot Anna Tremayne, her connection to some secret cooking club, and her blog post. And by the way, could Ms. Parisi please explain what was meant by the term—here the sheriff consulted his notes—"oh murder"? Fina, figuring it was how a non-Italian heard the word *omertà*, obliged.

And I noted she did not suggest any historic correlation between *omertà* and *oh murder.* Instead, she explained to the sheriff that *omertà* added to the mystique of their two-hundred-year-old secret all-female culinary society. Members just like to believe there's something terribly important at stake, otherwise why should they fork over—although she didn't actually use the words "fork over"—the two-thousand-dollar initiation fee?

This little gumdrop of information was the biggest one I had snagged since putting together that Georgia and Anna were one and the same. *Two-thousand-dollar initiation fee?* Clearly the Belfiere *B* tattoo alone wasn't enough pain. Had Maria Pia Angelotta already anted up?

"I thought you'd want to know," said Fina, wrapping up. "Invite me for some antipasto sometime," she said before we murmured goodbyes at each other. I hung up, and crawled out of my Volvo as though the poor car was incapable of protecting me from what was to come. I grabbed my pathetic new leather portfolio and weighed it speculatively in my hand.

Perhaps I could hedge my bets by slipping in a few flat stones? I tried swiping the air forehand and backhand with my portfolio, wondering just what kind of defensive damage I could cause. Yes. Yes. Very good. As I kicked around in the brown grass just past the curb of the parking lot, looking for some flat stones, I pondered the info Fina had given me.

So the cops knew about Georgia being Anna Tremayne, celebrity chef. And the cops also knew that Georgia/Anna was connected somehow to a very old and secret cooking society called Belfiere. And the cops had heard about Anna T.'s hysterical blog post that appeared to blow the whistle on Belfiere, laying bare a motive for murder . . . for someone. And finally, the cops knew the murdered "hotshot" Anna Tremayne had violated *omertà*, the code of silence that was somehow worth buying into for a mere two thousand bankable clams.

I slid ten nice, flat stones into my leather portfolio, then tried the backhand once again.

Very, very nice. On the one hand, not too heavy to slow me down. On the other hand, packs enough of a wallop to make Mitchell or Slash suddenly unsure of the difference between a roux and a rarebit. Satisfied, I stashed it in a cardboard box with the two special sauce pots I had brought from Miracolo just for today's lesson.

Somewhat more confident now, what with my weighty class materials, I headed toward the front of the Quaker Hills Career Center, slowing only momentarily as I strode though the doors . . . which was when I remembered one of the very first things Fina had said when she called. *The sheriff's department had received a call.*

An anonymous call.

Whoever had made that call knew better than to call the Quaker Hills PD. Knew that Belfiere was meeting out in the county, the jurisdiction of the sheriff's department. Knew that Chef Fina Parisi, who lived at 7199 Gallows Hill Drive, was the host.

The significance of this insight eluded me for some time, while I hotfooted it down the brightly lighted hallway ahead of that resident dragon Courtney Harrington. The term *strega*, while suitable for Belladonna Russo, whose own daughter kept her out of the club that represented the highest in culinary arts (here I couldn't help cackling), seemed somehow inadequate for that person known as Courtney Harrington. This I would have to ponder. But for now, I pretended not to hear her strident shouts of "Angelino! You! You, Evelyn Angelino!"

For some strange reason, the kitchen classroom was suddenly promoted from Tenth Circle to sanctuary. I oozed inside so seamlessly, so ectoplasmically, I found myself wondering why I didn't look into special ops in those months while I was recovering from a leg broken in two places and wondering how I was ever going to pay the rent. I clutched my stuffed portfolio to my chest and scanned the room. Only because it didn't know any better, the sun was shining in all over the place. Lighting up the stainless steel classroom tables, the sequins on L'Shondra's top, and the metal studs on Mitchell's face.

"Good morning, class," I said, flashing around a crocodilian smile.

Frederick Faust raised a hand high. "Is it true we're down a man?"

I blinked at him, possibly a twenty-two-year-old, with fair hair parted once and for all back in 1955, the bangs combed back over the top. He must have looked cute in lederhosen when he was three. The Faust kid was the anti-Mitchell, but I'm not sure I liked him any better. "That man would be Georgia Payne, yes." Where's a situation room when you need one?

Renay Bassett slung a braceleted arm over the back of her stool and favored him with a look that would braise beef without turning on the burner. "Listen, Adolf," she said, warming up, "the next time you—"

And from there the eight of us—minus the man down—got fast-tracked to chaos, what with Renay telling Frederick just what he could do with his whisk, Corabeth belting out "Castle in a Cloud" from *Les Misérables*, and Slash the K drumming his little black heart out on the table with wooden spoons. A couple of punches were thrown by L'Shondra, pushed over the edge by that wise guy wannabe Mitchell, who was trash-talking behind his hands. Poor little Will Jaworski was reminding me of a big-eyed Ewok, fastening me with a look that said he still had a stockpot full of faith, both in my ability to control the classroom and in the Mets' chances of winning the World Series that fall.

"Silence!" I bellowed. Then I shoved apart Mitchell and L'Shondra, flung apart Frederick and Renay, told Corabeth to save it for late night at Miracolo, grabbed the drumsticks out of Slash's mitts, and pulled Will Jaworski out of the fray and up to the stovetop burners, where I used him to demonstrate how to make a simple roux. At which point the word "Suck-up!" got whispered around the sunny classroom. I glowered at them all.

While Will measured out the milk to mighty snoring sounds from Mitchell, Frederick asked again about Georgia. In as dignified a manner as possible, I explained that Georgia Payne had died suddenly at Miracolo, and I was sure we were all going to miss her very much. Just when I thought we could move on to the addition of flour to the roux, Slash piped up that Georgia had been "whacked." Then he raised an eyebrow, no easy thing given the hardware in what I could only call his face assembly, and looked smugly around at the others.

A few of them blanched better than any broccoli I had ever known. Nobody moved. And Will's stirring hand was poised trembling over the saucepan. "That true, Chef A.?" said L'Shondra.

I temporized. "Georgia died under . . . mysterious circumstances, yes." I'm not sure that sounded any better than "whacked," but it was all I had.

Despite the clamor for full disclosure, more details, and vomit-producing gore, I told them all to get busy at their stations—"except for you two"—I pointed at Mitchell and Slash, jerking my head in the direction of the hallway. Giving each other the eye, they sauntered toward me. I stared at nothing in particular as they got their swagga on and passed through the door I held open.

As the door eased shut behind us, I took a quick look up and down the hallway—some late students loping off to Automotive Technology and Cosmetology classes, which I'm pretty sure were two separate courses—no sign of that *stregissima* Courtney Harrington—and subtly backed the slouching Mitchell Terranova and blinking Slash Kipperman up against the wall. How best to handle these two, short of introducing them to my lovely leather portfolio? I reminded myself that what I wanted was information.

"I spoke to Don Lolo" was my opener.

This news was met with such creepy joy that

Mitchell grabbed kind of ineffectively at his crotch and Slash actually high-fived himself. Then the two of them grooved to whatever music they heard in their own heads until I held up a warning hand. "First, before Don Lolo can bring you into the organization, you must pass the truth test."

In that moment Slash went cross-eyed and Mitchell developed a sudden underbite. Their eyes ripped around my face like they were trying to determine just how far I was pulling their skinny little legs.

I went on to explain that Don Lolo Dinardo has unimpeachable information about the death of his lady friend, Georgia Payne, so he already knows the truth. What he wants now is to see whether your story matches it exactly. At which point my two wise guy wannabes got very studious, like we were heading into Final Jeopardy! "It's all about that red purse, boys," I said finally, lifting a speculative eyebrow at them and crossing my arms. "You need to come clean about how you got it. And don't spin me any more lines, because Don Lolo knows the truth." Which was more than I could say for myself. "There will be no consequences to you, you have to understand. But only if you come clean."

So they bought it, while visions of black limos danced in their weird little heads, and their words spilled out. And I, Evelyn Angelino, reluctant sleuth, cooking teacher to the star-crossed, hit pay dirt. The boys went on to describe how they had paid Georgia Payne a visit late that night at Miracolo. She let them in the back door, and while Mitchell distracted her, Slash pinched the red purse from the counter. Slash slipped it under his Phillies jacket. They liked her well enough—hey, she gave them some leftover biscotti—but they figured what the hell, a purse is a purse. (At this bit of insight, they spread their hands wide and I nodded like it made perfect sense.)

When I asked them who else was on hand, they looked at each other and came to the same conclusion at the same time: "Nobody."

"Nobody." I felt thoughtful.

Slash's mouth twisted. "Yeah," he said.

"Place was empty."

Slash sheepishly admitted they scored some silverware. "Not that it was real," he snorted. "Still, a guy's gotta eat."

I couldn't make sense of any of this—how these kids knew silver from silver plate, or how utensils alone can fill a stomach—so I plowed on, trying really hard to keep my expression neutral. "Then what happened?"

They shrugged. "She told us to get lost—"

"Well," said Slash, "'Run along home' is what she said."

And Mitchell snorted, "Like we live in da hood."

What was I going to do wit dese gangstas?

"And . . . ?"

"We blew the joint."

And then they both remembered something that caused them to fall out laughing.

"Ssh, ssh, ssh." I patted the air, worried that any sound of human joy would invoke Courtney Harrington.

Slash the K and Mitchell Terranova started pushing at each other playfully. "Yeah, she was standing in the doorway, like, you know?" said Slash, confidingly.

"Yes, I know what a doorway is."

"Saying good night."

"Yeah, when Dummy here—" a good shove at Mitchell, who was trying so hard to keep from blaring with laughter that bubbles appeared at the tip of his nose—"let a fork and spoon slide right through his pants—"

"—and hit the ground."

This hilarity included some choice put-downs about which of the two of them had less in there to hold up their pants, which ended in a stalemate. "Then what?" I pressed.

"Old Georgia didn't see a thing."

"Just shut the door on us—"

And then, out of the mouths of troubled babes,

I got a key piece of information. Out of the corner of my eye I saw a glimpse of pink heading our way that could only be the muffler shop shirt of the misnamed Courtney Harrington. As my mind flew to a satisfying image of jamming one of the stools in the kitchen classroom up against the doorknob, Slash the K clicked his tongue stud against his back molars and repeated, "Yeah, she shut the door on us." He scratched his chin, recollecting the moment. "And locked it."

At 12:10 I sat inert in my trusty old Volvo, my box of my leather portfolio and sauce pots on the seat next to me. Never had making a béchamel sauce, a béarnaise sauce, and a simple brown gravy been so exhausting. Practically hunched over the steering wheel, and chewing the inside of my cheeks to keep myself awake—no way I was going to nap in the parking lot at Quaker Hills Career Center, where I could wake up suddenly in a ring of fire—I drove below the speed limit into town. There I found a metered spot that still had some time on it, in front of my favorite boutique, Airplane Hangers, and jolted back my seat.

When Courtney Harrington had caught up with me (having had no success trying to turn the doorknob to the kitchen classroom, much to everyone's stifled laughter), she had a question about office hours. As in: I was supposed to have some. So the students could meet with me outside the classroom to discuss their needs. For a *strega* wearing a muffler shop shirt, she seemed pretty sincere, but the notion that anything like office hours would meet any of those particular students' needs made me erupt into hysterics.

Leaving Courtney with her mouth hanging open, I headed out the door, wiping my eyes.

With my seat back, I saw the Kale and Kayla Organics van zoom by on its way to the restaurant, where the flaky Kayla was delivering the day's order of produce. Miracolo was reopening after the murder of Anna Tremayne, and I wondered what kind of dinner crowd we'd get that night, given the fact that it was our second murder in less than a month, even if my beef braciola was on deck as the special as a lure for the squeamish. If I could stay awake to make it.

I catnapped for what turned out to be ten minutes and pulled myself out of the car, whereupon I was cornered by Dana Cahill, who kept tucking her black bob behind her ears, while she took me on about Grief Week. No mere catnap could steel me to any of Dana's endless requests and suggestions. "Aren't we done with Grief Week?" I felt myself sag against the car.

"Cut short, Eve, what with sudden deaths and whatnot." This "whatnot" she punctuated with fluttering fingers. If she were honest, she'd just come out and admit she wasn't done making neighborhood beagles howl at her tuneful slayings of splatter platters. Then she froze her shoulders in a gesture that I think was supposed to be appealing, and bared her cosmetically whitened teeth at me in a hopeful smile: "One more night?" She nibbled a cuticle.

I said graciously, "Whatever."

Which would land us all in the *pasta fazool* later, but for now, at least, she kissed me and sprang back up the block. At least I was rid of her. As I headed down the sidewalk toward Miracolo, where Kayla was double-parked outside while she unloaded the van, I thought about what I (hated to admit I) had learned at the jumpy, knobby knees of Slash the K and Mitchell Terranova. The boys had left Georgia Payne alive at the restaurant—minus a purse—also some of our place settings—where she was alone. And as they left, she locked the door.

I passed some lunch crowd turistas and avoided a group of polo-shirted Jaycees who were self-importantly figuring out street decorations for the Fourth of July. They were trying to come to some agreement about just how many miles of red, white, and blue twinkle lights to string up—here they prowled around looking for outdoor out-lets—when I got the full impact of what Slash had said. If Georgia/Anna had locked the back door to Miracolo when the boys left, then her murder wasn't a stranger killing. Either she had known her killer and unlocked the door for him . . . or her. Or . . .

Whoever killed Anna Tremayne had a key.

My hand settled on the front doorknob to our beautiful family restaurant just as the implications hit me. I'd need more than a brass knob to keep me upright. How was I ever going to get through my workday with the shakes?

16

Brushing by cousin Kayla, who was dressed in her classic powder-blue shorts overalls, today with a preposterous silver bandeau top, I breathed a quick "Hi" and headed for the office at the back. She called something after me about needing to talk about potato blight—as long as whatever she had to tell me didn't involve office hours, I was okay— and kept on unloading bins.

I closed the door to the office, pulled out my cell, and dialed the Quaker Hills PD. When they put me through to Detective Sally Fanella, who sounded like she was wrestling with a twelve-inch sub with everything on it, and the sub was winning, I asked her about the anonymous call to the sheriff's department. "How do you know about that?" she asked with a certain amount of suspicion in her voice. Then I heard some rustling of paper napkins.

I told her Fina Parisi was a friend of mine. Which, the second I said it, I realized was true.

Sally Fanella grunted. "Sheriff brought us up to speed, of course, since it's our jurisdiction."

"And the caller?"

If I could see her, she'd be shrugging. "Male. Nervous. Clocked in at ten forty-five. What more can I tell you? But now you can tell me—why the interest? Got something to add to your statement?"

As if.

Did I need to put a call in to Joe Beck? And if so, was I calling on him to do his lawyer thing for me, whatever that was? Or was I accusing him of something—something other than questionable taste in women, if he was still sneaking around with Potato Blight Girl? Because it was Joe Beck who knew about Anna T.'s hysterical blog. And it was Joe Beck who knew about the suspicious "death" at the Belfiere meeting two years ago, after which a scared—okay, hysterical—Anna Tremayne disappeared underground, going so far as to have her tattoo removed.

And it was Joe Beck who knew that Anna was threatening to publish an exposé of the two-hundred-year-old secret cooking society called Belfiere. Had she waited it out, she might have discovered that the worst that could happen from the "poison game" was suspension from the club, and being cut off from the traditional homemade hooch.

It was Joe Beck.

But why? Why would he set the authorities on Belfiere—without telling me?

Did he have something to hide that did not include my cousin Kayla?

Could he have had something to do with Anna's murder?

Even worse: Was all that kissing part of a plot to throw me off the track?

And as I walked in circles around the office at the back of Miracolo, I felt colder than anyone had a right to feel in the third week of June in Quaker Hills, Pennsylvania.

"No," I said with a sigh a little bigger than I expected. "Nothing to add, Detective Fanella." Somehow I got through the routine workday at Miracolo Italian Restaurant without any detectable goof-ups. At one point in the prepping process for the beef braciola entrée special, I think I dozed off while I was rolling the sliced and pounded and seasoned flank steak. There was something just a little too lulling about the rolling action to keep me conscious. Fortunately, enough neurons fired off to jolt me awake before I slid off the stool and landed my face in a meaty patch of fresh diced garlic.

While Choo Choo worked, huffing, on some zabaglione for the dessert special, he called back to me that he had seen Lanners walking into the law offices of Patty Pantuso, Nonna's estate attorney, earlier today. When I pinned him down—always difficult with the mountainous but slippery Choo Choo—he thought it must have been before eleven o'clock.

"Guess he wasn't too sick for that," said Choo Choo in his uninquisitive way, then added: "Although not for nothing is Patty Pantuso called Hot Pantuso." At that, my cousin grinned and nodded, privately enjoying whatever visions of Patty were dancing in his brain. The fact that Landon is gay didn't seem to enter into his deliberations on that score.

I gnawed on some flavorful toothpicks while I considered this bit of information. Best-case scenario, Landon was just running an errand for Maria Pia. Yes, that was it. Only, when our Nonna arrived, slightly the worse for wear after her Belfiere induction, it wasn't the case. Nothing like homemade hooch topping off an evening of costumes and attention to make her facial features look like they'd slipped a little. Even her outrageously thick and buoyant hair looked like it didn't have the will to spring very far from her face.

Still, Maria Pia Angelotta was nothing if not a trouper, even when it wasn't required. She winced and kissed Choo Choo and me, fluttered a vague hand at Paulette, and cast a shuttered eye around the kitchen. Had it been in flames, she might have noticed. But as it was, she slunk down the hall to the office, where I followed her and poked in my head. "Hey, Nonna, been in touch with Patty Pantuso lately?"

As she sank into one of the leather couches, she sent me a look like I had just asked her to find the square root of a prime number. "No, why would I? She's a vegetarian." Which gives you a sense of just how much sense Nonna was making the day after. Still, I decided it meant she had not deputized Landon to pay a call on Hot Pantuso.

Which meant that Landon Angelotta had business of his own with her. First I'd ever heard of it. What could it be? Choo Choo, when questioned closely as he groaned over the zabaglione—he likes making desserts in inverse proportion to how much he likes eating them—didn't have a clue. But he shrugged, which on Choo Choo looks like the kind of mudslide villagers fear, and added that maybe it had something to do with Uncle Dom's estate.

Well, okay, but Uncle Dom, Landon's father, died several years ago and his estate had long been settled. It's what made my darling cousin/brother/ best friend a wealthy young man.

So, why now? And then my fingers paused mid-toothpicking the braciola when my brain flipped the whole thing and I saw a totally different possibility. Landon was out sick—maybe he wasn't malingering—he had too good a work ethic—maybe he was really and truly sick. As in very sick. As in seeing Hot Pantuso for a Last Will of his own.

After that extremely disturbing thought, I finished all my preps in a wooden way. No more dozing. All the servers—including Corabeth—turned up. So did the enigmatic Mrs. Crawford, a vision in pale yellow taffeta and a Kate Middleton kind of hat with a veil. I had a half-hour break before the customers showed up, and when Maria Pia did appropriate coddling things with Giancarlo Crespi—she had lured him back to Miracolo simply by reminding him with a kiss on his cheek just how far back they went—I closed myself in the office and paged through the documents of Anna Tremayne.

Dividing up everything into little piles across the desk, I had ended up with categories I loosely called Identity, Relationships, and Professional. The last was by far the least interesting, what with unenlightening résumés, clippings, publishers' replies, tax returns, and so on. Nothing new there. At the top of the Identity pile I set her birth certificate. And in the Relationships pile I put any correspondence that seemed more personal than anything else. I paused over a few jotted notes from a wine merchant named Claude, who seemed to be feeling her out about how she felt about his wines, his prices, his wonderful self. On top of Claude's feelers I set what was clearly a torrid love letter, dated nearly forty years ago. No envelope, just a one-page, handwritten, combustible kind of document that began with "My Darling." From there, it got more inventive.

Sadly, the only person ever mentioning "tender loins" to me was my butcher, and this fellow was always pretty clear that, make no mistake, what we were discussing was bovine. I waved the love letter I'd discovered in Anna T.'s things, gently cursing the writer for not naming names, but maybe I had never had the kind of relationship where names weren't necessary. This notion, plus the one that Landon's bucket list might include—"See Hot Pantuso about Last Will and Testament"—was downright depressing.

Setting down the love letter, I studied the birth certificate. From that pink, rectangular document I learned that Baby Girl Anna was born in Philadelphia County on October 4, 1975, mother Annelise Tremayne, father Donald Tremayne. I quickly checked the signature on the love letter from nearly forty years ago: scribbled, but it looked like "Don." So the love letter was written by Don to Annelise. And out of their romance came Baby Girl Anna, who went through changes, from celebrity chef to glove salesclerk, from Belfiere hysteric to . . . murder victim in the foyer of my Miracolo.

Was I getting anywhere at all in my investigation?

So her parents were crazy about each other.

So I had her birth date.

Were these even baby steps?

I was just about ready to clean up the piles until I could pore over them after my workday was done, when Paulette Coniglio knocked and entered. Looking for a quick, quiet update on my crashing of the Belfiere induction, she perched on the edge of the desk. When I told her I was busted by the zipper on the gown she had so kindly made me, Paulette slapped her forehead and muttered some Italian swear words not even my nonna knew. Then I filled her in on the moonshine and tinctures that were the biggest and baddest that Belfiere has to offer, which made her laugh that throaty laugh that always reminded me, first, of Lauren Bacall and, second, how stupid my father was.

Finally, I waved my hand over the piles of Georgia/Anna's documents and explained them with one word: "Georgia."

Paulette cast big, mascaraed eyes over the stacks,

and then they settled on the love letter, where her expression changed. She seemed startled. "Whatcha got here, Eve?" She turned the letter gently with her fingers until it was facing her.

"What do you mean?" I said, sitting up just a little bit straighter.

'Well," she shrugged, "Isn't this Georgia Payne's stuff? Isn't that what you just told me?"

"Yeah, but—"

And in the very next moment came a comment that gave me the lead I was looking for.

Paulette was smiling quizzically at the letter Don had written to Annelise. "What's Georgia Payne doing with an old letter from Dominic?"

Dominic?

My uncle Dominic Angelotta?

Landon's pop?

My guardian?

What was she talking about?

Could I trust a woman who would wantonly use a zipper instead of buttons?

Nay, I say, nay.

But she was unmovable. Certain that the letter—"Pretty steamy," she admitted, giving it a quick once-over, adding, "Jeez, Dom," to a guy who had been dead and buried lo these last eight years—had been written by the brother of her longtime squeeze, my dad, the great, disappearing Jock Angelotta. Paulette and Dominic had corresponded a lot after Jock had taken off from Quaker Hills and all his responsibilities, and Paulette, devastated, had moved out of town to forget. Dominic kept after her, trying to get her to come back to work at Miracolo, and finally, she relented.

"Sweet guy," she said softly, "made a total pest of himself." But it was handwriting she knew well. She pointed to the signature, "Even the splashy way he wrote his own name—it always looked like 'Don.'"

No one knew better than I did just how sweet Dominic Angelotta was. He took over the dad role when my real one couldn't stick it. But what about this Donald Tremayne that Annelise had listed as the father of Baby Girl Anna? Two different men? It had to be. Did Annelise have a passionate love affair with Uncle Dom? Was Aunt May still alive when it happened? Did I really want the answers to any of these questions? It's funny how more light—anywhere—just ends up looking like more dark. If Dominic Angelotta had written this letter to Annelise, it just felt like the key to a closet where inside there was only darkness and *l'uomo nero*. All over again.

We took our battle stations and got through the

dinner rush, deflecting as many questions about the murder as we could without getting annoyed or seeming unduly mysterious. Maria Pia had gotten a second wind and was circulating feverishly, stopping by each table, finding something to talk about everywhere she oozed. Corabeth came up with an answer about the origins of zabaglione I suspected she invented, but everyone was delighted.

Jonathan thought outside the wine bin and made some risky recommendations that paid off. Li Wei actually looked for extra things to wash whether they needed it or not. Mrs. Crawford stuck to jazz and, although I missed the "Hokey-Pokey," I was grateful for what was predictable. Enough surprises for one day. That evening, not a single dish broke, not a single customer argued about the bill, not a single menu item fell flat.

Miracolo, in a word, was back.

Just as the crowd thinned out, the way it usually did around 10 p.m., and Dana Cahill and the regulars came in, carting their instruments and their Grief Week shrine, I slipped off my shoes in the kitchen and positioned one of the stools against the one little bit of wall free of any counter space. Choo Choo left the kitchen to corner Vera Tyndall in the dining room, near the table where Jonathan stood with his elegant arms folded over his tight-shirted chest.

I closed my eyes. The happy clattering sounds

of Li Wei at work were soothing to me. As the regulars tuned up, making their nightly hunt for an A worth playing, they sounded different to my jaded ears. More acoustic, less electric. Maybe the tail end of Grief Week was entering a folksy phase that left out electrified music. Fine by me.

At the sound of the kitchen doors opening, I eased open one eye. Maria Pia. She fluffed her hair with all ten fingers, then pulled a small can of hair spray out of a dress pocket and spritzed it manically all around her head in a figure eight. I'm pretty sure some of it landed on what was left of the zabaglione. "Nonna," I said quietly, not making a big deal out of it, "do you remember someone named Annelise?" I wanted to keep it open-ended and just see where the name took her.

The spraying stopped and she got a blank look. "Annelise? Why, *cara*?"

I made a face. "No particular reason, just wondering."

"Annelise." Then, again: "Annelise." Saying the name the same way twice didn't seem to jog her memory.

We fastened each other with a neutral look.

So maybe Paulette Coniglio was mistaken. Maybe that forty-year-old love letter to Anna T.'s mother was written by her husband, "Donald," after all.

Just as I was beginning to find some comfort in that notion, Nonna said the fateful word, "Wait."

"Wait?"

"Wait, there's something. Annelise."

"That's okay, Nonna, you don't have to—"

She flipped a hand at me. I caught a glimpse of the Belfiere tattoo. "Do you want to hear or not? Why do you ask me if you don't want to hear? Are you Little Serena?"

"So tell me, Nonna."

Maria Pia Angelotta looked like she was attempting to communicate with the spirit world, all of whom were living in the twelve-inch jumbo fryer hanging from the rack suspended over Landon's prep table. "There was a girl who worked for Dominic . . ." With that, my heart slid south. "A long time ago. An employee in his plumbing shop. Nice girl." Nonna replaced the cap to the hair spray and seemed to reach the end of whatever she had to tell me about someone named Annelise.

"Is that all?" I tried not to sound as disappointed as I felt.

"Please," she barked. "Of course that's not all. It's never all when it's young love, and Dominic was young, just starting out. I remember being worried, now that I think about it." Her voice softened. "Annelise Tomaine. Beautiful girl. Very fair."

"What about Aunt May?"

Nonna made the half-cringing, Italian gesture that says *I'm warding off a vampire only I left my garlic at home.* "May! This was before Aunt May came into the picture."

"What happened?"

She widened her eyes at me. "Thankfully, *niente*—nothing," she said with a philosophical toggle of her head. "Before we knew it, Annelise was gone—some thought Baltimore, some thought Philly—who knew? And May Siever came on the scene, and"—she smiled—"my Dominic grew up."

So why did I feel so sad?

"Believe me, Eve, now that it comes back to me"—here Nonna gripped me by the shoulders in a way that said she was letting me think we were two women of the world—"we were grateful that the worst thing that came from the Annelise thing was a little bit of a broken heart for Dominic." She pulled experimentally at her hair and turned to head back to the music coming from the dining room. Maybe she could talk the Grief Weekers into thinking her signature song, "Three Coins in a Fountain," was about a girl who drowned in it. Over her shoulder she flung, "Dominic got some experience—and a boy needs experience—but"—she gave a little laugh—"no lasting reminders, if you know what I mean."

With that she swept invisible lint from her

charcoal-gray skirt with the pink belt, and murmured. "Little Annelise Tomaine. I had completely forgotten about her." And she disappeared through the double doors, never pressing to hear where I'd heard the name *Annelise*. Lucky thing. Until I did some more figuring, I didn't want to spring Uncle Dom's steamy love letter on her. Reading it, she might have to reconsider whether the lovely Annelise was her sonny boy's maiden flight into "experience." He mentioned things I found myself hoping Joe Beck knew. But not from Kayla.

I took a deep breath.

Annelise Tomaine was how Maria Pia remembered her. But it wasn't Tomaine, it was Tremayne. Which meant Tremayne was her birth name, not her married name. And as soon as I got home, I'd fire up the laptop and see how far I could get researching the elusive "Donald Tremayne," Baby Anna's father of record. Slipping off the stool, I went over to the double doors and peered into the dining room.

Dana Cahill, dressed for some reason in a catsuit, but without the ears, was trying out some patter on the four-person "crowd," muttering suggestively into her hand mike. The crowd pretty much shot her the flat looks that restaurant models get when they interrupt your lunch and private conversation to tell you where you can buy the overpriced getup.

If this four-person audience didn't like the patter, just wait till Dana started singing.

The regulars, Leo the mandolin player and the others, kept vamping while Maria Pia tried to talk everyone into "Three Coins." The only one it looked like she convinced was the dependable Giancarlo Crespi. Mrs. Crawford, who was packing up her sheet music and happened to look up— the woman always seems to know when she's got my attention—crossed her eyes. A terse review of the entertainment. I grinned at her.

Leo's mandolin, without the amps, sounded like, well, a mandolin, and the bass and guitar and clarinet were apparently performing three different songs. None of it, I decided, needed me, so I waved to Mrs. C., grabbed my little backpack, which held Anna's documents, and slipped out the back.

The back door Annelise's daughter had locked the night of the murder.

If she was living her life underground, as Georgia Payne, cat lover, former glove seller, cooking student, who knew her? Especially since she had changed her looks somewhat. Just what kind of enemies could under-the-radar Georgia Payne make in the last two years since she had taken on that fake identity? Not one violent enough to kill her, I was betting.

Which kept bringing me back to her true identity as Anna Tremayne. But, here again, who were the enemies, besides the Belfiere crowd she unreasonably feared and hated? Any moonshining, parlor-game clubbers piqued enough at her to commit murder? Not likely. I think they were happy to see her go, happy to slap an Inactive status on her, and brush the dust from their collective hands.

So the question was . . .

Who was still around from her old life—up to two years ago—as Anna Tremayne, celebrity chef?

And although that seemed to be the key question, I couldn't get around the fact that she had changed her looks. Changed her looks. As I hurried down the north side off Market Square to my car, hotfooting it around late-night amblers, I found myself stuck with what seemed like a truth I couldn't shake: even if someone hated Anna Tremayne enough to kill her, how would he even recognize her? *How?*

The night was muggy enough that I thought we'd have a storm by morning, so I folded my blue butterfly chair and carried it inside with me. As I felt for the switch that turned on the track lighting in my little house, Abbie swished me as though we'd been friends forever, and I crouched to pet her. Which seemed like an acceptable delay tactic from me, in her eyes, until I got down to the serious business of a platter of chicken and liver. I speed-dialed Joe Beck and, when he didn't pick up, left a message about helping me hunt down Donald Tremayne, who might be in his sixties by now.

As I set out a can of cat food on the counter and reached for a spoon, the breeze kicked up and sent something just a little bit moonlit and a whole lot floral through the screened window over the sink. Can the neighbor's honeysuckle travel that far? Abbie landed on the counter just in case I thought I was going to dive into that chow without her. And then I froze. A shadow swept by the window, maybe ten feet away from the Tumbleweed. Although every instinct made me want to drop to the floor, clutching the cat, trying hard not to whimper, I did something totally counterintuitive: I leaned in for a closer look.

But, at what?

And there it was again. The shadow moved easily toward the front of my house. Setting the cat food on the floor, I frog-walked below the level of the windows, and reached up to flick off the lights. And, like Anna Tremayne that night, locked the door. The problem with my 130 square feet of living space was that it really came up short on hiding places. Or exits. If I survived the night, I was going to fire off some suggestions to the good folks at Tumbleweed.

But, hair-raising moments being what they are, I crawled into the corner and sat up against the wall, just behind the locked door, considering the situation. Which was when I heard stealthy footsteps come up my steps, and I remembered the Belfiere motto, *Never Too Many Knives*. Suddenly this motto seemed to contain all the really useful wisdom in the world, but any knives I owned that could do anything more helpful at the moment than peel an apple were lined up on the magnetized rack over the sink—and in plain view of the open window.

Abbie chose that moment to start meowing some comments on the fare.

Cats have no appreciation for danger that does not directly involve them.

17

From my spot in the dark I watched the brass doorknob glint as the shadow tried it.

Seriously, had I rattled enough cages, yanked enough chains, spewed enough clichés, to warrant a midnight visitor who was presumably not Joe Beck?

Could those actually be fingernails scraping at the door?

It's fair to say my skin crawled.

And then I heard a deep whisper so close I'd swear the lips were touching wood: "Let me in, Eve."

And now my scalp joined my skin. Because horror most definitely likes company.

"Eve," it came again, "you've got to let me in!"

I sat up. "Landon?" I said in a fierce whisper.

Then came his characteristic knock in boogie-woogie time. At which point several things happened at once. I leaped up, Abbie leaped away, I slammed on the lights, and I opened the door to my cousin, who was getting an earful about scaring the bejeezus out of me. I grabbed him by the shoulder and pulled him inside. "Where have you been?" I yelled. "And what the hell's the matter with you?" And: "What do you think of the cat?"

Landon looked ragged, like he'd been living on the edge somewhere, if only in his own head. He was dressed all in black—what I think they call a muscle shirt—and jeans—and I was guessing he hadn't shaved in a couple of days. Most of his great hair was tucked up under a black knit cap. With a quick look out to the road, I noticed his BMW parked on my gravel drive just off the road. He collapsed on the window seat, clutching one of my cushions to his belly. Abbie jumped up to inspect the newcomer, padding cheekily over the clutched cushion.

"Nice cat," said Landon weakly, while I stood by shaking my head, not sure whether I should continue calling him out on his inexplicable behavior over the past two days . . . or make him a café mocha.

"It's Georgia's."

And then my beloved cousin Landon Angelotta

did something I had never seen in all my thirty-two years, not even when Uncle Dom died. He started to sob, his eyes shut tight. I was at his side in a flash, trying to hug him, but when that didn't work, because he was flat out on his back, I held his hands, which were trembling. "Georgia," was all he said through the sobs, his poor head turning from side to side like all he wanted to do was push away every bit of consciousness.

"Landon," I said, squeezing his hands. "Landon. Some Perrier? A café mocha?" Although, if he chose the mocha, I couldn't do anything more than tear open a packet and stir the powder into some hot water. Since a decision seemed beyond Landon at that moment, I grabbed a light comforter from one of my three shelves and spread it over him.

Abbie tried out the fabric with her claws as I pulled the Perrier out of the fridge and closed my fingers around half a lemon I still had. I sprinkled some ice into a glass, filled it with the carbonated water, and added a slice of lemon to the works.

With one hand I pulled over a chair and with the other I handed Landon this drink, coaxing him into sitting up. Abbie moved down to his feet while I plumped the cushions behind his back. Then I folded my hands between my knees and waited. For a few minutes, Landon sipped his drink and gazed out into the night. We both watched a set of headlights pass us out on the road and continue on to where it was headed. For all the unanswered—and maybe even unanswerable—questions we had between us about the murder of Georgia Payne, for a few quiet minutes it was just Landon and Eve all over again. And in those moments I actually believed nothing could touch us. He swiped the cap off his head, his fingertips touching the glass of the window like they were looking for cool air. Then he scooted over and raised a wing of the light cover, and as I snuggled in, I knew he was going to be all right. Because then I could lock my arms around him at least a little ways, and when he smiled faintly, I knew we'd be fine.

We shared the Perrier while he told me the story.

After we discovered Georgia Payne's body and the cops came, he could tell by the way Joe Beck was acting that Georgia's death wasn't from natural causes. So he hunkered down and spent the next couple of days online, where he followed the trail from Georgia Payne to Anna Tremayne.

He found the restaurant reviews and reread the hysterical Anna T. blog post about Belfiere. But could the cops seriously think a few old tepidly critical reviews from her old life as Anna Tremayne would lead to a murder suspect? And could the cops seriously think that one hysterical blog post about a meeting of some middle-aged chefs would lead to a murder suspect? As Landon let those points sink in, he started petting Abbie, who shot him one of those long, slow blinks that are always mysterious in a cat. But I sat there feeling kind of foolish, because what Landon had dismissed so easily in terms of the murder—anything, that is, arising from Belfiere or restaurant reviews—I had clung to like it was Maria Pia's original recipe for osso buco that she keeps locked in a safe deposit box at her bank, with no existing copies anywhere.

He went on, "I couldn't find a good alternative suspect anywhere I looked. Finally, I knew I couldn't put off the visit to Detective Fanella, so I went. Just yesterday."

"And—?" If it had been terrible, wouldn't I have heard?

Landon sat bolt upright—the cat clung to Landon, the comforter did not—and hugged his knees. "It went okay," he said with a tired little shrug, tucking his head into his knees for a brief moment. Then he shot me a quick, sad smile. "Only, as I sat there, saying as little as I could, Eve, without raising red flags for her"—he heaved a sigh—"I realized it was like waiting for the tsunami to hit your shore." What was he talking about? "It was headed my way and there was nothing at all I could do to stop it. Or head it off. Or change its course."

"Landon—"

He held up a hand, and I grabbed those same long fingers that used to be able to tag me out at first base back in our sandlot days, and I held on. "So here I am, Eve, because it's going to get bad, and . . ." He slung a quick, gentle arm around my neck and pulled my head close to his. "I need you in my corner."

Now I was scared. "Your corner? Why do you have a corner? There's no corner."

"I've run out of other suspects for the cops, Eve, and I can finally see the tsunami."

"Landon, what is it? What are you talking about?"

He pulled away from me but kept his eyes on mine. And all I can say is, it's a lucky thing I was sitting. "Anna Tremayne," he said quietly, "was my half sister."

So out came the Laphroaig.

And I lowered the white miniblinds at the window seat.

Abbie, unperturbed by these revelations, jumped down and sauntered back to the dinner bowl to work on the leftovers.

What followed was a whole mess of information sharing. I told Landon about the love letter from his dad to Annelise, which was news to him. As for what set him on what he was dramatically calling the path to prosecution, "It was the necklace," he said simply. Then he reached a thumb under his black muscle shirt and tugged out a chain with a pendant: a tourmaline in a finely wrought silver birdcage. Our eyes met. "Is this Anna's?" I whispered, remembering the one I saw hanging around her neck, the one that kept drawing Landon in for a closer look.

"It's mine. My dad made it for me when I was a kid. I just never wear it."

Uncle Dominic, plumbing supply baron and silversmithing hobbyist. "They're identical."

"Two of a kind," he said wryly.

"Anna's must have been her mother's. Annelise's."

"I remember Dad's telling me he had only made one other." Landon half laughed. "I was eight and I thought, lucky thing, no way I was wearing this stupid birdcage around. And I was sorry for whoever got the other one."

"Now we know." From the lover to the lover's only child. And there went Maria Pia's certainty that all her son Dominic had gotten out of the love affair with Annelise "Tomaine" was some experience. Without a word, in the soft lamplight, I motioned Landon off the window seat, which I pulled out into a bed, at which improvement Abbie gave me a look like I had been holding out on her. Landon stripped off his shirt while I climbed into the loft and grabbed a pillow, which he caught one-handed.

Back down on the main floor, I lowered the other blinds, stopping for a second by the screened window to listen to the crickets. "Did he ever know about her? Your dad."

"No," said Landon, shaking his head slowly. "I honestly don't think so." He looked at me. "If he did, he would have done right by her." I nodded. Uncle Dom had done right by me, and I wasn't even his own child. He was a man who had a pretty broad interpretation of what doing right meant.

As Landon stared into what was left of the Scotch, he added, "But that's not what's going to bring me down, Eve."

"What are you talking about?" I sat down on the edge of the bed.

"Anna Tremayne was my sister. My *older* sister."

"So? You only just found out."

He shook his head sadly. "That's not the point." Abbie was curled up and ready for the humans to get on with the business of sleeping. And she had chosen Landon. Cats always know. Besides, sacking out with the newcomer didn't involve any complicated loft access problems.

"Then what is?"

He let out a little laugh. "I'm the prime suspect, kiddo."

My heart started to pound. "Why?" I asked softly, ready to fight him on it.

"It's all about the money, Eve."

"What money? You were Uncle Dom's only heir. Even if he had known about Anna, which we don't think he did, he left everything to you."

Landon lifted an eyebrow at me. "Dad's everything, Eve, wasn't so much everything, as it turns out."

"What do you mean?"

"The company was tanking before he died, and yes, I got some inheritance from him . . ."

I opened my hands at Landon in the Italian gesture that translates as *Your brain is as thin a pomodoro sauce made without San Marzano tomatoes.*

"Most of my money, *carissima*, comes from Nonno."

"Nonna?" I was confused. "Who's still with us?" No comment.

"Not Nonna. Benigno. Nonno. Our grandfather." He shrugged. "Not a man ahead of his times. Or particularly, oh, astute. He thought the fact that I hung out with guys made me macho."

"Just because you're gay doesn't mean you're not also macho."

"But you get the point."

"And the money?"

"A big fat honking bequest in his will. I went to Patty Pantuso today just to be sure I was right on the terms of Nonno's bequest." He leaned back. "It's all come back to haunt me. Because now," he said quietly, "now it shows motive."

I could hardly get it out: "Motive?"

"The money, Eve. They'll say it was the money. And for the life of me—and I do mean the life of me—I don't know how to prove them wrong. I'll never be able to convince them I didn't know any of this until after she was already dead." All of a sudden my beloved Landon looked about a decade older than his thirty-three years. "The money that bought my condo, my BMW, my Dartmouth days, my rich-boy lessons all over the place, my trips, my investments, the money that allows me to play at sous chef with you instead of having to get a real job—"

"Landon, talk sense—"

"It was all Benigno's money, Eve. Not Dominic's. It was all money our nonno Angelotta left specifically to his 'oldest grandchild.'"

And suddenly—sitting there with him in the low light on a warm June night, where all I could handle listening to were the distant and dependable crickets—I understood.

"His oldest grandchild," Landon went on, "who, up until just two days ago, before Georgia Payne came into our lives"—he gave me a wry look, both hands spread wide—"was me."

That night I tossed so much I was surprised I didn't toss myself right out of the loft into a heap on the floor ten feet below. Maybe I'd earn a framed picture of myself on Giancarlo Crespi's polished mahogany bar next year for Grief Week at Miracolo. It's always nice when you wake up and a course of action is clear. But in terms of sleep as a prerequisite to clear thought, I have always considered it overrated. Things weren't necessarily any clearer on any given morning than they were the night before, only delayed.

By the time I had headed up my ladder to bed, I knew a couple of things for sure. To Landon, no one had a better motive than he did for the death of his half sister, Anna, which was understandably freaking him out. Which was why he placed the anonymous call to the sheriff's department, setting them at the Belfiere crowd, which seemed like a good place for finding the true killer. And taking the heat off himself. So I was making it my business to get Landon out of the line of fire.

I had been so wrapped up trying to prove a case

of motive against Fina Parisi or any of the rest of her Belfiereans—including Elodie Tichinoff—that I had dangerously back-burnered the other classic telltale clues of guilt for a murder—namely, means and opportunity. Much as it pained me to say the words, even silently in my own head, but Anna Tremayne had been killed at Miracolo, so it was back to the scene of the crime I would go.

But what really broke my heart were Landon's last words before he drifted off to sleep in the presence of me and his half sister's cat, Abbie. I slipped the cocktail glass out of his hand before it could slide from his fingers to the floor. I watched my beloved Landon shake his head dreamily. Then he murmured, "I never got to know her."

And I knew there would always be that, even after we figured out the crime, even after we made room for her memory in our family, even after we named a particularly delicious veal dish *alla Anna*, even after we set a framed picture of her on the bar next year during Grief Week. There would always be Landon's regret—"I never got to know her"— that nothing could make better. Even if it was shared. Because Anna Tremayne was as much my cousin as Landon was, more my cousin, a closer cousin, than Kayla. If it weren't for the pesky fact that our grandfathers were brothers and she grew the best eggplant in the Tri-State Area, I would delete her from my phone contacts. (And, possibly, Joe Beck's.)

I felt cheated.

In the morning, a quick glance to the front of my Tumbleweed showed me a pile of Landon and Abbie, asleep, so I slunk around getting ready for a day I could only praise for its not including a trip out to Quaker Hills Career Center in search of my daily dose of knives, sauces, and miscreants.

As I slipped out of my Tumbleweed, where I left kibble for Abbie—who gave me an arch look like she had everything under control—and a banana and some French-pressed coffee in a carafe for Landon, I felt a steely determination. Someone had killed my cousin Anna. Maybe this wasn't a violation of *omertà,* because this crime went way beyond any "code of silence" that, finally, just seems like nothing more than aching, teenage secrets. No, this crime was a violation of family. Suddenly I felt so Italian I might start yelling at everyone I loved.

In the meantime, I was heading back to the scene of the crime, where even if there weren't clues, there might be tugs to the imagination. I would figure it out. And I would figure it out before Detective Sally Fanella figured out the hidden blood relationship between Georgia Payne and Landon Angelotta—and before she slapped Hot Pantuso with a court order giving her a right to look at Benigno Angelotta's will.

I ask you: Where's a good busybody when you really need one?

It was 8:12 a.m. and I had already spent fifteen minutes crouched in the empty foyer at Miracolo, not registering anything new about the murder. Somehow, somehow, Anna Tremayne had been electrocuted and it was beginning to look like Zeus had flung a lightning bolt her way. I took a deep breath. Back it up, back it up. Anna hadn't just decided to hang out in the foyer; she was there, after the workday was over, to lock up the place. Lock up. I looked up. Aside from the brass light fixture on the ceiling, there was no metal anywhere in the foyer except for the doorknobs. The dead bolt, and right underneath, the regular knob.

Whatever happened to Anna Tremayne had happened right in that small space. Electric current had shot through her body and stopped her heart. Was it possible the current had hit her in the dining room and that she had crawled into the foyer, hoping to get outside for help? The mere thought made me sit back kind of helplessly right there on the tile floor. But from the little I had read on the grisly topic, I didn't think crawling for help was possible, not with a lethal hit.

As I sat frustrated on the floor, Anna's murder was beginning to seem like a locked-room mystery.

How did the killer get in? Either Anna knew him or he had a key.

But if he could get in, why the elaborate means of murder? Harnessing some death-dealing electric current takes more in the way of planning than, say, stabbing or strangling.

It was an interesting thought. Suddenly the killer possibilities could include women. And suddenly actually getting inside the restaurant wasn't necessary in order to commit murder . . .

When I heard some deep laughs coming from out on the sidewalk, I pushed aside the double-rodded curtain on the front door and saw the Jaycees were back, this time with flags and stepladders and boxes of twinkle lights. These were our bald, baseball-capped guys wearing identical cargo shorts, who firmly believe that civic life comes down to putting up flags and cutting your grass.

Once I figured out who killed Anna Tremayne, I'd ponder whether they had a point. In Quaker Hills, this cheerful crew of Jaycees was as much a part of the landscape as the garbage collectors and street cleaners and our very own wandering philosopher, Akahana Takei.

Scrambling to my feet, I unlocked the front door and stepped outside. The Jaycees were sharing stories about how one son was on the junior swim team and knocking 'em out of the water—spoken without irony—and how one daughter was in computer camp and available for babysitting. I approached them casually as they swarmed around the decorative streetlamp in front of Miracolo, and one of them went jauntily up the stepladder to unfurl what he called Ole Glory and jam it into the flagpole holder.

My exchanges with this group always begin with *Hey, fellas*, and today was no different. After they reminded me with hearty good humor that their names were Gene, Bud, and Drew, I laughed, "Right, right," and pumped them for information. Down to a man they came up short in the busybody department: nobody had seen any suspicious activity outside Miracolo on the night of the murder. Then they all had to make locker-room comments about just what they were at home doing with their wives at that hour. Which led right away to guffaws and more improv about what they *weren't* at home doing with their, uh, girlfriends. Those cutups.

I thanked them for making our street safe for

parades and went in search of Akahana, a reliable philosophizing night owl of the first magnitude. Her presence in Market Square at all hours had led to a petition drive to persuade town council to enact an obnoxious curfew law, but it was met with enough resistance from the rest of us that it failed. The fact that Akahana herself had signed the petition made the council wonder whether anyone quite that innocent was a threat to public safety.

I ran Akahana to ground on the west end of Market Square, our commercial district, where I learned she had been out of town at a Kierke-gaard convention on the night of the murder. And to boot, she had heard no scuttlebutt about the case. "Even your tone-deaf singer lady knows more than her usual nothing, and not in a Kierkegaard-ian way." With that Akahana went off to do some Dumpster diving.

So, another couple of busybodies bit the dust.

After collaring street cleaners, city service department workers, a couple of FedEx delivery guys, Quaker Hills' single cabbie, Joe Beck's florist brother James, and random dog walkers, I decided to quit before people started avoiding me like the Repent, the End Is Near guy, who wore a sandwich board around Quaker Hills for a while and then disappeared. We guessed that, when it came to himself, Repent must have been right. So I crossed back over to Miracolo, where only Bud was left. Gene and Drew had worked their way farther up the street with their flags.

I watched Bud work on the red, white, and blue twinkle lights. The cover to the outdoor outlet, down near the woodwork, stood open, just waiting for his handiwork. I watched him strip some wires—and if there's anything that interests me less than wires it's balancing my checkbook—because, apparently, the strands were too short and he had to splice them. With his fingernails he peeled back the insulation, exposing the copper wires inside the cords of the twinkle lights. "What would happen if you plugged in the cord?" I asked him because it wasn't even 10 a.m. and I had run out of ideas.

It was a question that got a big reaction. "As long as I kept my hands on the insulation here, nothing."

"And if you don't?"

"Well, let's put it this way," said Bud, widening his billiard-ball-blue eyes at me, "I'd complete the circuit." Then he added: "Only I wouldn't be around to know it."

Welcome to Electricity 101. I crossed my arms. "So you actually have to touch the wires to complete the circuit?" A hazy image of Georgia/Anna was shimmering at me just out of reach, there in the Miracolo foyer as she went to lock up at midnight on the last night of her life.

"Nope." Bud shifted on his haunches just enough to pull out his keys. His big fingers nimbly held up one, which he brought close to the exposed wires. "This would do the job pretty good, too. Metal's great for that." He waggled the key at me.

"Thanks, Bud," I said, eyeballing the distance between the covered outdoor outlet and the locks on Miracolo's front door. Five, six feet? Leaving him to his alterations on strands of twinkle lights, I let myself into the restaurant and very slowly closed the door behind me. My breathing felt shallow as I stared at the locks, the dead bolt, and the regular Schlage. Oh, Anna, you were just doing your job, and that's what somebody was counting on, waiting. And then . . . you completed the circuit. Which sounds like some kind of achievement—but only for the killer.

I was pretty close to understanding how Anna Tremayne had died, but I didn't have the whole picture yet. Not the details. Not the face on the other side of the door. All I had for sure was the method, and for now I was keeping that to myself. Maybe there was something to be said for *omertà*, after all. Maybe the code of silence has something to do with self-preservation in the shadowy company of a killer I couldn't yet identify. I'd let what I discovered simmer along with the Bolognese sauce for my tagliatelle entrée special.

For now, toting the box with my two special pots from home, I walked through the empty dining room, where the natural daylight filtered through the curtains and dust motes drifted. Everything around me seemed unfamiliar, like I was suddenly a stranger in a place I had known all my life. Everything seemed charged with mystery and poised for something—some final explosion of truth . . . and whatever else it would bring. The terrible thing is that this kind of alarm doesn't make any noise, doesn't give us a heads-up. Objects look sinister. People seem hostile. And trust is nowhere to be found.

Once through the double doors, I entered my little chrome and stainless steel kingdom, ready to begin my workday, but distracted by thoughts of Anna's murder. Setting down the box, I pulled out the pots and discovered my Instructor Eve leather portfolio there—rocks and all, which I wouldn't be needing again until tomorrow—and left it on the junk counter, along with catalogs and bills. I took a deep breath, my fingers clamped on the box. Just how far into my prepping could I get before somebody commented on my shaking hands?

18

If you can't find a busybody to help solve the crime, then go for a string of nuisances. Their distraction value for you goes way beyond rubies. Throughout the afternoon on a day where all my trust was gone, maybe for no good reason, but gone nonetheless, a string of nuisances turned up and really went a long way toward keep me preoccupied. First came Kayla, who needed to be paid then and there for the bins of organic produce because she had to buy a new dress she'd just seen at Airplane Hangers.

Then came Maria Pia, who declared she had her eye on a lovely fellow who worked on the road crew out on Highway 8. He was the handsome, burly one who held up the stop sign. Landon— who turned up telling me he might as well cook before he gets arrested for murder—and I sighed at this announcement, predicting even a lustier version of "Three Coins" that evening.

Then came the carpet cleaning service, who declared they might have to sue us for providing them with a soiled carpet that probably clogged their cleaning equipment. Then off they went with more soiled carpets.

Then came Mitchell Terranova and Slash the K, shirtless, demanding to know whether Don Lolo was a stand-up kind of guy who would honor their underworld ambitions. I threw them out before they could poke around and discover Choo Choo in his maître d' suit at the podium, taking dinner reservations over the phone.

Meanwhile, as the Bolognese sauce simmered, the primo nuisance in my life in Quaker Hills turned up early for want of anything better to do: Dana Cahill, what Akahana called our tone-deaf singer lady. Her husband, Patrick, was out of town on a business trip and she was extravagantly bored. So she wandered around my kitchen, yapping, in a white tank top and turquoise shantung Capri pants and wedge slip-on sandals with ghastly pink plastic bows. Landon and I pretty much ignored her and prepped silently for dinner.

Dana helped herself to some tonic water and pulled a stool up to the center prep table, where she perched, circling her glass reflectively—which

was about as reflective as Dana Cahill ever got—
and talked about what a difficult day she was having. "Professionally," she added, shooting us looks
like we two would understand.

I gave her my standard, "Oh?" which is all she
ever needs to whip her into a conversational gallop.
The only thing that was helping me at that moment in the afternoon was the image of drowning
Dana in a blender of pulverized pesto. Finally, a
practical use for the mess . . .

And at that moment I got a call from Joe Beck,
so I turned away from Dana and listened to his
glum report that he hadn't come up with a Donald Tremayne who wasn't either older than thirty-
nine or downright dead. I felt a little frisson of
guilt, having forgotten to head him off, what with
sorting out Anna Tremayne's true paternity with
Landon. So I thanked him prettily and left it that
I'd fill him in on anything new in the case (I made
it sound like "new" was just a remote possibility)
tomorrow.

Dana was still talking, explaining to a glassy-
eyed Landon that what she really needed for the
end of Grief Week—"One last song!" she pleaded
when we got agitated and reminded her that Grief
Week ended last night—was a really good dead-
on-the-road kind of piece. Did we know any?
Landon threw out the ever-sappy "Teen Angel,"

which he said he was pretty sure she had already performed, no?

"Hit by a train, Landon." Dana smiled, her hands open wide like these differences mattered terribly. "And I feel Leo didn't get to hear anything truly close to the, well, facts."

"Leo?" said Landon.

"The facts?" said I. Then, to Landon: "Leo's the mandolin player. The regular. You know. Leo."

"Okay."

Dana sighed. "He seems to be needing more, and if I can help him with my vocal gifts, you know I will." While Landon offered me a spoonful of Bolognese sauce, which I tasted with my eyes closed, just to savor it fully, Dana leaned her elbows on the prep table and went to describe the hit-and-run accident that killed Matt Cardona, Leo's son. Matt was twenty-eight and a marathoner, training out on county roads when he was hit. Dusk. Reflective stripes, but didn't do him any good at that turn when the speeding car came along. There was a witness, who called 911, and the poor kid lived a little while.

Sad, no denying it. Landon and I widened our eyes at each other. Kind of blew the death of Dana's dog, Booger, right out of the water. Still, one man's grief is one man's grief, and that's enough. At that moment, Jonathan turned up looking like he'd just come from a haircut and a particularly nice coffee date, decked out in the Miracolo "look." Landon sent him a tight-lipped smile—he seemed to be getting nowhere with his crush—and turned quietly back to the almonds he was toasting.

Setting down a new bottle of Barbaresco he had discovered in Philly and wanted us to try, Jonathan rolled up his sleeves and jumped into the conversation. "Oh, yeah," he said, "didn't it come up the other night, before Maria Pia's big dinner here? Remember?" He actually slung an arm around Dana.

"When?"

"You, me, Vera, Georgia—poor Georgia—Leo, maybe Corabeth."

"Oh . . . right," she said, leaning into Jonathan, but probably not remembering what he was talking about at all.

"We were talking about cars, and from there it went to road accidents—"

"Leo mentioned Matt, right, I remember."

Jonathan lifted his very attractive shoulders. "Then, what with too much Grief Week—"

"—to lighten the mood," put in Dana, with a quick smile that was meant to show us how good with people she was—"I mean, there's just so many dead wives, dogs, and kids we can handle." Ah, the sensitive Dana Cahill.

"But then it got fun, right?" Jonathan squeezed her shoulder, at which Landon started knocking back toasted almonds with a grim look, and I began to wonder about our sommelier's sexual orientation. And taste in women. His other hand sketched a marquee in the air: "'Worst Loser Cars We've Ever Owned.'"

Dana burbled.

Landon rolled his eyes, thinking maybe he was learning more about Jonathan than his crush could take in order to survive.

Me, I found myself strangely riveted. Between the two of them, Dana and Jonathan remembered that Georgia Payne had mentioned having owned a white Cadillac Escalade, at which conspicuous consumption all the rest of them groaned. "If you want a big-ass old-rich-white-lady car, why not just buy a Land Rover?" That was Corabeth.

And Georgia said what made her get rid of it was that it didn't corner well, practically going off country roads—okay, okay, even if she was doing 55 in a 35 mph zone, still. There were just so many mailboxes and raccoons a girl could take out, said Georgia, making them all laugh, before changing her wicked ways and getting more reliable wheels. Then the rest of them offered up stories about an Optima, a Yugo, and an Aztec from yesteryear.

It turned out to be a packed dining room from

the time we opened the doors until the last diner stuffed her credit card receipt into her purse and toddled out. There were still a few stragglers, happy just to kick back and watch the regulars set up their instruments. Dana was warming up with lame repartee with Leo, who switched to guitar and left the mandolin in an open case, and the lanky, long-haired social studies teacher, who seemed to be engaged in an athletic event just tuning his bass.

The splats of Dana's jokes went right over the head of Giancarlo, who was smiling benevolently in every direction as he poured after-dinner liqueurs—mainly because Maria Pia was flirting with him. Which was always Nonna's default when she sensed fences needed mending.

Mrs. Crawford, a vision in knee-length, mint-green chiffon with a gold-colored flapper's cloche pulled down around her ears, packed up and left to meet a friend for a nightcap. Choo Choo, Vera, Landon, and I were intensely interested in this friend, since it was her first mention in the month she had been our pianist that she had a life outside our four walls. Not that any of us ever doubted it. But this was the closest she had let us come to knowing anything. In a bit of a hurry, off she went at a brisk clip in her towering heels.

I circled behind the bar, brushing by Giancarlo and Nonna, who was ladling it on thick about his

passionate nature, and finding something to interest me in the stack of dirty barware stashed under
the bar. It was the closest I could get for staking
out the regulars. They had been doing this gig-
of-their-own-devising at our restaurant for a few
years, but I'd never paid them any attention.

Leo was replacing a mandolin string as I looked
up from the fascinating dirty glasses. "Any mandolin tonight, Leo? I just love the boost you give
it with the juice." When he gave me a mild look,
I said with some dizzy spirit I hoped would come
across as disarming, "Wired for sound!"

"No, not tonight. The wire broke." And he
went back to turning a tuning key.

Dana pulled a bar stool in front of the little
clutch of musicians, at which Maria Pia practically
trembled, waiting to hear the opening bars of her
signature song. As I bent to pick up a stray cocktail
napkin from where it peeked out half under the bar,
something small glinted at me. My fingers brushed
it forward, and then I palmed it. Sure enough,
Dana Cahill, acting more like she was announcing
the semifinalists in the Miss America Pageant, introduced Maria Pia Angelotta—and her very own
self—in that classic song about young Italian love . . .

The music began.

Giancarlo pressed a seemingly reluctant Maria
Pia out from behind the bar.

And I opened my palm. What I held looked like the end of a black electrical cord. Maybe two inches, that's all, cut cleanly through with a pair of scissors. Staring at the cut, all I saw was what was left of two copper wires.

You know the expression *My blood ran cold*? Well, by me, that's not quite how it goes. For blood to run cold, you have to have blood. What I was feeling in that moment was that I had morphed into some other kind of being, something bloodless, something even kind of mineral. I felt beyond a racing heart, beyond prickling skin, beyond even a cold sweat. All I had were eyes, and mine slid to the right by about four feet and settled on the mandolin lying in the open case. Cordless.

The wire broke.

My breath came in rough little pops drowned out by the song. What was left of the cord sat like a motionless black insect in my palm. At that moment, I slowly looked up and found Leo noodling away on the guitar, his eyes on mine.

By 11:30 Miracolo had emptied out, and a tired staff was wandering off home. It was my turn to lock up, so I made myself scarce in the kitchen, polishing prep tables that had already been polished, trying very hard to keep an open mind about murder. Maria Pia had patted my cheek and then actually let Giancarlo drive her home instead of Choo Choo.

Landon gave me a weary kiss and went home to feed Vaughn and wait for the law. This was spoken with big-eyed paranoia, which I countered with an eloquent eye roll. Corabeth flashed me a peace sign and went out with Li Wei in tow. Paulette prowled around the entire restaurant, which—with only a little bit of irony— she declared a terrorist-free zone, and departed.

While the regulars packed up, chatting in tired mumbles about the set, I slipped a Linda Ronstadt CD into the sound system for a shot of the anti-Dana. Even though Dana herself was still swanning around the dining room long after the onlookers (truer word than *audience*, really) had left. Right after I set a doorstop against one of the open double doors, to clear the kitchen of the last of the dinner aromas, I texted Detective Sally Fanella, hoping she was somewhere conscious with her phone turned on. *Cn u give me date of hit skip on county road third week in June 2 yrs ago.*

No immediate answer. I wasn't sure how everything pieced together—or even whether it would—but I was curious about that information. As I flicked off the switch to the A/C, Dana came running toward me stiff-armed, with tiny little scooting steps in her wedge sandals.

"How was I?" She gushed at me as though she was the one delivering the compliment.

Then she caught my hands and bit her coral-glossed lips.

I went to my default answer—"Same as always"—spoken with enough gusto that it was all she needed.

"Eve, Eve, Eve . . ." She gave me a fond, sidelong look. "My biggest fan."

Which was really saying something.

Then I slung an arm around her and jogged us girlies on over to the Sub-Zero fridge and pulled out my private stash of coconut water (I am not immune to trends). As I poured us both a short one, since I really didn't want to encourage Dana to hang around much beyond my pumping her for info, I asked her about poor Leo, keeping it out of earshot of the musicians as I kept one eye on them, still packing up. What was the date of the hit-and-run? Where did it happen? Somewhere out on a county road?

But Dana came up empty of everything except coconut water.

And Sally Fanella was silent.

Then Dana held my face, kissed both cheeks, and loped back out to the dining room to leave with her "boys." I kept Linda Ronstadt on an endless loop as they all cleared out, the bass clunking through the front doorway, followed by the ghostly Leo, with his two instrument cases, and the clarinetist.

A laughing Dana, slipping into a sparkling little shrug, was last, hard on their heels. Then gone. I dimmed the overhead globe lights, feeling like some kind of minor restaurant god that could change things in my very own firmament. I stared for a rough moment at the two locks on our front door, then got over it and quickly locked up.

Turning back into the dining room, where one of my last official acts of the day was to blow out the votive candles, I saw a stack of papers on the piano. Mrs. Crawford's sheet music. In her hurry, she'd forgotten it. I put the sheet music on the piano stool, then headed to the closest table, where the votive candle burned low. Suddenly something occurred to me, so I pulled my phone out of my pocket and texted Fina Parisi. *Hey, need date of Anna's induction night she ran out on you. Antipasto together this Friday?*

I pinched out a couple of candles, snapped up a forgotten set of keys, danced to Linda's demanding to know "When Will I Be Loved?", when a soft one-two chime made me grab my phone. It was Fina, texting me back. *June 21 two years ago at dusk never forget it. Yes to Friday.* So Georgia Payne had torn out of the Belfiere meeting, freaked out, at high speed in her white Caddy Escalade, cornering badly, almost slipping off the country road, taking out a mailbox. Maybe a raccoon. Maybe a runner—

Which was when my phone chimed softly again.

Sally Fanella. For some reason—maybe at those times when we feel the presence of a weighty inevitability, something we wonder we didn't notice earlier, although it's hard to say what good it ever does—I swallowed hard before reading her text. In the dim lights of Miracolo, I held up my phone and read: *Cold case county hwy 8 runner left 4 dead 9:21 p.m. June 21. Witness saw white SUV couldn't catch plates. Y?* County Highway 8 ran through Pendragon, Pennsylvania. How far from Fina's house was Anna Tremayne when, in the failing light, she hit Matt Cardona? Did she even realize it? Would we ever know?

What I knew for certain—and here my whole body felt like the weighty inevitability that had only skulked around outside me until that very moment—was that Georgia Payne had shown up, as luck would have it, to work at Miracolo. And miracle it was for a father still grieving his dead son when casual conversation about loser cars solved for him what the cops had filed under cold cases. There she was, his for the killing.

First the cutting of the power cord for the mandolin, then the stripping back of the insulation, then pulling apart the wires, then the wait. The wait outside on the sidewalk, finding what shadows he could, until he saw her just inside the front door, ready to lock up. All he had to do was plug the cord into the outdoor outlet, and at just the right moment—

My phone rang, startling me. I looked: Dana.

—all he had to do was touch a wire to each metal lock as Georgia's hands met them on the inside, where she completed the circuit—

"Eve?"

"Dana."

Just to stay busy, my trembling fingers pinched out the final candle, near the center of the empty dining room.

"Eve, just to let you know, I told Leo about all your interest in Matt and what happened. How you were asking about things I couldn't answer—I always hate letting you down—you know, like the day, the time, the place. He'll get back to you. It's always good to go straight to the source, don't you think?" And then: "Eve?"

Which was when I realized I saw a shadow in the kitchen, and, with a tumbling heart, I eased closer to the nearest table and slipped the phone—leaving it on—out of sight behind a candle holder. I heard a faint "Eve?" coming from it, hoping to hell Dana would just, for once in her life, shut up. Through the open kitchen door came Leo Cardona. I used to joke that Dana Cahill was going to be the death of me, but I never thought she was going to be the *death* of me.

"Leo!" I said loud enough to alert my phone that I wasn't alone.

Leo Cardona was backlit by the bright lights of the little chrome and stainless steel kingdom I was missing already. It wasn't quite like having the burly, menacing Raymond Burr swaying in the doorway at the end of *Rear Window*, but I wasn't about to underestimate a man who could cold-bloodedly electrocute someone. I was taller and younger than the mandolin player, but he outweighed me by about a pound and a half was my guess, and it was hard to gauge just what kind of advantage that would give him.

"Why couldn't you leave it alone?" he asked softly.

Too late to play dumb. No *Whatever do you mean?* was going to fly. I debated screaming outright, but it was possible Dana had gotten bored and hung up, and I needed to conserve my strength. As he took a step toward me, hands in his shapeless pockets, saying something about Matt, something about the driver who ran him down and left him for dead, all I could see was the way the lights from the kitchen threaded through the white wisps of his thin wavy hair that seemed to be standing up in shock at what he did. And at what he was about to do. He was closing fast when I finally got out, "So you killed Georgia Payne," talking loud enough for dead phones and extinguished votive candles and a piano I would never hear again.

He was close enough to me now that I could see his pale, doughy face and light, limpid eyes, a face where I could never read the extent of the grief because it had always looked like it was grieving, anyway. "Didn't you?" I yelled just as he leaped at me, screaming, "You're damn right I did!" At the last second, I turned just enough that the weight of him didn't knock me over, but I got pushed into a violent back bend against a table as a chair fell over and I saw a glint of wire in his hands. The wire. The stripped cord. The murder weapon.

We were caught in a fierce, total-body struggle of snarls and yelps. As the cord went around my neck, I realized with horror that I couldn't throw him off. I couldn't angle my legs in any position to cause him pain. I couldn't jam my fingers into his determined eyes. Overhead the beautiful dim globes of Miracolo seemed hazy as I worked my desperate fingers under the tightening cord around my neck.

Landon will never get over it.

With that, I heard my strangled roar, and I tried sinking my teeth into this surprisingly strong mandolin player. No luck. Cardona. *Cardona.* If he was

Italian, then Maria Pia would never get over it. I jerked my body just enough to overturn the table, and the weight of an insane Leo Cardona and me pushed the table screeching across the tiled floor until we hit another table. And still he hung on.

My fingers were clutching at the cord as I ran out of breath and the last thing I felt was the beginning of tears. I guess, when it comes right down to it, you never know when you've had your very last saltimbocca. Or kiss . . . I was just letting my mind stray to the image of Joe Beck to block out a killer that was filling my field of vision. Just as I felt my fingers slacken on the cord, another shadow eclipsed a hazy globe of light, and in a wide, dark arc an arm swung toward us and I heard the air knocked out of my assailant. Again the dark arc swung, this time downward, once, twice, like faceless fate, and the killer of my cousin Anna Tremayne fell off me and slumped in a heap to the floor.

I gagged attractively for half a minute, clutching my throat, my fingers plucking at the cord. When my vision cleared, I looked up. It was Mrs. Crawford, still in her mint-green flapper girl dress and gold cloche. She stood looking down at me, one hip thrust out, in something like amusement. "I forgot my music," she said in that deep, nasal voice. Then she extended an arm to flourish her weapon at me. It was my leather portfolio stuffed full of a class roster and ten good rocks. She seemed philosophical. "He was a terrible musician," she drawled. Together we turned to look at the inert form of Leo Cardona. "Consider this"—she held up the portfolio to the unresponsive Leo—"my review."

Within the hour I had more company. First a couple of uniformed cops carted off Leo Cardona, which helped my trembling a lot. Maria Pia gave me one of her strands of pearls to cover the bruises on my neck, and she kept her composure admirably. She had Giancarlo to hold and pat and squeeze her hand, because, no matter what the crisis, for her faithful Giancarlo, it was always about her.

And I had Landon, who was so manically relieved about so many things that he chattered incessantly and made up some canapés of cream cheese, cilantro, hot pepper jelly, and caviar. When I told him his sister Anna's cat, Abbie, was now his to keep, he was radiant. I watched Paulette discuss the fine points of effective blows with rock-loaded cases with Mrs. Crawford. And Choo Choo, who had come running, bare-chested, in his striped pajama pants, hummed while he pulled espresso shots.

Then there was Detective Sally Fanella, taking

down the fine points of the story from Dana Cahill, who was plenty jazzed that she had stayed on the line, heard threats from Leo—"*Leo!* You think you know a person!"—and called Quaker Hills finest. I had a bad moment wondering if I was going to have to be indebted to Dana Cahill for the rest of my natural-born days. I guess it showed on my face, because Joe Beck whispered, "It's okay, Eve, Mrs. Crawford was your first responder."

We clinked espresso shots, and looked each other in the eye. I felt tired, but as I sat there with everyone I loved around me, sat there in my new pearls, I smiled. Joe Beck brushed the hair out of my face, and if we weren't all suddenly singing a rousing crackpot version of "Those Were the Days," I'm pretty sure he would have kissed me. Tomorrow I'd invite him over for drinks . . . and some pesto.

Definitely some pesto.

Choo Choo Bacigalupo's Recipe for Gorgonzola and Spiced Walnuts in Port Wine Syrup

SERVES 4

"How hard can it be?"–Choo Choo Bacigalupo

3 cups port wine

1 tablespoon unsalted butter

½ cup walnut halves

½ teaspoon cayenne

½ teaspoon black pepper

½ teaspoon salt

2 teaspoons sugar

8 oz. Gorgonzola cheese

In a saucepan, bring the wine to a boil. Cook over medium heat until reduced to ½ cup, about 12–15 minutes. Allow to cool.

In an 8-inch sauté pan, melt the butter over medium heat. Add the walnuts, cayenne, black pepper, salt, and sugar. Sauté until well coated and lightly toasted, 2–3 minutes. Set aside to cool.

Divide the cheese among four plates and spoon nuts over each portion. Drizzle the wine syrup over each plate and serve with crusty bread.